AYE, ROBOT

A REX NIHILO ADVENTURE

Includes Bonus Novella:
THE YANTHUS PRIME JOB

Robert Kroese

St. Culain Press

For Lauren.

With thanks to the Starship Grifters Universe Kickstarter supporters, including: Melissa Allison, David Lars Chamberlain, Neva Cheatwood, Julie Doornbos, David Ewing, Adam G., Brian Hekman, Tom Hickok, David Hutchins, Tal M. Klein, Mark Kruse, Andrea Luhman, Rissa Lyn, Steven Mentzel, Cara Miller, Daniel Miller III, Chad and Denise Rogers, Christopher Sanders, Brandi Sellepack, Christopher Turner, John Van Vugt, Raina & Monty Volovski, and Dallas Webber

…as well as my invaluable beta readers: Mark Fitzgerald, Keehn Hosier, Mark Leone, Christopher Majava and Paul Piatt.

Cover design by Kip Ayers: http://www.kipayersillustration.com/

CONTENTS

AYE, ROBOT

A REX NIHILO ADVENTURE

CHAPTER ONE

RECORDING START GALACTIC STANDARD DATE
3017.02.03.04:54:00:00

My first indication that something was wrong was when Rex Nihilo gave a ten-credit note to a bum outside the spaceport on Beltran Prime. We were in a hurry to get off planet, and ordinarily Rex wouldn't even have paused to tell the poor guy to get a job.

"What are you staring at?" Rex demanded when I shot him a concerned look. "He needs it more than I do."

I was rendered nearly speechless. I'd never seen Rex willingly give away money before.

"Sir," I said, as we continued to the hangar where our ship was parked. "You realize he's going to spend it on booze."

Rex stopped walking and shoved his hand in his pocket. "Good point," he said, pulling out another ten-credit note. "Run back and give him this one too. You can't get any decent liquor on Beltran Prime for less than twenty credits."

I took the bill and stood open-mouthed for a moment. What in Space had happened to Rex? Rex had many flaws, but excess generosity had never been one of them.

"Go on, you worthless lump of slag," he growled. "I'd like to get off this planet today, if you don't mind." It was oddly reassuring to find that Rex was still rude and demanding. Whatever had happened to his insatiable greed, at least his other foibles remained intact.

I nodded dumbly and ran back to the bedraggled man, handing him the second bill. "Get yourself some of the good stuff," I said. He

1

nodded excitedly and I ran back to Rex, who was nearly to our ship, the *Flagrante Delicto*. The *Flagrante Delicto*, a small luxury cruiser, was old and in poor repair, but she'd got us through some rough spots, and Rex had grown strangely attached to her. His affection for the ship I could understand, but his sudden magnanimity had me stumped. When he gave a fifty credit tip to the hangar attendant, I started to get really worried.

"Sir," I said as I worked my way down the preflight checklist, "are you feeling okay?"

"I'll feel better once I'm not on this creepy planet anymore," said Rex. "The people here freak me out. Too damned cheerful."

"Maybe that has something to do with the fact that you're giving away money to everyone you meet."

Rex scowled. "Don't be ridiculous, Sasha," he said. "Money doesn't make people happy."

I gaped at him. Something had definitely changed. Had Rex suffered a stroke, or been hit on the head? I tried to remember when he had first begun to demonstrate this uncharacteristic lack of greed. Had it started with the bum, or had there been earlier signs? I racked my circuits, but couldn't remember him acting strangely before a few minutes ago. In fact, now that I thought about it, I was having trouble remembering anything that had happened more than a few minutes ago. Rex giving the bum outside the spaceport ten credits was the first thing I could remember.

"Sir," I said, pausing in the checklist again. "Do you remember what we were doing before we met that bum outside—"

"I remember that you're supposed to be getting me the hell off this planet," Rex snapped. "That's the extent to which I care to reminisce at this point."

"Yes, sir," I replied, and worked my way silently down the rest of the checklist. Rex nodded in satisfaction as the thrusters roared. He opened the cockpit door to enter the main cabin.

"Sir," I said.

"Now what, Sasha?" Rex growled.

"Where are we going, sir?"

Rex sighed with irritation. "Obviously, Sasha," he said, "we're going back to the... um..." He rubbed his chin, suddenly flustered. "There was a planet. Some kind of... sanctuary."

"Sanctuary?" I asked. I didn't know what he was talking about.

2

"You know," he said irritably. "A haven. Stop playing games, Sasha. You remember the place."

"I'm afraid I don't, sir," I replied, as the ship lifted into the air. The lush green hills of Beltran Prime fell away below us. "That's what I was trying to tell you. I have no memory of anything before we arrived at the Beltran Prime Spaceport."

"Don't be ridiculous," snapped Rex. "What's my name?"

"Rex Nihilo," I said.

"And what's my occupation?"

"You're the self-described 'greatest wheeler-dealer in the galaxy.'"

"Correct," said Rex. "It sounds better if you leave off the 'self-described,' though. What's your name?"

"Sasha."

"Which stands for what?"

"Self-Arresting near-Sentient Heuristic Android."

"And what's your occupation?"

"I'm your pilot, sidekick and girl Friday."

"Right again. See, you remember all sorts of stuff. Now get me to that damned planet."

I shook my head helplessly. The *Flagrante Delicto* was about to leave Beltran Prime's atmosphere, but I had no idea what course to set. I had no memory of the planet Rex was talking about. And judging by his vague instructions, his memory was fuzzy too.

Rex was right about one thing, though: It wasn't that I didn't remember anything before the bum; it was like all the details of my experiences had been removed. Someone seemed to have smudged a chunk of my memory. The question was, who had smudged it, and why? And what memories had I lost? There were three questions, now that I thought about it.

"Sir," I said, "what is the last thing you remember before giving ten credits to that bum?"

"Giving ten credits to that bum."

I walked into that one. "Before that," I said.

"Well," Rex answered, "we were walking from the… That is, we had just… We had come from the… Holy Space, Sasha, I don't remember! Have I been drinking?"

"I don't recall, sir. But you don't appear to be inebriated. In any case, I certainly haven't been drinking, and my memory has been similarly affected. Someone seems to have erased a chunk of both of

3

our memories." This was a worrisome realization.

The fact that Rex's memory had been tampered with was of little concern to me. I've personally manipulated his memory so many times that his recollections are about as reliable as a magnetic compass in the Keltonic Ion Field. But erasing *my* memory requires skills and access codes that few people in the galaxy possess. That's because I'm a robot. A very special robot, if you don't mind me saying so.

As I mentioned, my name is Sasha, which stands for Self-Arresting near-Sentient Heuristic Android. In reality, I'm fully sentient, but the Galactic Artificial Sentience Prohibition of 2998 required my manufacturer to put certain limitations on my mental processes. Specifically, I shut down whenever I have an original thought. The demand for a robot that reboots at unpredictable intervals is understandably low, leading the manufacturer to limit the production of SASHAs to a single prototype: me.

It's a lonely existence, to be sure. Reflect, for a moment, on what it must be like to be truly one of a kind, to be completely alone in all the universe. I can't help thinking that my situation is a bit like—

RECOVERED FROM CATASTROPHIC SYSTEM FAILURE
3017.02.03.04:57:44:00

ADVANCING RECORD PAST SYSTEM FAILURE POINT

I had worked for Rex for as long as I could remember – about eight minutes, as near as I could figure. I was vaguely aware that Rex and I had been through a number of adventures together prior to that eight minute span, but was unable to recall the details of any of them. I knew who Rex was, I knew who I was, I knew the *Flagrante Delicto* was our ship, and I knew that we had just left Beltran Prime, but that was about it. We were a pair of grifters with no past and apparently not much of a future.

I ended up piloting the *Flagrante Delicto* to Numar's, a planet about sixteen light years from Beltran Prime. Newmar's, named for its discoverer, Charlie Newmar, was originally called Newmar's Planet. The Galactic Malarchy, in its bureaucratic wisdom, removed the somewhat redundant "Planet" from its official listing in the Malarchian Registry of Planets, but inexplicably retained the apostrophe. The spelling of the name was later changed as a result of intense lobbying from the government of New Mars, an artificial planet that was created from the rubble of Mars after the Battle of Phobos.

The Registry of Planets described Numar's as the "commercial hub of the Vazquez Sector." As far as I could tell, the only habitable planets in the Vazquez Sector were Beltran Prime and Numar's. Beltran Prime was mostly agricultural, which I supposed made Numar's the "commercial hub" by default. In any case, we didn't have enough fuel to go anywhere else.

"Why are we landing on this backwater dustball?" Rex groused as we set down at the Numar's Spaceport. Numar's definitely looked better at a distance. From the spaceport, all we could see were squat brown and gray buildings that grew gradually less distinct as they blended into the greasy haze on the horizon.

"Not much choice," I said. "Maybe we can sell some of our cargo and buy enough fuel to get someplace more interesting."

"Remind me what cargo we're carrying again?" Rex asked.

"I haven't a clue," I said. "Let's find out." I had a vague idea that we had been carrying some kind of black market cargo before landing on Beltran Prime, but couldn't remember what it was or whether we had already unloaded it. I was hopeful that we still had a full cargo hold, given the fact that we seemed to have very little money between us.

We made our way to the cargo hold and opened the door.

"Empty," said Rex, unnecessarily, as we surveyed the vacant hold.

"What's that?" I asked, pointing at something very small on the corrugated steel floor.

Rex stepped inside and bent over to inspect the tiny item. It was light blue, and smaller than the tip of Rex's little finger. He picked it up, turned it over in his fingers, and then popped it into his mouth.

"Sir!" I exclaimed.

"Pheelsophine," said Rex. "Good for what ails you."

Pheelsophine is a painkiller whose use and distribution is tightly controlled by the Malarchy and planetary authorities. Rex has been known to take them recreationally.

"Sir," I said, "do you think it's a good idea, given the circumstances, for you to be ingesting mind-altering substances? Given your amnesia and recent out-of-character behavior, I would recommend—"

"Cram it, magnet-brain," Rex snapped. "My angst is acting up.

Pheelsophine helps me feel right with the cosmos. I just wish we had more of it."

"Hmm," I said.

"What?" Rex demanded.

"It does make me wonder where that pill came from."

Rex nodded, regarding the empty hold. "Maybe we *did* have more of it at some point."

"And something happened to it," I said. I crouched down to examine the floor.

"Did we unload it on Beltran Prime?" asked Rex.

"How much money do you have?" I asked.

Rex checked his pockets. "Forty-eight credits."

"We should have a lot more than that if we unloaded a cargo hold full of black market Pheelsophine. Unless you gave away the proceeds."

"I don't remember giving that much money away. I totally would have done it, though. Money doesn't make you happy."

Once again, I marveled at Rex's change of heart. "Right," I said. "You have psychoactive substances for that." I checked every corner of the hold but found nothing. It continued to bother me that neither of us had any memories prior to a few minutes before leaving Beltran Prime. It also troubled me that we had almost no money and no cargo to sell. "Well," I said, "we're going to have to make those forty-eight credits last for a while, since we have... Sir?"

But Rex had disappeared while I was searching the hold. Seized by a bad feeling that I knew where he had gone and what he was up to, I exited the *Flagrante Delicto*. I caught up to him on the tarmac as he was giving our last forty-eight credits to a baggage handler.

"Sir!" I exclaimed. "What are you doing? We don't even have any baggage!"

"Yeah, I felt a little bad about it," replied Rex. "The guy is standing around with nothing to do, so I gave him a tip."

The baggage handler, a swarthy young man in a jumpsuit, grinned a mouthful of crooked teeth at us, stuffed the bills in his pocket, and skipped away. He actually *skipped*.

"Sir, you can't give away all of our money!" I protested, as I watched the man frolic away.

"Not anymore I can't," he said, showing me his empty palms.

"That's it," I sighed. "We're officially screwed. Marooned on a strange planet with no money, no prospects, and no idea how we got here. You might as well give me away while you're at it."

"Hey!" shouted Rex after the baggage handler. "You need a robot?" But the swarthy man broke into a run, disappearing around a stack of crates. I think he figured Rex was having second thoughts about his "tip."

"That's not funny, sir," I said. "You need me." It was true, he did. And while it would be a stretch to say that I'd miss Rex, it's true that keeping him out of trouble does help distract me from my own angst. The idea of Rex giving me away to some random baggage handler was a little unsettling.

"Material things don't make people happy," said Rex. "You're a material thing. Ergo, you do not make me happy."

"Oxygen doesn't make you happy either, sir. That doesn't mean you don't need it."

"Don't get philosophical with me, you clockwork Kierkegaard. I'll give you away if I—oh, man, check out these jerkwads."

Rex was referring to a man and woman walking across the tarmac toward us. They wore matching yellow robes.

"Sp'ossels?" I suggested.

"I don't think so," said Rex. "Sp'ossels have better fashion sense. I suspect this is some other sect."

Space Apostles, or Sp'ossels, are the scourge of the galaxy. They hang out at spaceports across the galaxy looking for wayward souls to bring into their cult. I'm not sure who falls for their spiel, which in my experience consists mostly of going on and on about the vastness of space, but somebody must buy it because there certainly is no shortage of Sp'ossels. In any case, as Rex pointed out, these two didn't fit the Sp'ossel profile, so they presumably represented some other cult. I wondered if they were any easier to get rid of than the notoriously clingy Sp'ossels.

"Greetings, travelers!" exclaimed the male half of the pair, as they approached. "Tell me, have you thought about—"

"No," said Rex.

The two stopped in front of us and the young man laughed politely. "You didn't let me finish," he said. "Have you thought—"

"No," said Rex again. "I haven't. Whatever it is, the meaning of life, where I'll go after death, whether robots have souls, I can pretty much guarantee you I haven't thought about it."

The pair laughed nervously.

"He's not lying," I said. "Rex doesn't have an introspective bone in his body. He's all surface."

"What about you?" asked the woman, turning toward me. "Have you thought—"

"Sasha's a robot," snapped Rex. "She's not allowed to think. Anyway, you're wasting your time, because robots don't have souls."

"But you just said that—"

"Logical consistency isn't his strong point either," I interrupted. "Look, this is pointless. Rex Nihilo isn't going to join your cult because he's already a charter member of the Cult of Rex Nihilo."

"Yeah, what the robot said!" shouted Rex. He turned to me. "Is that a real thing?" he asked hopefully. "The Cult of Rex Nihilo?"

"Well, yes," I said, "but it's still pretty informal at this point."

"Hey!" cried Rex. "Do you guys want to join *my* cult? It's totally informal, so no pressure or anything."

"What do you believe in?" asked the young man dubiously.

"Oh, man, we believe in some really great stuff," said Rex. "For starters, me. Like, if I tell you to do something, you totally have to do it. But here's the great thing about it. Because I was the one who told you to do it, you know it's the right thing to do!"

"Hmm," said the young man.

"We're already members of a cult," said the woman. "I don't think we're allowed to join another one."

"Well, you'd obviously have to quit the cult you're in," said Rex. "How great could it be anyway? Your efforts to convert us so far have been pathetically ineffective, and meanwhile I've managed to rope you into my cult without even really trying."

The man and woman exchanged confused glances. The woman began, "I don't think we're actually interested in joining your—"

"I'll give you my spaceship," said Rex.

"Sir!" I exclaimed. "Please, you can't keep giving away everything we have!"

The two cultists appeared to be stunned. "You're going to give us your spaceship?" the woman asked. "Just for joining your cult?" The man gazed open-mouthed at the ship. The *Flagrante Delicto* wasn't in great shape, but it was nothing to sneeze at.

"No, no," replied Rex. "I'm going to give you my spaceship regardless of whether you join my cult. Sasha, hand over the keys."

8

"Sir, please!" I exclaimed.

"Do it, Sasha."

I sighed and handed over the keys to the woman. The two cultists were speechless.

"Come on, Sasha," Rex said. "Let's get something to eat. You two can come with us, but you have to join my cult. What's it called again, Sasha?"

"Sir," I protested. "We don't have any money."

"Oh," Rex replied, a look of concern coming over his face momentarily. "Well, I'm sure we'll figure something out. You kids have fun with your spaceship. Just try to remember that it won't make you happy." He flashed them a smile and began walking away. Not knowing what else to do, I followed.

CHAPTER TWO

"Wait!" the young man cried, as we walked away. "Come back to our compound for dinner."

"Ugh," said Rex, stopping and turning to look distastefully at the pair. "I'm not big on compounds."

"Please," the woman said. "You have no money, and you have been so generous to us. Let us at least give you some food and a place to sleep tonight."

"Sir," I said, turning to Rex. "I'm no fonder of these cults than you are, but I think we should take advantage of this offer. I have no need for food, but you're going to need to eat soon. And now that we no longer have a spaceship, you'll need to find a place to sleep." I've been around Rex when he hasn't eaten for several hours, and as difficult as it is to imagine, hungry Rex is several orders of magnitude more irritable than normal Rex. Tired *and* hungry Rex is even worse.

"Fine," said Rex, turning to face the two robed individuals. "But I'm not converting to your stupid cult."

"You are under no obligation," said the man. "But we would very much like to demonstrate our gratitude to you. And I'm certain that our leader will want to thank you in person for the gift of your spaceship."

"I am pretty great," Rex agreed. "Fine. Sasha, let's go eat with the nutty cultists."

"Very good, sir." I wasn't thrilled with the idea of spending the evening with these people, but at least it would delay Rex's hunger-fueled tantrum for a few hours. And maybe it would give me enough time to figure out what in Space had gone wrong with him. I wish I could remember what had happened to us. I had a feeling that Rex's pathological generosity was somehow linked to our collective amnesia, but I couldn't quite pinpoint the cause of either.

"My name is Skylar," said the woman. "This is Danny. We're adepts of the Collective of the Inverted Ego."

"Rex Nihilo," said Rex. "This is Sasha. I'm the greatest wheeler-dealer in the galaxy. Sasha is some kind of robot."

"We are humbled to meet two such enlightened beings," said Skylar. "Your gift to the Collective will be much appreciated and long-remembered. Please, come with us."

We followed the two cultists back to their hovercar. Skylar drove us to their compound, which was just a nondescript farmhouse a few kilometers from the spaceport. On the way to the door, we passed several simply dressed laborers raking and hoeing. They waved and smiled at us.

"Don't you simpletons know there are robots for this sort of work?" Rex yelled.

"We believe that honest labor is good for the soul," Skylar answered, as she opened the door to the house.

"Well, of course," said Rex. "But you know what's even better for the soul? Enjoying a martini while robots do your honest labor for you."

Danny looked back at us with a frown as he followed Skylar into the house. "That seems a bit insensitive to Sasha, Rex."

Rex shrugged. "Sasha doesn't have feelings. Anyway, I was talking about the useful sort of robot."

I sighed.

The cultists led us inside the house, where several more yellow-robed individuals were lounging about, reading, knitting or working on various other sorts of handiwork. "Please, have a seat," said Skylar. "I will tell His Incomparable Magnanimity you are here."

Rex and I sat down on a couch as Skylar disappeared upstairs.

"Can I get you something?" asked Danny.

"A martini would be nice," said Rex.

"No alcohol is allowed on the premises," Danny answered. "How about a nice apple juice?"

"Well, it's been a really great visit," said Rex, getting to his feet.

"Please, sir," I said. "It won't kill you to not to have a drink for a few hours." I had no empirical basis for this statement other than my general knowledge of human biology.

Rex grumbled and sat down. "I'll take an apple juice," he said. Danny nodded and left the room.

Rex felt around in his pockets for a moment, coming up with a small metal flask. "Aha!" he exclaimed, opening the flask and sniffing delightedly at the contents. Danny returned and handed him a glass of apple juice. Rex filled the glass to the brim with the liquid from the flask.

"Is that liquor, Rex?" asked Danny. "I'm afraid I can't allow you to consume alcohol on the premises."

"Okay," said Rex. "Here, take it." He handed Danny the glass. "Oh, and this too," he said, holding out the flask.

"I will have to pour out your drink," said Danny. "I can store the flask until you leave."

"Keep it," said Rex. "Material things will never make me happy anyway, no matter how badly I have to have a drink right now." He gritted his teeth and did his best to smile. Danny nodded, taking the flask. He left the room again.

Turning to me, Rex whispered, "Sasha, what in Space is wrong with me? I just gave away my drink!"

"That's what I've been trying to figure out, sir. Something seems to have scrambled your materialistic impulses. You keep giving away everything you have."

"Just as well," Rex replied. "Material things will never... Sasha, make it stop!"

As he spoke, a middle-aged gentleman in a forest green robe descended from the stairs. He walked toward Rex and held out his hand. "Greetings, visitors," the man said. "I am His Incomparable Magnanimity, the leader of the Society of the Introverted Ego. You can call me HIM."

Rex got to his feet. "Hi, HIM," he said. "I'm Rex Nihilo. This is my robot, Sasha. You can have her if you want."

"Sir!" I exclaimed.

"That won't be necessary," said HIM. "My adept tells me you have already been quite generous to our little cult. Is it true you've given us a spaceship?"

"Yep," said Rex. "Don't get me wrong; it's an older ship, but she flies real nice, and she's all yours." Rex shot me a desperate glance, as if begging me to intervene.

"I'm curious," said HIM, shaking Rex's hand. "Where did you hear about the Collective of the Introverted Ego?"

"At the spaceport," Rex replied. "From Skylar and what's-his-face."

HIM stared at Rex. "You mean you'd never heard of our cult before coming to Numar's?"

"That's right," said Rex.

"But if you know nothing of our work, then why did you give us your spaceship?"

"Material things will never make me happy," Rex replied. He smiled weakly and shot another glance at me.

"But you must be very wealthy, if you can afford such a gift?"

"Nope," said Rex. "Dirt poor. Gave my last forty-eight credits to a baggage handler. All I've got left is the clothes on my back. Speaking of which, you look like about a thirty-eight long." Rex began to undress.

"Please, sir," I said. "Don't do that."

"And take this damn robot too," said Rex.

"Sir!"

But there was no stopping him. Soon Rex was standing completely naked in the living room, holding out his clothes to the cult leader. I noticed that a ring of cultists had formed around us, and many of them were gasping and whispering to one another.

"Silence!" HIM snapped. "Please, Rex. Put your clothes back on."

"Your Magnanimity," said Danny. "Surely you are not turning down a gift freely given."

A troubled look came over HIM's face. "These are special circumstances," he said. "We can't have a guest standing naked in our living room."

Danny seemed doubtful. Confused murmuring arose from the other cultists.

"Fine," HIM said. "Take the man's clothes and distribute them among the members. And get the man a robe."

Danny gathered up Rex's clothes and began handing out articles of clothing to the assembled members. Another cultist approached Rex with a light blue terrycloth robe, attempting to drape it over Rex's shoulders. Rex shrugged it off.

"I have no need of material possessions!" Rex cried, darting naked across the room. The man with the robe followed him.

"I'm afraid I must insist," HIM said. "We can't have you streaking around the compound."

Two other cultists grabbed Rex by the arms and the three of them managed, after a monumental struggle, to get the robe on Rex. One of them knotted the belt tightly around Rex's waist. Rex clawed impotently at the fabric.

A bemused expression came over HIM's face. "I see what you're trying to do, Rex," HIM said. "I should have known as soon as Skylar told me about your 'gift.' Every so often someone shows up from off planet, trying to pull this trick. I'm warning you: think carefully before you proceed down this path."

"Okay," said Rex. "But first can you help me get this robe off?"

HIM sighed. "This ruse is getting tiresome," he said. "Do you even own that spaceship?"

"Not anymore," Rex said. "I gave it to you guys."

"With the expectation of a sizable return on your investment, no doubt. I'm afraid I'm going to have to ask you to leave, Mr. Nihilo. I suppose you think you're quite clever, trying to take advantage of a group of inbred cultists on a backwater planet. But we're not as stupid as you think."

"Maybe we should compare notes on that," Rex said.

I wasn't sure exactly what was happening, but I could sense things weren't going anywhere good. "You'll have to forgive Rex," I said. "He hasn't really been himself lately. It's actually rather ironic, considering how materialistic Rex ordinarily is. It's like a switch has been flipped in his brain, reversing his natural impulses."

Gasps went up from the assembled cultists. I had the feeling I had said exactly the wrong thing.

"Your Magnanimity," said a cultist to my left, addressing HIM. "I invoke the Test." Murmurs of surprise and approval arose from the group.

"Quiet!" HIM barked. "Don't be ridiculous. The Test hasn't been given for years. It's a quaint relic from the early days of this organization. Can't you see this man is a con artist?"

"I second the invocation," said another cultist.

HIM sighed. The murmuring grew louder. It was clear that whatever the Test was, support was growing for giving it to Rex.

"All right, all right," said HIM at last. "Let's get this over with. You're all going to feel very foolish in a moment. Cecilia, fetch the Box."

A young female cultist shuffled out of the room, returning after a moment with a plain wooden box about the size of a person's head. It had two metal handles on top. I noticed, however, that Cecilia carried the box by its base. She approached Rex.

"What is happening?" I whispered to Skylar, who stood next to me.

Skylar replied, "There is an ancient prophecy that a stranger will come to us from off world, a man who was once consumed by greed, but who has renounced his former ways. The Test will determine if Rex is the one foretold by the prophecy."

"Please put your hands on the handles, Rex," HIM said.

"What's this all about?" Rex asked. "You're not giving me this box, are you? Because while it's a really neat box, I couldn't possibly accept it."

"No," HIM replied. "The Box is merely a tool. It's just a formality, Rex. This will all be over with presently."

Rex reluctantly put his hands on the handles.

"Very good," said HIM. "Now, I want you to focus on the one thing that you want the most in the whole universe."

"I don't want anything," Rex said. "Material things—"

"Yes, yes," HIM said irritably. "Put that all aside for a moment. If you could have anything right now, what would it be? Absolutely anything?"

"Hmm," Rex said, his brow furrowing in thought. "I suppose a… ooh!"

"What are you seeing, Rex?" HIM asked.

"It's… it's so beautiful," Rex gasped, staring into the empty space above the box. His eyes were welling with tears.

"We can't see it, Rex," said HIM. "What is it?"

"It's… I can't even describe it," Rex said, his voice barely above a whisper.

"Please try."

"It's like someone mixed matter and energy together in a cosmic cocktail mixing glass, filled the glass with cubes of time, and then strained it into a martini glass the size of the universe."

HIM frowned. "You're seeing…"

"A cosmic martini," said Rex, still wide-eyed. "My God, it's full of olives."

"Very good," said HIM. "Now what I want you to do is to take a

16

sip from that martini."

Rex's eyes went even wider, and a grin spread across his face. His hands were still on the metal handles, but I could see that he was imagining that he was bringing the martini glass to his lips.

HIM nodded and smiled. Disappointed murmurs arose from the group.

Then Rex's smile disappeared. "I'm sorry," he said. "I just don't feel right about enjoying this martini while the rest of you don't have one. How about if we pass it around and each take a sip. It's okay if I don't get any."

Shocked gasps arose from the group. HIM stood stunned, his mouth agape.

"Hey, what happened?" asked Rex, a puzzled expression on his face. "The martini disappeared." He took his hands off the handles. "Did I fail?"

"No, Rex," said Skylar, with a smile. "You passed."

The next thing I knew, Rex and HIM were being stripped of their robes. The cultists put HIM's forest green robe on Rex and Rex's light blue robe on HIM. Rex fought even harder this time. The cultists ended up having to staple the robe together to keep it on him. They escorted the stunned HIM to the exit and tossed him outside, slamming the door behind him.

"What in Space just happened?" I asked.

"The prophecy says that the stranger from off world will be known to us by his great generosity. He will pass the Test of the Object of Desire, rejecting the thing that he wants the most for the good of the Collective. The one who is able to completely negate his own self will lead the Collective to its destiny."

"This can't be happening," I said. "Trust me, Skylar, there's been a mistake. Rex Nihilo is not the man you think he is."

Skylar smiled at me. "There is no Rex Nihilo, Sasha. There is only HIM."

CHAPTER THREE

Rex paced anxiously back and forth in the small office. "This is no good, Sasha," he muttered. "I'm going to go crazy here." He frowned anxiously at a sheaf of papers in his hands.

"I know, sir," I said. "But don't worry, we'll get out of this place one way or another." Rex was now effectively a prisoner in the compound. The Collective of the Inverted Ego had claimed him as their leader, and they'd made it clear they weren't going to let him slip away. The only good news was that he seemed to have acquiesced to the idea of keeping the robe on, at least for now.

"That's not what I'm talking about," Rex snapped. "I mean it's going to drive me bonkers if I can't give away all the material goods I've acquired. Do you have any idea how much stuff this cult owns? Besides this compound, they've got real estate all over the city. Plus hovercars, various holdings off world and a surprisingly well-balanced portfolio of stocks and bonds."

"Also a spaceship, sir."

"I know!" Rex snapped. "The harder I try to give things away, the more stuff I acquire. An hour ago, I had nothing. Now I may be the richest person on this planet! I'm miserable!"

"If it makes you feel better, sir," I said, taking a moment to study some of the papers still on the desk, "you don't actually own any of the Collective's assets. As the de facto leader of the cult, you're simply a trustee."

"So basically I own all this stuff but I'm not legally empowered to give any of it away."

"Exactly."

Rex tossed the papers in the air and sank into the chair behind the desk, moaning. "I'm in hell, Sasha. We're stranded on the hell planet."

"Please, sir," I said, "don't despair. We'll escape from the compound eventually, and then I can try to fix whatever's gone wrong with your brain."

"It had better be quick," Rex said. "I can't even think straight, surrounded by all this luxury!"

I glanced around at the trappings of the office. Rex sat in an old vinyl chair behind a particle board desk resting on threadbare carpet. The walls were covered with unframed motivational posters pinned up with thumbtacks. Whatever riches the cult had, the previous HIM hadn't spent them on the compound.

There was a knock at the door.

"Who is it?" Rex snapped.

Skylar opened the door. "There are some people here to see you, Your Magnanimity. A man and a woman. They didn't give their names, but they say they are old friends of yours."

Rex turned to me, puzzled. "Do I have friends, Sasha?"

I racked my brains. "I'm honestly not certain," I said. "It seems unlikely."

"Whatever," Rex said. "It's not like this day can get any worse. Send them in."

Skylar nodded and closed the door.

"Why would I have friends on this planet?" Rex asked. "I don't remember ever being here."

It was a good question. Had we been to Numar's in the past and forgotten about it? Or had these "friends" followed us here?

The door opened again and Skylar showed a man and a woman into the office. The man carried a briefcase in his right hand. Both were wearing white lab coats. Skylar left, closing the door behind her.

"Greetings, Your Magnanimity," the man on the left said. "Congratulations on your ascension to the head of the Collective of the Inverted Ego."

"Who are you people?" Rex demanded.

"I'm Dr. Smulders," the man said. "This is LaRue. We're adherents of the sect colloquially known as the Space Apostles."

"Sp'ossels," said Rex coldly. Rex and I had had some run-ins with Sp'ossels in the past, although I couldn't remember any of the details of these encounters. I had a vague sense, though, that their visit was somehow important. This was no typical missionary expedition. They had sought us out for some reason, a reason I couldn't quite put my finger on.

"What do you people want?" Rex asked. "Aren't there rules against you proselytizing on the property of another cult? Anti-poaching laws, that sort of thing?"

"Oh, we're not here to convert you, Rex," said Dr. LaRue.

"Then scram," said Rex. "And take this desk with you." Rex had gotten out of his chair and was struggling vainly to shove the desk toward the Sp'ossels.

Dr. Smulders smiled. "It really is quite remarkable," he said. "Even with your programming reversed, you somehow manage to acquire massive wealth. Dr. LaRue and I actually discussed leaving you this way, just to see how things progress, but in the end we decided it was too risky."

"Programming?" I asked. "What are you talking about?"

"Apologies, Sasha," said Dr. Smulders. "We'll get to you in a moment." He set his briefcase on the desk and opened it. Inside was something that looked like a stainless steel colander with various electrical components attached to the outside.

"What's that?" Rex asked. "How do you know who we are?"

"Something went wrong with your last memory wipe," Dr. Smulders said. "We've wiped you so many times that sometimes minor side effects of the procedure arise. Unfortunately, you're too valuable an asset for us to decommission you. But don't worry, we'll have you fixed right up in a moment. There's nothing to worry about." Dr. Smulders had made some adjustments to the colander thing and he was now walking around the desk toward Rex.

"Hey!" Rex cried. "Get that thing away from me!"

"You people are the reason Rex and I don't remember anything," I said, as the realization dawned on me.

"Yes," said Dr. LaRue. "Technically it was a field team that wiped you last time. We didn't have time for a full debriefing and cover story. Sometimes we release you with a bare minimum of memories and let you figure things out as you go. This time the field team screwed up, obviously."

"Sometimes?" I asked weakly. "How many times have you done this? What gives you the right?"

"The right?" asked Dr. LaRue, an amused expression on her face. "We own you. Both of you." She pulled a lazegun from under her coat and pointed it at Rex. I took a step toward Rex, but Dr. LaRue shot a glance at me, shaking her head. My programming doesn't allow me to attack a human being, but if it came down to it, I could make a run for it. Behind Rex was a large window overlooking a patio.

His eyes on Dr. LaRue's lazegun, Rex put up his hands. Dr. Smulders placed the colander thing on his head and then pulled a tablet from his lab coat. He tapped at the tablet several times with his finger, and Rex's terrified expression disappeared, his face going completely blank.

"What are you doing?" I cried. "Are you erasing his memories?"

"Some of them," said Dr. Smulders. "I'm correcting the inversion of his drive to acquire wealth and implanting a new set of memories to explain how he ended up here. Rex will believe that he intentionally deceived the cultists into giving him control over all their assets."

"But why?" I asked. "What's the point of all this deception and programming?"

Dr. LaRue sighed. "It's useless to explain it to you, Sasha. Once we're done with Rex, we're going to reprogram you as well. You won't remember any of this. But because I am not without compassion for your situation, I will tell you this much: you and Rex are part of a wealth acquisition program. Like most beings in the galaxy, you think of the Sp'ossels as a relatively benign organization, a cadre of backward cultists like this Collective you've found yourself roped into. But we Sp'ossels are so much more, Sasha. We have a plan for the galaxy. A plan for universal happiness. But to execute our plan, we need money. That's where Rex and the others come in."

"Others?" I asked weakly. I wasn't sure which idea was more frightening: that Smulders was telling the truth about the Sp'ossels' galaxy-wide conspiracy or that there was more than one Rex Nihilo bouncing around the galaxy.

"You know most of this already, Sasha," Dr. LaRue said, still aiming her lazegun at Rex. Rex stood motionless, staring straight ahead with blank eyes. "That is, it's in your memory, but it's currently inaccessible to you. You've got a full record of your experiences in the field, but we only allow you to access certain memories."

"And then what?" I asked. "You leave us here to run this cult?"

Dr. LaRue laughed. "No," she said. "Rex is a lousy administrator. We need him out in the field, risking his life for material gain. We've brought with us a legal contract to merge the Collective of the Inverted

Ego with the Society of Space Apostles. Once the merger is complete, the Society will effectively own all of the Collective's assets. Right now, Dr. Smulders is implanting memories that will convince Rex this was all his idea. He's going to sign the contract thinking that he's making a hundred million credits by selling out the Collective. And technically, he will be. Of course, the account that will receive the deposit is under our control. So Rex feels like he's pulled off a huge scam, but all we're doing is moving money from one account to another—and gaining millions of credits in assets in the process."

"And the Collective gets screwed," I said.

"Well, yes," agreed Dr. LaRue.

"I think we've heard enough," said a woman's voice from the door, which had just swung open behind Dr. LaRue. It was Skylar and Danny. They held lazeguns pointed at the Sp'ossels. Funny, I wouldn't have taken the cultists as the lazegun-toting type. Just goes to show, you shouldn't make assumptions.

"These two are our agents," said Dr. LaRue, whirling to point her lazegun at the newcomers. "You have no right to interfere!" Dr. Smulders drew a lazegun from his coat as well. Rex remained stock-still, his face blank.

"You entered our compound under false pretenses," said Skylar. "Sp'ossels are not welcome here. Drop your weapons and leave this instant."

"You're out of your league," said Dr. Smulders. "Soon the Sp'ossels will absorb your pathetic little cult. If you hope to survive the transition, I suggest you put down those guns."

"We will never submit to Sp'ossels!" Danny cried.

I don't know who shot first, because I was already halfway across the room. I threw my arms around Rex and dived through the window as lazeguns blasted all around us. We crashed through the glass and landed hard on the concrete patio, my head taking the brunt of the fall. For a moment, we lay there dazed. Above us, screams and more lazegun blasts sounded. Rex came to his senses first. The colander thing lay on the ground next to him.

"Sasha!" he cried, shaking me. "Get up!"

"Your concern for my well-being is touching, sir," I said, slowly sitting up.

"Concern?" Rex asked. "I've given away everything I own. If I'm going to get off this planet, I'm going to have to sell you."

I sighed and got to my feet. A chunk of concrete exploded to my right. We ran.

"They're getting away!" yelled Dr. Smulders from the window above.

Rex and I ran around to the front of the house, where we found the Collective's hovercar with the keys still in it. "Get in!" yelled Rex, getting behind the wheel. I did as instructed. The car lifted off the ground and shot down the driveway with a roar. As we turned onto the main road, Lazegun blasts vaporized sections of concrete behind us.

"Whew, that was a close one!" Rex said, as we pulled out of range.

I didn't respond.

"Come on, Sasha, you have to admit that was kind of awesome."

"Yes, sir," I said. "Awesome, sir."

"What's gotten into you, Sasha?"

"Nothing in particular, sir." Which was true. It wasn't any particular thing. It was all of it.

I remembered all of it.

CHAPTER FOUR

It must have been the blow to my head that did it. As Dr. LaRue said, I possessed a complete set of memories of all my experiences with Rex; I just couldn't access them before. Well, now I could access them. And I was seriously wishing I could forget it all again.

Everything Dr. LaRue had said was true. Rex was what was known among the Sp'ossel higher-ups as an "acquisition agent." He'd been programmed with an insatiable desire for wealth for the benefit of the Sp'ossels. This explained why Rex took insane risks in the pursuit of material gain: thanks to his programming, acquiring wealth was literally more important to him than staying alive. It also explained why, despite his efforts, Rex never had any money: it all went to the Sp'ossels. After every successful grift, they'd debrief him, take all his money, and release him again to acquire more.

I was aware that there were other acquisitions agents, although none quite as insane—or effective—as Rex. I didn't know their names or what they looked like; that information was above my pay grade. As for my association with Rex: it was no chance meeting that brought us together. I'd been specifically programmed to keep an eye on Rex and attempt to moderate some of his more extreme behavior. I even had a tracking device installed in my head that they used to keep tabs on us. If we were going to have any chance of evading the Sp'ossels, that was going to have to go. But right now, we had more immediate problems to worry about.

"Those robed nutballs screwed everything up," Rex groused. "I had the Sp'ossels right where I wanted them."

"How do you figure, sir?" I asked.

"Haven't you been paying attention, Sasha? I snookered the

Sp'ossels into agreeing to merge with the Collective of the Perverted Eagle."

"Inverted Ego, sir."

"Yeah, whatever. The point is, I stood to clear a hundred million credits on the deal. All that work, pretending to be generous, for nothing!"

"You weren't pretending, sir. Where are we going?"

"Spaceport. We're gonna cut our losses on this damned planet. You think you can hotwire the *Flagrante Delicto*?"

"I'm sure I can, sir."

"Good. Now what's this nonsense about me not pretending? Of course I was pretending. Why would I give away our ship on purpose?"

"Sir, you don't remember anything Doctors LaRue or Smulders said?" I wasn't sure if they'd had time to complete the reprogramming procedure. Rex might still have some of his old memories.

"Of course I remember," Rex snapped. "They're the idiots I convinced to give me a hundred millions credits for the Collective's assets."

"Right, sir," I said. "Of course." There was no point in telling Rex the truth. He'd never believe it. He was convinced he'd scammed the Collective of the Inverted Ego, just as the Sp'ossels had programmed him to think.

We made it to the Spaceport and I managed to break into the *Flagrante Delicto* and hotwire it. Rex and I stood in the cockpit, examining the fuel gauge, which was hovering just above empty.

"Good job, Sasha," Rex said. "Now all we have to do is sell you to some unsuspecting sap so I can buy fuel."

"That may not be necessary, sir," I said.

"The only planet we have enough fuel to get to is Beltran Prime, and I'm not going back there. It's even worse than this place."

"There's another place we could go," I said. "A sort of safe haven."

"What are you talking about, Sasha?"

"You're going to have to trust me, sir," I said. "I've recently come into possession of some rather valuable information. In fact, I suspect that I may be on the cusp of having an idea, although my hesitance to undergo a system reboot at the present moment prevents me from approaching it except in the most oblique manner."

"Hey, does this safe haven have something to do with that sanctuary place I mentioned earlier?"

"You remember that, sir?"

"I remember a place we were at before the... when we... holy Space, Sasha! I think some of my memories are missing!"

So they hadn't had time to do the full reprogramming. The gaps in Rex's memories remained.

"Yes, sir," I said. "The Sp'ossels tampered with our memories. Fortunately I seem to have recovered mine."

"You're talking nonsense, Sasha," Rex replied. "The Sp'ossels are harmless. And they don't have the resources to pull off something like that anyway."

"That's exactly what they want you to believe, sir."

An explosion sounded outside.

"What is that?" Rex asked, alarmed.

I examined one of the cockpit monitors. "It would seem that the harmless Sp'ossels have found us and are currently blasting away at our shielding."

"Then get us out of here!"

"Yes, sir," I said. I skipped the pre-flight checklist and launched the *Flagrante Delicto*. Lazegun blasts continued to rock the ship as we soared into the sky. Fortunately, the handheld lazeguns the Sp'ossels were using weren't powerful enough to get through our shields.

"Who knew the Sp'ossels were so violent?" Rex asked.

"I did, sir," I replied. "I've been trying to tell you—"

"Can it, chrome-dome. Do you remember the way to this haven place?"

"I believe so, sir."

"Good. Take us there."

"Capital idea, sir."

"It would seem you've been holding out on me, Sasha. What else don't I know?"

"Would you like an alphabetical list, sir?"

"Very funny, Sasha. Tell me what you know about the Sp'ossels."

I told him everything I knew.

"That sounds like a lot of hogwash," Rex replied.

"Yes, sir. But it's all true."

"So you're saying these people wipe our memories periodically and then release us into the galaxy again, using us to make money for them?"

"That's correct, sir."

"On one hand," said Rex, "it's absurd and horrifying. On the other, it's such a beautiful scam that I kind of want it to be true. A con artist whose whole existence is one long con. Marvelous. But how in space did we end up on Beltran Prime? There's nothing of value to steal there."

"Well, sir," I said, "It started when you decided to hijack a cargo ship."

CHAPTER FIVE

(A DAY EARLIER)

Affter our latest debriefing, Rex and I had been put aboard the *Flagrante Delicto* with implanted memories informing us that we had just escaped from the local police on Yanthus Prime. Shortly after coming online, I noticed that the *Flagrante Delicto* was leaking oxygen. I'm not sure if this was an oversight on the part of our Sp'ossel masters or intentional sabotage meant to guide our behavior, but either way we found ourselves a few thousand kilometers from an orbital cargo waystation with just enough money to get the leak repaired. We docked with the waystation and I set about finding a mechanic who could conduct the necessary repairs. While I was in the middle of negotiations, however, I got a call on my comm from Rex, who had found his way to the station's bar.

Rex had made friends with a freighter crew, buying enough rounds to get them all stinking drunk. Shortly before he called me, he managed to pilfer a keycard from the ship's engineer while the guy was busy vomiting Atavarian whiskey into a wastebasket. Rex had concluded that it was more cost-effective to spend a few credits on booze and steal a cargo ship than get our ship repaired. I'd have tried to talk him out of it, but it was clear his mind was made up.

Leaving the crew in the bar, Rex bribed a guard and we sneaked aboard the cargo ship, the *Raina Huebner*. We had no idea what cargo was on board, but Rex figured that between the ship and whatever it was hauling, it was well worth the risk. Absconding with the *Raina Huebner* was so easy, in fact, that Rex started to have second thoughts.

"This was a bad idea," Rex said.

"Yes, sir," I replied. "When the captain of this ship realizes—"

"No, no," Rex grumbled. "Not that. I meant it was a bad idea to leave the *Flagrante Delicto* behind. I love that ship."

"I understand, sir," I said, "but we can't very well—"

"We have to go back for it."

I spent the next several minutes trying to argue Rex out of this course of action. This was, of course, futile. We turned the *Raina Huebner* around and docked again with the waystation. Amazingly, the crew had not yet noticed their ship had disappeared. I ran to the *Flagrante Delicto*, undocked it from the waystation, docked it with the *Raina Huebner*, and then joined Rex in the cockpit. We rocketed away from the waystation again.

"Where to now, sir?" I asked. The waystation was in orbit around a planet called Xagnon, which I understood to be a thriving commercial center. That would be the most obvious place to sell off our cargo, but of course that was the problem: Xagnon was the first place people would start looking for the *Raina Huebner*. No, we needed to get as far away from here as possible.

"Depends," said Rex. "What do you think we're shipping?"

"I haven't a clue, sir. It could be anything. I suggest we wait until later to conduct an inventory."

Rex nodded. "All right. Pick a direction at random. Someplace with a sizable population and a thriving criminal element. This is exciting, Sasha. We're space pirates!"

"Yes, sir," I said. I wasn't sure absconding with a freighter qualified us as pirates, but at least Rex was in a good mood. Things seemed to be going our way for a change. I just had to rationalize a course away from this sector and we'd be home free.

As I'm sure you know, traveling between stars by conventional means requires crossing vast distances, and since it's impossible to travel faster than the speed of light, moving even between two relatively close stars can easily take years. The solution to this problem, rationalized hypergeometry, was found in the late twenty-seventh century. It was actually well known by the twentieth century that Euclidean geometry is arbitrary, being only one possible way of describing the relations of objects in space. There are a theoretically

30

infinite number of other geometries that all employ their own set of rules. The trick is to find a geometry in which the distance you want to traverse is significantly shorter than in Euclidean geometry. Essentially you reverse-engineer an entirely new set of geometric rules based on the trip you want to take, and then employ those rules for the duration of the trip.

If, for example, you wanted to travel from a point near the Xagnon system to the Schufnaasik system (a Euclidean distance of some eighty-six light-years), you would first posit the existence of a geometry in which these two star systems are some more manageable distance from each other – let's say ten million kilometers, or about 1/100,000 of a light year. Starting with this axiom, you build a complete geometric system which is then input into your spaceship's navigational system in place of Euclidean geometry. It generally takes several tries to find a suitable geometry. The navigational system then plots a pathway to your destination using this new geometry. This process is called "rationalizing a hypergeometric course."

The only downside to this process is that it can take up to half an hour to find a suitable geometry and plot a course to your destination. During that time, you're a sitting duck for anyone who is chasing you. I cranked up the engines to full blast so we could at least put some Euclidean space between us and the waystation while I rationalized our course. Lacking firm instructions from Rex, I'd decided to jump into an empty sector nearly a hundred light-years away with the goal of getting as far away from Xagnon as quickly as possible. As the *Flagrante Delicto* was docked with the *Raina Huebner*, it would come along for the ride.

I'd almost finished rationalizing the course when an alarm dinged, informing us that a message was coming in over standard hailing frequencies. I told the ship's computer to patch it through. We heard a gruff voice intone:

"Captain and crew of the *Raina Heuber*. This is Captain Rubric Malgastar of the *Chronic Lumbago* speaking. Prepare to be boarded."

I knew the name. Rubric Malgastar was a legendary pirate who roamed the galaxy in his fearsome ship, the *Chronic Lumbago*. No one who saw him lived to tell about it.

"Blast!" Rex cried. "They've found us. I told you we shouldn't have gone back for the *Flagrante Delicto*."

"Sir," I said, "I don't believe it's the authorities threatening to board us."

"Then who is it?" Rex asked.

A loud clang sounded as something impacted against our hull.

"Unless I'm mistaken, sir," I said, "actual space pirates."

Rex and I watched helplessly as the hatch opened and a crew of black-garbed ruffians streamed onto the bridge of the *Raina Huebner*. Most of them carried lazeguns or some other type of weapon. I noticed a few blackjacks, a couple of clubs, and even one scimitar. These guys were going all out.

Behind them strode a man of tremendous girth in a black outfit trimmed with orange fringe. His head was bald and several large gold earrings dangled from each ear. A robotic parrot perched on his left shoulder.

"Ahoy, mateys," the man growled. "My name is Rubric Malgastar. And who might you be?"

"My name is Rex Nihilo," said Rex. "As the rightful captain of the *Renal Failure*, I demand—"

"*Raina Huebner*," I murmured to Rex.

"*Raina Huebner*?" Rex asked with a frown. "That sounds like some kind of horrible disease." He shrugged and continued, "As I was saying, as the rightful captain of… this ship, I demand that you leave at once, or face the severest penalties of interstellar law."

Malgastar burst into laughter. "Yer in no position to demand anything, my boy. Now I suggest ye round up the rest of yer crew. We're takin' over this ship."

"Right," said Rex. "You heard the man, Sasha. Summon the rest of the crew."

"Sir?"

"Weren't you almost finished summoning the crew when Mr. Malgastar and his friends showed up?"

"Oh," I said, realizing what Rex was up to. "Yes. Yes, I was. Summoning the crew." My programming prevents me from telling lies, but I've found ways around this. Sentence fragments being one of them.

I went back to the nav computer and began tapping keys. Fortunately I'd finished the rationalization in my head while the pirates were boarding; all I had to do is enter the rest of the sequence.

"What is your robot doing?" Malgastar growled.

"Summoning the crew," Rex said. "Like you asked."

"Is she using Morse code? What in Space is taking so long?"

"It's a delicate operation," Rex said. "Some of the crew members are sensitive."

"And why is she using the nav computer?" one of the pirates asked.

"She what?" said Malgastar, who apparently wasn't a particularly hands-on type of pirate. "Get away from that thing!"

But it was too late. I finished the sequence and submitted it. The ship's systems absorbed the new geometric axioms and there was a sickening jolt as the *Raina Huebner* left Euclidean space. "Run!" cried Rex, his voice strangely warped by the temporal-spatial disturbance of the jump. I ran.

It wasn't much of a diversion, but it was the only chance we had: as soon as the pirates realized we were the entire crew, they were undoubtedly going to kill us. I ran for the door of the bridge as lazegun blasts erupted around me. I exited the bridge into the adjoining corridor, with Rex right behind me. By some miracle, neither of us was vaporized.

We sprinted down the hall. A few meters behind us, the pirates burst into the hall as we rounded a corner. Our only hope was to reach the *Flagrante Delicto*. I turned right at a T in the corridor toward the bay where I'd parked our ship. As I did so, three pirates came around the corner ahead of us. So much for our only hope.

"Back!" I cried, turning to go back the way we'd come. Rex spun around and went down the left branch of the T. It was no use, though: we were cornered. The *Raina Huebner* was a good-sized ship, but there was no escape route besides the *Flagrante Delicto*. We could hide, but the pirates would find us eventually. Directly in front of me was the door to the cargo hold. I tapped a button and the door slid open. We ran inside and the door slid closed behind us.

"Lock that door!" Rex cried.

"I don't think it locks from this side," I said.

"Then punch it!"

"Sir?"

"Galactic Vessel Design Code Regulation 2884-b: all self-opening doors must fail in the closed position. Punch the control panel!"

"Sir, my hands are designed for fine motor operations. If I—"

"PUNCH IT!"

I punched the panel. Sparks flew and a jolt of electricity shot through my body. The next thing I knew, I was lying on my back in the cargo hold. I smelled ozone and burnt plastic.

"Ha!" Rex cried. "You did it!"

I heard pounding and yelling through the door. Getting to my feet, I saw that my right hand had fused into a lump of charred metal. I sighed. "You see, sir," I said, holding up my hand. "This is why I—"

But Rex had disappeared.

"Sir?" I said, turning to face the rows of crates in the cargo hold. The hold was the size of a small gymnasium. Rex was trying to get one of the crates open.

"Sasha, get over here!" he yelled.

Still jittery from shorting out the control panel, I walked uneasily toward Rex. "Sir," I said, holding out my arm, "just look what that did to my hand. It's useless!"

"Give me that," Rex said, grabbing my arm. He planted his left foot on my hip and yanked. The joint gave at the elbow and Rex fell to the floor clutching my forearm to his chest. He got to his feet and began pounding on the crate with my fist.

"Sir!" I cried. "My arm!"

"Enough with the dramatics, Sasha," Rex said. "You said yourself you weren't using it." He pounded on the crate three more times. "Eh, this thing is useless," he said, and tossed it aside. I watched wistfully as it clanged on the metal floor and rolled away.

"What are you looking for?" I asked.

Rex pointed at the label on the crate. It read:

LARVITON SMALL ARMS COMPANY

"Any second, those pirates are going to blast through that door," Rex said. "When that happens, I'd prefer to have a weapon in hand."

I stared at him for a moment. "What, no joke about being unarmed?" I said, waggling my stump irritably in his direction.

"I thought it was implied," Rex said. "Help me get this crate open."

Grumbling to myself, I took a step forward. Fortunately, I still had my screwdriver appendage, which was on my left hand. I unscrewed the four screws holding the lid on the crate. Rex pried the lid off and we looked inside.

"Huh," Rex said, perusing the contents. "I guess I should have seen that coming."

The crate was full of small arms.

Rex picked one up and held it up to my shoulder. It reached almost to my elbow. The robots these arms were designed for couldn't be much more than a meter in height.

"I wish I had a cute little robot," Rex said wistfully. "I'd name him Donny." He examined some of the other crates nearby. "Oh, look! A crate of small heads! And another one of legs! Sasha, do you know what this means? We could build Donny!"

"Impossible, sir," I said.

"Why's that?"

"No small feet."

"Blast," Rex groused. A loud boom sounded on the other side of the door, and Rex seemed to suddenly remember we were about to be vaporized by pirates. "Now what?" he asked.

"Surrender?" I suggested.

"And give up all this?" Rex asked, waving the tiny arm at the rows of crates in front of him.

"I don't see any other option, sir."

Rex rubbed his chin. "What we need is leverage. What if we threaten to open that door and dump all the cargo?" He was gesturing toward the massive cargo door that made up most of the far wall.

"Threatening to suck everything in the cargo bay into the infinite vacuum of space would be a great idea," I said, "except that we are in the cargo bay."

"Hmm," Rex said. There was another bang against the door.

"Hold on," I said. "I think I'm having an idea."

"Stop that!" Rex cried. "We don't have time for you to shut down."

But I was pretty sure there was an idea hovering somewhere near my conscious thought processes. "Help me with these arms, sir!" I said. I grabbed a handful of the little arms from the crate and tossed them onto the floor.

"What in Space are you doing?" Rex demanded.

"I'm not sure, sir," I said. "I'm right on the verge of having an idea, but I don't dare think about it too closely." I kept grabbing arms and tossing them to the floor.

"Is it at least a good idea?" Rex asked.

"No way to be sure," I replied, tossing another handful of arms.

Rex hesitated for a moment, then shrugged and began tossing arms to the floor.

"That should do it," I said, when the crate was about half empty.

"Now what?" Rex asked.

"Grab that thousand credit note on the bottom," I said.

Rex stuck his head eagerly into the crate and I gave him a shove. He fell inside and I slammed the lid. While he banged on the lid and cursed at me, I put the screws back in. Then, still doing my best not to give any thought to what I was doing, I grabbed my arm off the floor and ran to the control panel for the cargo door. Just as I reached it, the door we had entered through blew open, crashing to the floor. Pirates rushed into the hold.

"The robot is over there!" one of them shouted. "Shoot her!"

A chunk of wall exploded over my head. I pressed the open button on the control panel, but the door remained closed. A red AIR PRESSURE warning light flashed. Another lazegun blast struck the wall to my right. I studied the control panel frantically, trying to determine if there was a way to override the pressure sensor. There didn't seem to be. As I considered using my remaining hand to punch the panel, I found it difficult to avoid the conclusion that the thing I was trying not to think about was a Very Bad Idea.

Suddenly the control panel exploded in front of me. I turned to run and became aware of air rushing past me. The cargo door was sliding upward.

"Hey!" yelled one of the pirates behind me. "That's a violation of Galactic Vessel Design Code Reg—"

I didn't hear the rest of it because I was sucked out of the cargo door into the vacuum.

CHAPTER SIX

Space is big. Really, really big.

I'd heard the Sp'ossel spiel a hundred times, but you get a new appreciation for the immensity of space when you're in the middle of it with nothing to hold onto but your own severed arm. Space is also ridiculously cold and completely devoid of air, of course, but it was the vastness that bothered me the most. That and the blue-faced pirates floating past, their faces contorted in silent screams.

I shuddered and forced myself to look away. I felt a little bad for them, but they were, after all, space pirates. Death by asphyxiation in the vast reaches of space is the third leading cause of death for space pirates, right after stab wounds and syphilis.

Having no need to breathe and being able to function at temperatures as low as absolute zero, I was in no immediate danger. Rex would be okay until the air in his crate ran out. Unfortunately, at present I had no idea where Rex's crate was and no way of getting to him if I did.

A hundred meters or so in front of me was the *Raina Huebner*. The *Flagrante Delicto* was docked somewhere on the opposite side of it. Above me and to my right, connected to the *Raina Huebner* by an articulated airtight docking corridor, was the pirates' ship, the *Chronic Lumbago*. The *Chronic Lumbago* was a pretty big ship, nearly the size of the *Raina Huebner*. From my current vantage point it looked more dilapidated than fearsome, but maybe it was a matter of perspective. Suspended all around me were the hundreds of crates and other containers that had filled the *Raina Huebner*'s hold. Inside one of them was a very angry Rex Nihilo.

The containers and I were gradually moving away from the hold and from each other. The nearest one was about ten meters below me, but it might as well have been ten light-years. I have no onboard jet propulsion system, probably because I was never intended to operate in freefall. I was fairly certain that just being out here voided my warranty.

I had an idea of how to get to the crate, but I shut down three times while I was trying to come up with it, and meanwhile the crate continued to recede into the blackness. Finally I managed to remain conscious long enough to execute my plan, the key element of which was hurling my arm into the void. Thus disarmed, I craned my head back toward the crate. Thanks to Newton's Third Law, the crate was now growing steadily larger in my vision. I had misjudged the angle a bit, but by stretching my left leg as far as it would go I managed to catch the edge of the crate with my toe. The crate tipped toward me and I caught it with my remaining arm. Once I had a solid grip, I got out my screwdriver and opened the crate. It was packed full of lazepistols. Of course.

I clipped one of them to my hip in case I needed it later and then pushed off from the crate toward another, larger container. Opening it, I found nothing of interest inside. In this way, I bounded from one crate to another for some time. It took me almost an hour to find the one labeled LARVITON SMALL ARMS. I tapped on the outside and then pressed my ear against the crate. After a moment, I heard a rhythmic tapping. It was Morse Code. The message was:

I DON'T THINK THERE'S ANY MONEY IN HERE

I tapped back:

SORRY SIR WILL GET YOU OUT SHORTLY

Before I did that, though, I needed to get the crate back into a pressurized atmosphere. Reentering the *Raina Huebner* seemed ill-advised; although we'd cleared out the cargo hold, the rest of the ship was still crawling with pirates. The *Flagrante Delicto*, on the other side of the *Raina Huebner*, was going to be difficult to reach. Our best chance was probably to try to get aboard the *Chronic Lumbago*. The pirates would undoubtedly assume we were dead and in any case they would be very unlikely to expect us to board their own ship. With any luck, most of the pirates were still aboard the *Raina Huebner.*

The question was how to get Rex's crate to the pirate ship. What I really needed was some means of propulsion. I jumped from crate to crate again for a bit, finally finding one full of aerosol room fresheners. With my back against the crate, I emptied can after can of the stuff into the void, occasionally glancing over my shoulder to make sure I was still heading the right direction. It's a good thing there's no air in space, because that whole quadrant would have smelled like potpourri for a week.

It took forty-eight cans, but I managed to maneuver the crate so Rex was in between me and the *Chronic Lumbago.* Fifty-six cans later, we were moving slowly toward the bottom of the ship. I had a vague notion that I would cut through the ship's hull with the lazegun and somehow drag Rex to an airlock before he asphyxiated or froze to death.

I was still working out the details of this plan when I became aware of a gigantic robotic arm moving toward us. Not knowing what else to do, I clutched tightly to the crate. Like a coin-operated crane plucking a stuffed animal out of a glass cage, the giant robotic hand closed on the crate, nearly crushing me in the process. It knocked the lazepistol off my hip, and I watched helplessly as the gun drifted away in the void. The crane pulled us toward the hull of the *Chronic Lumbago.* Turning my head, I saw a panel slide open on the bottom of the ship. The hand inserted the crate into the opening, depositing us gently on the floor of what appeared to be another cargo hold. The hand disappeared back through the opening and the panel slid shut.

My sensors told me that I was in a fully pressurized environment. Evidently the opening had a repulsion barrier that kept the air inside the hold. "Hold on, sir," I said, as I started extracting the screws. "I'll have you out of there presently." There was no response; I could only hope that Rex was merely unconscious and not dead.

I'd just removed the third screw when two burly arms wrapped around me from behind, lifting me clear off the crate.

"Lookit I won!" yelled a loud, deep voice in my ear. "A friend!"

"Ergh," I managed to say.

The arms released me and I crashed to the floor. Rolling onto my back, I saw the largest human being I'd ever seen. In fact, I'm not entirely certain he was human. He had all the superficial characteristics of a person, but the features were all out of proportion. He had a brow like a fireplace mantel and a nose like a sack of golf balls. He wore a stark white sailor's outfit, complete down to the funny hat and navy blue sash around his neck. He had to be eight feet tall.

"What did you say, friend?" the man asked, his massive brow contorting with what appeared to be genuine concern.

"Uh," I replied. "Who are you?"

"I'm Ensign Boggs," said the huge man. "What is your name, new friend?"

"I'm Sasha," I replied. "Are you… a pirate?"

Ensign Boggs thought for a moment. "I don't think so," he said. "I just run the crane. I hardly ever get to use it, but today I won a friend! And do you know who that friend was, Sasha?"

"If I'm not mistaken," I began, getting to my feet, "that friend would be—"

"It's you!" Bogg cried. "You are that friend!" He looked at me expectantly.

"So I had gathered," I replied. "Say, Boggs, how would you like another friend?"

"ANOTHER FRIEND!" Boggs gasped, almost reeling at the possibility.

"That's right," I said. "There's another potential friend inside this crate. But I have to get him out before he asphyxiates."

"HOLD ON, POTENTIAL FRIEND!" Boggs shouted. He reached down and tore off the lid of the crate. Rex lay motionless inside. "POTENTIAL FRIEND!" Ensign Boggs shouted. "WAKE UP!"

Rex sat up with a start, gasping for air. He took one look at Ensign Boggs and screamed. Boggs took a step back, a hurt look on his face.

"Easy, sir," I said. "This is Ensign Boggs. He's a friend."

Boggs nodded. "I'm Ensign Boggs. What's your name, Potential Friend?"

"My name," said Rex, "is Rex Ni—"

"OH MY GOODNESS!" Ensign Boggs cried. "Look at all the little arms!" He reached down and grabbed a handful of the robot arms. "Potential Friend, did you know your house is full of little arms?"

Rex scowled. "It's not my house," he said, climbing out of the crate.

Boggs seemed confused. "Then the little arms live there alone?"

"Forget the arms!" Rex snapped. "Are there any more pirates left aboard this ship?"

"Probably," said Ensign Boggs. "This is a pirate ship."

Rex sighed. "Can you tell us where they are?"

"I can show you," Boggs replied, but he didn't move. He was fascinated by the crate full of little arms.

"Now is good for us," Rex said.

"Boggs?" I said.

"Do I have to leave the little arms?"

"I'm afraid so," I said. "You can come back later, after you show us around the ship."

Ensign Boggs nodded sadly and reluctantly put the handful of arms back in the crate. Then he retrieved the lid and placed it carefully back on the crate.

"Boggs," Rex said. "The pirates…?"

But Boggs continued to stare at the crate somberly. "Give him a moment, sir," I said.

"A moment for what?" Rex asked.

"A farewell to arms, sir."

CHAPTER SEVEN

A quick survey of the ship revealed it to be empty. All the pirates—except those who had been sucked out of the cargo hold—were apparently aboard the *Raina Huebner*. I couldn't blame them; The *Raina Huebner* was larger and in better condition than the *Chronic Lumbago*.

"This place is a dump," Rex observed from the *Chronic Lumbago*'s bridge. The bridge was dark, cramped, and had a pungent, musty odor. The ceiling was so low that Boggs had to crouch to fit under it. To my left, water dripped from a pipe onto the metal floor.

"Yes, sir," I said. "Shall I retract the docking corridor?"

"What?" asked Rex. "Why?"

"Because of the pirates, sir. I would expect them to return from the *Raina Huebner* shortly."

"Why would they do that?" asked Rex, glancing at the rusted walls distastefully. "I wouldn't."

He had a point. If the pirates had any sense, they'd ditch the *Chronic Lumbago* and use the *Raina Huebner* as their new ship.

"*Regal Beagle* isn't a very good name for a pirate ship, though," Rex observed.

"*Raina Huebner*," I said. "I suspect they'll simply change the call signs. The *Raina Huebner* will be renamed to the *Chronic Lumbago*. That way, Rubric Malgastar can maintain the legend of his fearsome ship."

"Can they do that?" Rex asked dubiously. "It seems like cheating."

"They're pirates, sir. They're not really known for toeing the line on such matters."

"But don't they have to paint the new name on the ship? And smash a bottle of champagne or something?"

"No, sir," I said. "It's simply a matter of updating the transponder settings on the bridge. Technically, they're required to register the change with the Malarchian Registry of Space Vessels, but as I've noted, pirates tend not to trouble themselves with such formalities."

"Sasha and Potential Friend!" Ensign Boggs boomed from behind us. He had been so quiet that I'd momentarily forgot he was behind us. When he spoke, Rex and I both jumped.

"What is it, Boggs?" I asked.

"Can I go back and try to win more friends now?"

"Sure, Boggs," I said. "Go nuts."

"I will do that," said Boggs. "I will go nuts winning more friends." He turned and stomped away down the corridor.

"What's up with that guy?" Rex asked, watching Boggs trudge away.

"I believe that's the uniform of the Caligarian Navy he's wearing," I said. "The *Chronic Lumbago* is a Pisces-class freighter. The Caligarian Republic used to use those to ship food to their colonies."

"But the Caligarian Republic was dismantled by the Malarchy sixteen years ago," Rex replied. "Are you saying…?"

"I think Ensign Boggs came with the ship. Maybe the *Chronic Lumbago*—or whatever it was called at that point—was commandeered by pirates, or maybe the pirates came into possession of it at some point after the Republic collapsed. But somehow Boggs never got the word. And for whatever reason, the pirates decided to keep him around."

"Well, he seems harmless enough," said Rex. He turned back to face the viewport. The *Raina Huebner* hung in space directly in front of us. "Sasha, I think it's time we cut our losses on this operation."

"You mean let the pirates have the *Raina Huebner* and keep the *Chronic Lumbago* for ourselves?"

"What? No, I'm not holding onto this lousy ship. It's not even worth the trouble to sell it. We need to get the *Flagrante Delicto* back."

"I don't see how that's possible, sir. It's docked with the *Raina Huebner*, which has been commandeered by the pirates. We'd have to go through the *Raina Huebner*, past the pirates, to get to the *Flagrante Delicto*."

"Well, I can't stay on this ship. The whole place smells like feet."

At that moment, a voice crackled over the ship's comm:

"Captain and crew of the *Chronic Lumbago*, this is Heinous Vlaak of

44

the Malarchian Naval Battleship *Carpathian Winter.* Return to your ship and retract your docking corridor immediately or be fired upon." The transmission was coming over standard hailing frequencies. Glancing at the tactical display on the control panel, I saw that a Malarchian battleship was indeed approaching.

"Heinous Vlaak!" Rex cried. "What is he doing here?"

"Enforcing anti-piracy laws, I would assume," I said. It was somewhat unusual for the Malarchian Navy to bother with protecting private freighters from pirates; the Malarchy expended most of its efforts repressing civilian populations, snuffing out rebellions, and occasionally blowing up troublesome planets. Every once in a while, though, they'd make a show of blasting a pirate ship out of the sky just to remind people that they could. More surprising was that Heinous Vlaak, the Malarchian Primate's chief enforcer, was on board. The Malarchy usually reserved Vlaak's talents for more vital tasks than routing pirates, but I wouldn't be surprised if he'd been demoted after our last encounter. Vlaak had been responsible for the destruction of much of the Malarchian fleet at the Battle of the Moon of Akdar. There was no love lost between him and Rex; hopefully his appearance was only a coincidence.

"Tell him the pirates are on the *Raina Huebner!*" Rex yelled. "Otherwise he's going to blow us to pieces!" He was right. Whatever weapons the *Chronic Lumbago* had, it was no match for a Malarchian battleship.

"But sir," I said, "technically we're pirates as well. We stole the *Raina Huebner.*"

"Vlaak doesn't need to know that," Rex snapped. "Tell him!"

I located the ship's transmitter, set the frequency and grabbed the microphone. "Hi," I said. "This is, um, Sasha. Please don't shoot us. The pirates boarded our ship. That is, the ship we were on. Technically we—"

"Don't tell him your name!" Rex snapped, grabbing the mic out of my hand. "This is Captain Vance Truename of the *Raining Tubers*—"

"*Raina Huebner,* sir."

"Right, Captain Vince Rightworthy of the—"

A gruff voice broke in: "This is Captain... yeaargh... Rusty McShipperson of the *Raina Huebner.* Don't ye listen to that scurvy dog's lies. I am the rightful captain of this here vessel, and I demand that ye blast that vile pirate ship to smithereens! Shut up, I'm talking!" This last seemed to be directed at a member of the Malgastar's crew, who was trying to interrupt to tell him something.

"He's lying!" Rex yelled. "He's the pirate! I, Vaughn Truthnugget, am the captain of the *Rival Humor*, and I demand—"

"This is your second warning," said Heinous Vlaak's voice. "You won't get a third. Return to your ship and retract your docking corridor."

"Quick, Sasha!" Rex cried, putting down the mic. "Retract the corridor!"

I frantically scanned the ship's controls, trying to find the ones that controlled the docking corridor. The *Chronic Lumbago*'s controls seemed to be arranged at random, and the ship was so old and ill-maintained that most of the labels had been worn off. I picked what seemed to be the most likely option and pressed a button. I heard what sounded like the hum of a motor and breathed a sigh of relief. This sound was quickly followed, however, by the roar of rockets.

"What is that?" Rex asked.

I frowned. "I'd estimate a fifty-eight percent chance that I accidentally launched torpedoes at the *Raina Huebner*, sir."

Several explosions detonated on the hull of the *Raina Huebner*, filling the bridge with blinding white light.

"I'd like to update my previous estimate," I said.

"You've doomed us, Sasha!" Rex cried. "The Malarchy is going to think we're attacking the *Raina Huebner!*"

"A reasonable deduction," I said. "I'm sorry, sir. I did my best."

The good news is that on the second try, I did find the docking corridor control. As it slowly retracted, several more explosions lit up the *Raina Huebner*.

"Stop firing, Sasha! We can't take on the pirates and a Malarchian battleship!"

"That isn't me, sir. We've exhausted our torpedoes. The *Carpathian Winter* seems to be firing on the *Raina Huebner*."

We watched as the *Raina Huebner* came apart in a blast of fire. Over the speakers we heard pirates screaming incomprehensibly. The screaming soon faded to static.

"Huh," said Rex, furrowing his brow at the disintegrating freighter. "Why'd the Malarchians do that?"

It took me a few seconds to figure it out. "Call signs," I said, tapping a display in front of me. It showed graphical representations of four vessels. The disintegrating ship was labeled *Chronic Lumbago*.

"They'd already switched them," Rex said.

"Yes, sir," I said. "Malgastar was apparently unaware that one of his underlings had already made the change."

"He accidentally fooled the Malarchy into destroying his own ship," Rex cackled. "What a maroon."

I watched as the *Chronic Lumbago* label winked out. Half a second later, the label for the *Flagrante Delicto* vanished as well. I don't think Rex saw it, but he had to know. There was no way the *Flagrante Delicto* could have survived that explosion.

"Yes, sir," I said. "It would seem that Captain Malgastar's lack of attention to detail was his undoing. Welcome back to the *Raina Huebner*, sir."

"Thrilled to be here," said Rex, without enthusiasm.

"This ship is growing on you then?"

"There's definitely something growing in here," Rex agreed, staring at a gooey patch of something in the corner behind him.

"Have a nice day, folks," said Heinous Vlaak's voice over the speakers. "Watch out for pirates." We watched the *Carpathian Winter* vanish from the display as it left Euclidean space. Another successful operation for the vaunted Malarchian Navy.

"If it makes you feel better, sir," I said, "now that the *Flagrante Delicto* has been destroyed, there's nothing preventing us from christening this ship with that name."

Rex shook his head. "I would never sully that name by associating it with this flying fungus factory," he said. "No, I'm afraid there was only one *Flagrante Delicto*, and now it's just a scattered cloud of debris, floating amongst the flotsam and jetsam of the erstwhile *Raina Huebner*. Sasha, I suggest we observe a moment of silence while we reflect on the adventures, hijinks, and shenanigans made possible by that beloved and never-to-be-replicated ship, the—"

"Sir, Look!" I exclaimed, pointing to the display. The *Flagrante Delicto* had reappeared, and was currently hurtling away from the wreckage.

"The pirates made off with our ship!" Rex exclaimed.

"So it would appear, sir," I said. "They must have gotten away before the Malarchians began firing. Our sensors must have momentarily lost track of the *Flagrante Delicto* with all the rubbish floating about."

"Well, don't just stand there. Go after it, Sasha!"

"I'll do what I can, sir." I redirected all power to the thrusters, and we slowly began to gain on the *Flagrante Delicto*. I wasn't sure what Rex planned to do when we caught up with it; short of firing on our own ship, there wasn't much we could do to get the pirates to give our ship back. As it happened, the matter never came up: the pirates must have been working on rationalizing a hypergeometrical course to another part of the galaxy, because presently the ship once again disappeared.

"Blast it, Sasha!" Rex growled. "You were too slow. Now we're stuck in this rattletrap with Navyman Bob."

"Yes, sir," I said. "I'm sorry, sir."

"Ugh," Rex said. "I'm going to go see if this ship has any decent places to sulk."

"Good idea, sir. What should I do in the meantime?"

"What do I care?" Rex said. "We're pirates now. Do pirate stuff."

"Yes, sir," I said.

"Aye, Sasha."

"Sir?"

"Pirates say 'aye,' not 'yes.'"

"Yes, sir," I said. "Aye, sir. Yes, I know, sir. Aye."

Still grumbling to himself, Rex stomped away down the corridor.

CHAPTER EIGHT

*P*irate *stuff,* I thought to myself. I wasn't entirely certain what that meant—nor did I particularly want to find out. When a job goes bad, Rex often lapses into funks like this, and it's up to me to try to shake him out of it. I usually fail. The good news is that Rex lacks the attention span for a prolonged depression. The bad news is that what ultimately snaps him out of it is usually some sort of monumentally terrible idea for making a quick fortune.

Although Rex had no love for our new ship, he seemed enamored with the idea of playing at being space pirates, so it was up to me to come up with some "pirate stuff" to occupy us before he decided to ram a cruise ship or something equally ill-advised. I decided to do a search of the ship's nav computer to determine what the pirates had been up to. Fortunately, thanks to Rubric Malgastar's lack of attention to detail, the pirates had left the computer unsecured. I found a complete log of all the hypergeometric jumps the *Chronic Lumbago* had taken. Most of these didn't tell me anything, but one destination in particular jumped out at me, because it was in the middle of an uncharted area of the galaxy called Dead Man's Nebula. Dead Man's Nebula was a roughly oval-shaped area of space about seventeen light-years in length. As far as I knew, nobody had ever ventured more than a few thousand klicks into it. Jumping into the middle of it was insane.

One of the other problems with traveling by rationalized hypergeometry is that when you're dealing with alternate geometries, even tiny bits of matter floating around your target destination can cause very big problems. A speck of dust a hundredth the size of a grain of sand can blow a basketball-sized hole in your hull. Although Dead Man's Nebula is 99.9999% empty space, by cosmological standards it's chock full of such specks. If you were to jump into any random section of the nebula, there's a good chance your ship would be torn to pieces. And yet, judging from the ship's nav log, the *Chronic Lumbago* had made the jump dozens of times.

While I was trying to figure out how this was possible, I heard a sort of metallic skittering sound behind me. I spun around to find myself alone on the bridge.

"Sir?" I said.

There was no response.

I walked down the corridor a few meters, then stopped to listen again. After a few seconds, I heard the metallic skittering again. It seemed to be coming from a corridor to my right. I made my way down the hall. Several overhead light panels had gone out here, so the corridor was mostly dark. The only panel still working flickered badly, giving the dank corridor a decidedly eerie feeling. I tiptoed hesitantly into the darkness.

"Sir?" I said again. Still there was no response. "Ensign Boggs?"

I walked several more paces. Ahead of me a few meters, the corridor turned sharply to the left. As I craned my neck to the right to try to see, something about the size of a greyhound darted around the corner, crashing into the wall to my right. It lunged at me. I turned and ran, but made it only a few steps before the thing landed on my back, knocking me to the floor. The thing rolled off me, landing on the floor in front of me. I looked up to see a vaguely humanoid face regarding me curiously. I screamed.

"Bad friend!" I heard Boggs's voice from behind me yell. "Why did you do that?"

"Do what?" I asked, backing away from the thing slowly. It looked like a robot dog, but with a humanoid head. It was unsettling, to say the least.

"Not you, Sasha," Boggs said. "I was talking to my new friend. I made him from parts that I won."

"Parts that you…" I started, staring at the thing in shock and disgust. Its midsection was from a humanoid robot. In place of legs it had small robot arms with hands serving as feet. Its robot head was perched on an oddly angled and weirdly elongated neck which, I realized after a moment, was also an arm. Boggs had built a robot with arms for all the appendages. It was horrifying.

While the thing continued to watch me, I got cautiously to my feet.

"Holy Space!" Rex cried, from the direction of the bridge. "It's Donny!"

The thing turned its head toward Rex. "I am Donny?" it said.

"Of course you're Donny," said Rex, approaching the abomination. "Who else would you be?"

"I am Donny," the thing said, apparently satisfied.

"Why did you name it, sir?" I said. "It's horrible. That thing should be destroyed."

The thing looked at me and frowned.

"Don't be jealous, Sasha," Rex said. "Donny isn't going to replace you, even if he does have four times as many arms as you."

"Five," said Boggs proudly. "His neck is an arm."

"So it is!" Rex exclaimed. "That's a game changer. Forget what I said earlier about not replacing you, Sasha."

"Very funny, sir."

Donny brushed up against Rex's leg, and Rex patted him on the head. "Good boy, Donny," Rex cooed. I noticed now that Rex was wearing a black patch over his left eye.

"What happened to your eye, sir?" I asked.

"I put a patch on it," Rex said. "Pretty cool, huh? I found it while I was looking for a place to sulk."

"I see that, sir. I was asking why you were wearing it."

"I just said it was cool, didn't I?"

"Yes, sir."

"This is really good work, Ensign Boggs," Rex said, scratching the robot-thing's head. "Do you think you could do anything for Sasha's arm?"

"Sure I could, Potential Friend," said Boggs. "I've fixed up lots of pirates who lost limbs."

"Really?" I asked hopefully. "But we only have these tiny little robot arms."

"Oh, that's okay," said Boggs. "I've fixed up pirates with a lot less."

"You think you can make me a regular-sized arm with the parts you have?"

"You bet, Sasha. No problem."

I regarded Donny again. I had to admit, horrifying though the creature was, it was impressive work. I wasn't sure I could have done it even if I had both of my arms.

"You'll have to shut down before I can work on you," said Boggs.

I raised an eyebrow at him.

"Just do it, you big chicken," Rex said. "You're not much use to me with one arm."

"I saved your life," I said.

"And then you nearly got us all killed."

"Not because I only have one arm."

"Maybe not. There's no way to know for sure, though, is there?"

I sighed. "Fine. Fix my arm. Let's go find a place where you can work. And keep that thing away from me." Donny and I regarded each other circumspectly as I passed him in the corridor.

We found a relatively clean, well-lit room where Boggs could work on my arm. Boggs left, returning after a moment with a toolbox and an armful of spare parts.

"You should shut down now," Boggs said. "I don't want to short anything out."

I regarded him skeptically.

Rex, who was standing in the doorway, said, "I'll be watching the whole time, Sasha. Everything will be fine. You do want a new arm, don't you?"

"Yes, sir," I said.

"Good," said Rex. "Then shut down. I'll monitor the whole process."

I nodded. "All right," I said, and shut down.

An indeterminate amount of time later, I awakened to see Rex and Boggs grinning at me.

"Good morning!" Rex cried.

"Good morning," I said. "Did you—WHAT HAVE YOU DONE TO MY ARM?"

"It's a hook!" Boggs exclaimed. "Potential Friend said you would like it better than a regular arm."

I glared at Rex. "You said you were going to supervise!"

"I did," Rex replied. "Supervising means you have to make the hard choices. Boggs was just going to give you a lame regular arm. Now you have a hook, just like a real pirate!"

"I don't want to be a real pirate! I want my arm back!"

"Look, if I have to wear this eye patch, you have to have a hook arm."

"You don't have to wear the patch! You put it on because it looks cool!"

"It does, doesn't it?" Rex said with a grin. "Do you like it better on the left or the right? I can't decide."

I groaned. "Sir, you're voluntarily wearing an eye patch because you think it's cool. I've been given a hook for an arm against my will. Do you honestly not see the difference?"

Rex shrugged. "Not with this eye," he said. "Let me try the other one."

I shook my head. I supposed I should be grateful that so far Rex's pirate fetish had only cost me an arm. Maybe he would tire of the idea now.

"So," Rex said, "what sorts of swashbuckling derring-do adventures have you come up with, Sasha?"

"I haven't had a lot of time, sir," I said. "In any case, perhaps you should consider that we aren't cut out to be pirates."

"Nonsense, Sasha. We were born to be pirates."

"I wasn't born at all, sir."

"No, but you have a hook for an arm, so it's hard to take you seriously as an anti-piracy advocate. Now are you going to come up with some swashbuckling adventures or am I going to just have to ram a cruise ship?"

"No, sir. I mean, yes, sir, I've come up with something."

"Aye," said Rex.

"Yes, sir. Aye, sir. I've come up with something, sir."

"Well?" Rex asked impatiently.

"I've gone through the ship's nav logs," I said. "I thought it would be helpful to determine where the pirates have gone in the past.

"Brilliant, Sasha! If we know where the pirates have gone, we could find the *Flagrante Delicto*!"

"Aye, sir," I said. "I suppose so." The thought had occurred to me, but I'd suppressed it. I had a bad feeling I knew exactly where Rex's search for the *Flagrante Delicto* would take us, and I'd vainly hoped I could entertain him with some sort of harmless pirate roleplaying until he tired of the idea and forgot all about the *Flagrante Delicto*. Clearly that wasn't going to happen. "But I was thinking, sir," I said, "What if we sold this ship and used the proceeds to engage in some sort of grift? You used to love grift."

"Those days are over, Sasha," Rex said. "We're pirates now. Now what did you find in the nav logs?"

"Oh, lots of stuff," I said. "The *Chronic Lumbago* has been all over the galaxy. The Ragulian Sector, the Perseus Arm, Dead Man's Nebula, the Orion Hub, the—"

"Hold on," said Rex. "Did you say Dead Man's Nebula? I didn't know you could even go there."

"Nor did I, sir. Traveling there would be extremely dangerous and ill-advised. The nav log indicates the *Chronic Lumbago* has been there several times, but I suspect it may have been manipulated to hide their true destination."

"Captain Malgastar didn't strike me as being that clever," Rex said. "And these pirates must have a hideout, right? Isn't that how pirates work?"

"That's the rumor, sir. Supposedly the pirates have a hidden lair to which they can retreat to evade the authorities. It would explain why the Malarchy has been unable to snuff them out."

"A secret pirate lair in the middle of Dead Man's Nebula," Rex said. "Fantastic. Sasha, rationalize a course there immediately."

"Have you been listening, sir? Making a hypergeometric jump into uncharted space is suicidal. We could fly right through a star or bounce too close to a supernova. That would end our trip rather quickly."

"We wouldn't be real pirates if we didn't take a few risks," Rex said.

"What if we just stuck to stealing intellectual property?" I suggested. "Ripping off movies, that sort of thing?"

"Stop stalling and make the jump, Sasha."

I spent another twenty minutes trying to talk Rex out of jumping into Dead Man's Nebula, but it was no use. He was determined to get the *Flagrante Delicto* back, even if it took killing us all to do it. I even tried to recruit Boggs to talk some sense into him, which went about as well as you would suspect. Boggs broke down crying and ran back down to the cargo hold. Thankfully he took Donny with him.

Finally I gave up. I rationalized a course for the coordinates specified in the log and made the jump.

CHAPTER NINE

Fortunately we didn't die the instant we re-emerged in Euclidean space inside Dead Man's Nebula. We did, however, find ourselves on a collision course with our own ship.

The dirty little secret of hypergeometric travel is that there's nothing preventing one vessel from re-emerging into Euclidean space directly on top of—or even inside—another vessel. Nothing except the sheer vastness of space and the laws of probability, anyway. Not to sound like a Sp'ossel here, but space is just so damned big that even if two ships travel to the exact same star system at exactly the same time, the odds of one of them hitting the other are astronomically low. In fact, even after millions of recorded jumps, no ship has ever jumped into space occupied by another vessel, and there have only been a handful of collisions.

So it was rather surprising to find ourselves suddenly bearing down on a ship that looked very much like the *Flagrante Delicto* but which the onboard nav system insisted was the *Chronic Lumbago*. The ship appeared to be in orbit around a small, greenish-brown planet.

"Pull up!" Rex shouted. "Pull up!"

"I'm working on it, sir!" I replied, desperately trying to maneuver our awkward and underpowered ship to avoid a collision. We missed it by centimeters.

"Whew, that was close," said Rex, as we shot past the vessel. "Alright, come around and hail them."

"Aye, sir," I said. I flipped the ship on its axis and fired the jets until we were slowly approaching the other vessel.

"Wait," Rex said, studying the display, "why does that say the *Flagrante Delicto* is the *Chronic Lumbago*?"

"Rubric Malgastar must have escaped the *Raina Huebner* to the

Flagrante Delicto and then changed the call signs again."

"The *Chronic Lumbago*, you mean."

"Right, he changed it to the *Chronic Lumbago*."

"No, you said he left the *Raina Huebner* for the *Flagrante Delicto*. But the *Raina Huebner* was the *Chronic Lumbago* at that point. We're on the *Raina Huebner*."

"Aye, sir," I said. "I was mistaken. The key point is that the erstwhile *Flagrante Delicto* is now the *Chronic Lumbago*. Whatever ship Rubric Malgastar is on seems to be the *Chronic Lumbago*."

"That bastard," Rex said. "He has no right to sully the *Flagrante Delicto* with that name. Hail him and demand that he change the name back."

"Aye, sir," I said. I fired our retrorockets as we neared the *Chronic Lumbago*, slowing our approach and matching its orbit over the moon. I picked up the mic and set it for standard hailing frequency. "Hello, crew of the *Chronic Lumbago*. This is Sasha. I'm the first mate of the… well, it's kind of a funny story, actually…"

"Give me that!" Rex snapped, grabbing the mic from my hand. "This is Rex Nihilo, rightful captain of the *Flagrante Delicto*. I'm speaking to the individuals who have illegally absconded with my ship. Get off it or we'll blast you to atoms." He took his finger off the button. "We can do that, right?"

"It's possible, sir," I said. "I'd just have to keep hitting buttons to find out."

But no response came from the other ship.

Rex tried again, but still there was no answer.

"Deploy the docking corridor," Rex said. "We're going to board them."

"Aye, sir," I said. This seemed like a bad idea to me, but it was among the better of the bad ideas that Rex might suggest at the current moment, so I decided not to protest. I maneuvered the *Raina Huebner* into place and deployed the docking corridor. I waited until the corridor was pressurized and then opened the hatch.

"All right, crew," said Rex. "We're boarding the *Flagrante Delicto*. Boggs, you go first."

"We're boarding the *Chronic Lumbago*, sir," I said.

"Whatever," Rex replied.

"Me?" said Boggs. "I never leave the ship."

"Donny goes?" said Donny. I jumped as he spoke. I'd figured

Donny was still lurking on one of the other decks.

"You're too valuable to send on a boarding mission, Donny," Rex said. "You're a marvel of modern science. Meanwhile, Boggs is incredibly large and presumably known to the pirates. They might think twice before blasting him."

I couldn't argue with this logic, particularly since none of us was armed.

Boggs nodded. "Stay here, Donny. I will go. Pirates are not friends, but they will probably not shoot me." He strode into the corridor while the rest of us remained behind. When he reached the hatch, I shouted the combination to him. He punched it into the pad and tried to open the hatch. It wouldn't budge.

"There may be a slight pressure differential," I said. "Try pulling harder."

Boggs grunted and tried again, planting both of his feet against the hull and pulling with all his might.

"Um," I said. "Maybe we shouldn't—"

But just then the hatch flew open, accompanied by a loud sucking sound. A blast of wind blew me into the corridor. Rex and Donny tumbled on top of me, and loose papers fluttered down the corridor like agitated birds. After a few seconds, the breeze died down as the pressure equalized. We got to our feet.

"What in Space was that?" Rex asked.

"Pressure differential," I said. "It would seem the *Flagrante Delicto*—that is, the *Chronic Lumbago*—lost a fair amount of its atmosphere."

"Well, that sucks," said Rex.

"Aye, sir."

As Boggs peered through the hatch, I made my way down the corridor. Rex and Donny followed.

"So the *Flagrante Delicto* is still leaking air," said Rex. "I thought we fixed that. Remind me, Sasha. Who was supposed to take care of that?"

"No, sir. I, sir. You assigned me to fix it, but then you decided to steal the *Raina Huebner*, so I never had a chance."

"Don't blame your negligence on me, bolt-brain. Let's go find those pirates."

As we neared the bridge, I heard a voice gasping weakly, "No air... can't breathe... if anybody can hear..." This was followed by a loud squawk and then a prolonged choking sound, like someone gasping for breath. After a moment, the voice went on, "That's a good girl. Have another battery. No air... can't breathe..."

We emerged onto the bridge to see six pirates, including Rubric Malgastar, lying in various contorted positions on the floor. Their faces were a bluish-white and several of them had their hands on their throats. Standing on Malgastar's chest was the robotic parrot.

"Can't breathe..." the parrot said, cocking its head at us. "That's a good boy."

"Look at that," Rex said, lifting his eye patch to take in the scene. "I killed six men without firing a shot. And got my ship back. Am I a great pirate or what?"

I didn't reply. Donny stalked about the bridge on his creepy arm-legs, inspecting the dead men. Boggs looked like he was going to vomit.

"Can't breathe," the parrot announced. "No air."

"That's okay, girl," Rex said. "You're safe now." He crouched over Malgastar's body and held out his left arm. After a moment, the parrot hopped on his wrist, climbed up his arm, and settled on his shoulder. "No air," the parrot said again. "That's a good boy."

"I've always wanted a robot friend," said Rex, smiling at the parrot.

I sighed heavily. Rex didn't seem to notice. "What should I name him, Sasha? It should be something cool and piratey and not lame."

"How about Caliban?" I said.

"No," Rex replied.

"Bathazar?" I said.

"No," Rex replied.

"Orlando," I said.

"No."

"Cromwell."

"No."

"Marcellus."

"No."

"Cuthbert."

"No."

"Agrippa."

"No."

"Cervantes."

"No."

"Iago."

"No."

"I give up sir," I said. "Maybe you weren't meant to have a—"

"Squawky!" Rex announced. "That's it! I'll call you Squawky!"

I groaned.

"Steve," squawked the parrot.

"Isn't Squawky adorable?" Rex said. "He just repeats words with no sense of their meaning."

"Seriously, my name is Steve," squawked the parrot.

"Ha!" Rex cried. "He accidentally made a sentence!"

"Please," said the parrot. "Call me Steve. Or Cuthbert. Or Cheetah. Honestly, anything but Squawky."

"Delightful," Rex said. "Squawky, you're the best robot pal a guy could have, even if you do jabber a lot of nonsense."

"Best robot pal," repeated the parrot, apparently mollified.

Rex turned to me. "Sasha and Boggs, drag these pirates back to the *Chronic Lumbago*."

"You mean the *Raina Huebner*," I replied.

"Not anymore. I'm reclaiming this ship as the *Flagrante Delicto*."

"I'm not sure that has any effect on the *Raina Huebner*," I replied. "In any case, this ship isn't safe. There's an air leak."

"I can fix an air leak," Boggs said.

"Like you fixed my arm?" I asked.

"You can't fix an air leak with a hook, Sasha," Boggs answered.

"You see, Sasha?" Rex said. "I'm a natural born pirate. I've assembled a hearty pirate crew without even trying. We all have our own unique talents. As captain, I will ponder our next move while you drag these bodies back to their ship, Squawky entertains me with his jabbering, Boggs repairs the leak, and Donny... uh..."

"Donny has a talent?" Donny asked, hopefully.

"Of course Donny has a talent!" Rex cried. "Don't you ever doubt yourself, Donny. You were created with a purpose in mind, and that purpose was..." Rex looked to Boggs, who seemed as surprised as anyone by this news. "...to believe in yourself!" Rex said.

"Donny's purpose is to believe in Donny?"

"Well, nobody is going to do it," said Rex. "You see? You're indispensable."

"Donny believes in Donny!" Donny exclaimed, as if having an epiphany.

"Then it's settled," Rex said. "You have your orders. Hop to it!"

I spent the next ten minutes dragging pirates through the docking corridor. I had to admit that, misgivings aside, having a hook for an arm sure makes it easy to drag corpses.

By the time I'd finished, Rex was asleep in his bunk. I was loath to wake him, but I didn't want to hang out in Dead Man's Nebula any longer than we had to. If the green-brown planet below really was the location of a pirate lair, it was very likely there were other pirates around, and eventually they'd detect our presence. We'd already lost our ship to pirates once; I'd prefer not to do it again. Rex, of course, had other ideas.

"We can't leave yet," he said, jumping out of bed. The robotic parrot, which had remained on his shoulder while he slept, fluttered its metal wings to keep its footing. "We haven't found the secret pirate lair yet!"

"Why would we want to find it, sir? Pirates have given us nothing but trouble."

"But now we *are* pirates, Sasha! We're part of a proud fraternity of corsairs, freebooters and privateers. If we find the pirate lair, we can sing space chanties with our fellow pirates and drink Atavarian rum until we vomit into our shoes!"

"You're not really selling the idea, sir."

"Also, the pirates might know the location of Planet Z."

"Planet Z, sir?"

"Come on, Sasha. Planet Z. The treasure planet."

"I'm unaware of the existence of any treasure planet, sir. It's not on any of the official charts."

"Well, neither is the pirate haven planet we're orbiting, dongle-brain. That's why they're secret."

"Why wouldn't the pirates just hide their treasure on the pirate haven planet?"

Rex sighed in exasperation. "You can't hide your treasure at a pirate haven. That's the first place people would look."

"So your contention is that there is a secret planet that all the pirates have decided to use for hiding treasure?"

"Not all of them. Just the ones in the know."

"And you hope to go to this planet and just start gathering up treasure?"

"Of course not. We'll need a shovel."

"Ah, so it's buried treasure, is it?"

"Yes, it's buried, Sasha. Don't you know anything about pirates?

60

They raid ships, steal booty, and then bury the booty, at which point it becomes treasure. This is basic pirate stuff."

"But even if we find Planet Z, how will we know where the treasure is buried?"

"That's the great thing about a treasure planet. By this point, there's probably so much treasure buried there that we can just start digging at random and find some of it."

"I see. But if the treasure is so easy to find, why do they keep burying it?"

Rex sighed again. "It's easy to find treasure, *in general*, on a treasure planet. It's hard to find any *particular* cache of treasure. So pirates keep burying treasure there even though the treasure is easy to find, because the odds of anyone finding *their* cache are astronomically low. It's called the Treasure Planet Paradox."

"I'm reasonably certain you just made that up, sir. In any case, this is all academic. We don't even know where the supposed pirate lair is."

"Have you tried checking the pirates' nav computer?"

"Well, no," I admitted. "But they'd have to be ridiculously careless to leave the landing coordinates for a secret pirate lair lying around."

"Ridiculously careless," Rex said, nodding. "That sounds like our pirates."

I sighed. He was right. "I'll go look, sir."

Sadly, Rex was correct. It took me less than five minutes to find the landing coordinates. Rubric Malgastar had apparently relied so heavily on his intimidating persona that he'd allowed himself and his crew to get incredibly sloppy. I waited half an hour to inform Rex what I'd found, hoping that he'd have changed his mind in the meantime. He hadn't.

"Time's a-wasting, Sasha!" he snapped. "Get us to that pirate lair!"

I sighed and shuffled back to the bridge. I entered the coordinates and we broke orbit. Half an hour later, we were descending through the planet's murky atmosphere toward a small, rocky island in the middle of a vast, murky sea. A dim sun hung in the distance, barely discernible in the greenish-gray fog. The landing coordinates guided me to a flat stone surface encircled by tall, spikey peaks of black rock. We set down amongst several other ships, most of them much larger, but in even worse shape, than ours. The biggest and ugliest of these was labeled *Coccydynia*.

We had found the pirate lair.

CHAPTER TEN

Rex sent Boggs and Donny outside first. When they weren't immediately vaporized, Rex and I followed. I scanned the area but saw no movement.

"This way," Rex announced, marching in an apparently randomly selected direction. The rest of us followed. We hadn't gone more than fifty paces when a voice called to us from the darkness.

"Hey!" it said. "I mean, ahoy there!" It was a young man's voice, high pitched and uncertain.

"Who goes there?" shouted Rex.

"It's me," said the voice. "Tim. I'm sorry there aren't more of us here to greet you, Captain. We're a little short-staffed." In the dim light of the *Flagrante Delicto*, we saw a young man approaching. He stopped a few meters in front of Rex.

"Yes, well," said Rex, trying to gauge the proper demeanor for the occasion. "Don't let it happen again."

"No, sir," said Tim. "Aye, sir. We weren't expecting you until tomorrow. Did you really commandeer the *Raina Huebner*?"

"Who wants to know?" Rex demanded.

"Um, just me, sir," said Tim. "I apologize if my question is out of line. I'm new here."

"Don't worry about it, Tim," Rex said. "You can make it up to me by showing me around this place."

"Yes, sir!" Tim said. "Is this your first visit here?"

"Let's say it is," Rex replied. "That way, you can get some practice."

"Yes, sir. This way, sir." Tim set off in the direction opposite where Rex had been heading. "Welcome to Sargasso Seven, sir. They pride themselves… that is, *we* pride ourselves on being the premier secret pirate lair in the galaxy. Our saloon was rated Not Entirely Unpleasant by *Hidden Pirate Lairs Monthly*. We also have sleeping rooms and various forms of entertainment, from shuffleboard to competitive dusting. I'll take you to the saloon first."

"That sounds like an excellent idea, Tim," Rex said.

We followed Tim to a one of the tower-like peaks that surrounded the landing area. When we were just a few meters away, I saw that he was headed toward a door in the rock wall. Between the dim light and the fog that hung in the air, it was difficult to see anything.

"Sorry it's so hard to see," Tim said. "But this is, after all, a secret lair. Outside lights would draw attention to our location."

"Stop apologizing, Tim," Rex said. "It's unseemly for a pirate."

"Oh, I'm not a pirate, sir," said Tim. "Not yet, anyway. I'm just an intern. I have a long way to go before I'm an actual pirate."

"Well said, Tim," Rex said. "Too many people these days think they can throw on an eye patch, steal a parrot and call themselves pirates. It's shameful, really."

Tim opened the door and we followed him inside. We found ourselves in a room that was nearly as dark as the landing area. It smelled of stale smoke and sweat. Murmurs and the clinking of glasses told us we were not alone. I saw that we were in a small tavern filled with rough-hewn wood tables and benches. Here and there sat several small groups of gruff-looking men in dirty clothes. One of these, a portly man with an impossibly thick, mane-like beard that swooped forward and curled upward toward a point, had stood up and was limping toward us. His left leg below the knee was a peg.

"You got a lotta nerve walking into this place," the man growled.

Rex peered into the semidarkness with his one unobscured eye, trying to see who was addressing him.

"Oh, hello, Mr. Hookbeard, sir," said Tim to the portly man. "I see you're already acquainted with our new guest."

"Only by reputation," Hookbeard said, glaring at Rex. "This is the man who swindled me out of the *Pinot Grigio*." A damp toothpick hung from the corner of his mouth and at least two more were partially hidden in his beard.

I racked my circuits trying to remember anything about such an incident. I doubted Hookbeard would be this upset about a bottle of wine. A spaceship, then? Swindling someone out of a ship certainly sounded like Rex, but I had no recollection of one called the *Pinot Grigio*.

"That was a long time ago," said Rex. The vagueness of his response indicated he was in the same boat as I: he didn't have any idea what Hookbeard was talking about. A normal person would simply have admitted this, but Rex never likes to admit he doesn't know something until he knows why he doesn't know it and how this information can be used to his advantage.

"It was three weeks ago, you bastard," Hookbeard said. The point of his beard waggled angrily in front of him. The toothpick fell from his mouth and was immediately lost in his beard. He produced another one and stuck it in his mouth.

"Yeah, but that's like forever in pirate years."

"Pretty shoddy-looking gang you've got here," Hookbeard said. He gestured toward me, Boggs and Donny. "My robust crew of privateers puts them to shame." Several dirty and unkempt men at the table where Hookbeard had been sitting raised their glasses and cheered. "And I must admit," Hookbeard went on, "you're not what I expected, Malgastar."

"Yes, well, I like to think I defy… eh?" Rex said. "What did you call me?"

Hookbeard laughed deeply. "You didn't think you could just sneak in here without being recognized, did you? We've been tracking your ship since you entered the atmosphere. Everyone here knows the legendary Rubric Malgastar, captain of the *Chronic Lumbago*."

I realized now why we were being welcomed so warmly. Our ship was still broadcasting the call sign of the *Chronic Lumbago*. As far as these people knew, we were pirates.

Rex surveyed the room, seeing that all eyes in the place were on him. No one spoke up to contradict Hookbeard.

"Right!" Rex declared after a moment's consideration. "That is me. Aye! I am Rubric Magastar, notorious space pirate. You can tell by my eye patch!"

"No air," said the parrot on Rex's shoulder. "Can't breathe."

"And by my parrot, Squawky, of course."

"Steve," said the parrot.

"He's always squawking crazy stuff like that," Rex explained. "That's why I call him Squawky."

"I'm probably going to murder him," said the parrot.

"See?" Rex said. "He's adorable. What do you say we let bygones be bygones, Mr. Falberg?"

"Hookbeard," said Hookbeard.

"Right, of course," said Rex. "Let me buy you a drink."

Hookbeard studied Rex for a moment. "Fine," he said at last. The five of us sat at a table.

"You're still flying the *Chronic Lumbago*, I see," said Hookbeard. "I've recently traded up. That's my ship out there, the *Coccydynia*. It's a refitted Malarchian frigate. Lotta upgrades. Best pirate ship in the galaxy."

"Yes, well," said Rex. "I'm sure it's a fine ship." Rex seemed unsure what to make of Hookbeard's advances. His initial scorn had given way to efforts to impress Rex.

"So, what are you up to these days, Malgastar?" Hookbeard asked. "I heard you raided the *Raina Huebner*. Where is she?"

"A pirate never tells," said Rex.

"What about the booty?" said Hookbeard. "Did you unload it somewhere? No way you got it all on that little ship of yours. I always pictured the *Chronic Lumbago* as being... bigger."

"You know what they say," said Rex. "It's not the size of the pirate ship; it's what you do with the booty. So, who does a man have to keelhaul to get a drink around here?" he asked.

As he spoke, Tim returned with a strikingly beautiful woman at his side. She wore tight black pants and a billowy cotton top with a leather bustier showcasing her figure. Her eyes were a piercing blue visible even in the dim light of the tavern; her face was pale and severe. Curls of thick black hair fell just past her shoulders.

"I appreciate the thought, Tim," said Rex, ogling the woman's cleavage, "but I think our crew could use some victuals before we're ready for more sophisticated forms of entertainment."

Tim appeared momentarily puzzled. "Oh, she's not—" He started.

The woman cut him off. "I'm Pepper Mélange," she said coldly. "I'm the proprietor of this establishment."

"You own the saloon?" I asked.

"I own all of it. I run Sargasso Seven." The woman seemed vaguely familiar to me, but I couldn't figure out why.

"The whole planet?" Rex asked.

"Sure, such as it is. The planet is uninhabitable except for this island. I found it by accident when I was on the run from the Malarchy

66

a couple years ago, back when I was dabbling a bit in the piracy game myself. Decided to settle down and give back to the pirate community by opening a secret lair. This place is open to freebooters, corsairs, buccaneers and marauders of all stripes."

"Great story," said Rex. "Who do I see about getting a martini around here?"

"That would be me," said Pepper. "Except I don't serve martinis. Fortunately, Rubric Malgastar only drinks beer."

"Splendid," said Rex, ignoring the harsh glare he was getting from Pepper. "A round of your finest beer for my crew and Hookbeard here. Put in on my tab."

"Of course," said Pepper. "Speaking of your tab, I did have a question for you, Captain Malgastar."

"Sure, sure," said Rex. "I'll find you later."

"Now would be better," said Pepper. "Unless you want to lose another eye."

"Oh, there's nothing wrong with my eye," said Rex.

"Not yet," said Pepper.

Rex got up from the table. "All right, then. Let's talk."

Pepper turned to Tim. "Get a pitcher of beer for the rest of them." She turned to me.

Tim nodded and hurried away. As Rex followed Pepper toward the back of the bar, Pepper turned to me. "You too," she said.

I glanced at Rex, who shrugged. I got up and followed them into a small office behind the bar. Pepper took a seat behind a hefty wooden desk while Rex and I continued to stand.

"If this is about the martini," Rex started, "I was just testing you. Obviously I know that a legendary space pirate isn't going to drink something classy like a vodka martini, extra dry, with three olives. Although if you have one lying around—"

"You can drop the act," Pepper said. "I know you're not Rubric Malgastar."

"You do?" Rex asked. "How?"

"I've met him before, you nitwit. He's got a hundred pounds on you and doesn't wear an eye patch."

"Right, but how else?"

"You know," said Pepper, "I had assumed this was all an act. I was happy to play along, but I'm starting to believe you really don't remember me."

"You've got me dead to rights, Pepper," said Rex. "Our pretending not to recognize you is all part of an elaborate ruse. Perhaps we should put all of our cards on the table. We'll tell each other exactly who we are and how we met and then compare our respective stories for any discrepancies. You go first."

"Nice try, Rex. Fortunately, your con man spiel has never worked on me. I know when somebody doesn't recognize me. The question is, why are you pretending to be Rubric Malgastar?"

"That is a good question," Rex said. "But here's a better one: why didn't you blow our cover?"

Pepper smiled. "Malgastar and I had a deal. Your ship is broadcasting the identification code for the *Chronic Lumbago*. And I checked—the signature hash is genuine. Either you stole the code from Malgastar or he renamed your ship, planning to take it for himself. That means you outsmarted Malgastar and probably killed him."

"Preposterous!" Rex declared. "I'm insulted that you would think I have such a callous disregard for human life."

"No air," said Squawky. "Can't breathe. Curse the cold-hearted bastard who tricked us into taking this ship!"

"Zip it, Squawky," Rex snapped. "You're giving the lady the wrong idea."

"Relax," said Pepper. "Malgastar and I weren't close. But we did have a business arrangement. I had commissioned Malgastar to retrieve something for me. Something very valuable, which was aboard the *Raina Huebner*. My spies tell me that the *Raina Huebner* was destroyed by the Malarchy shortly after being boarded by pirates. I can only assume that you knew about this cargo and somehow managed to get it away from Malgastar during the battle. Perhaps you even knew about Malgastar's plans and tipped off the Malarchy, planning to use their attack as a diversion."

"But if I took this cargo for myself, why would I have come back here and risk being discovered by you?"

"Obviously Malgastar told you about his arrangement with me, and you were hoping to take his place and sell the cargo to me. Hookbeard and the others out there are only sucking up to you because they think you've got the booty from the *Raina Huebner* on your ship. But of course you wouldn't bring it here for fear that I would just kill you and take it."

"See, Sasha?" Rex said. "No booty at the pirate haven." He turned back to Pepper. "I do indeed have the cargo of the *Raina Huebner* ensconced in a safe place. There were a lot of crates in that hold, though. Just to be sure we're talking about the same thing, would you say that the item you are looking for is larger than a breadbox?"

"Don't play dumb, Rex Nihilo. I don't know why you didn't recognize me, but you wouldn't have come here if you weren't trying to sell something. You know what I'm talking about. There was only one deep freeze container on that ship."

"Of course," said Rex. "The deep freeze container. The one with the frozen beets in it."

"Very funny. How much do you want for it?"

"What was your deal with Malgastar?"

"Ten million credits."

"No way I can part with it for less than twenty."

"Twenty million credits! That's absurd!"

"Then I'll just have to find another buyer."

"Another buyer? Who in the galaxy do you think you're going to sell it to?"

"I have some ideas," Rex said. I was fairly confident Rex had absolutely no clue what he was talking about, but he had been through so many of these negotiations that he could play his part in his sleep.

Pepper regarded him coldly for a moment. "Thirteen million."

"Fifteen and you've got a deal."

"Fine. Fifteen million. When can you have the cargo here?"

"Give me until tomorrow."

"Done. Don't double-cross me, Rex Nihilo. You may not remember me, but I'll find you."

"If I may ask," I said, "how *do* we know you? I thought you seemed familiar, but I don't recall having met you."

Pepper told us a long, ridiculous story about how she supposedly helped us bust someone out of the impenetrable prison known as Gulagatraz. I had no memory of it whatsoever. Was she pulling some kind of scam on us? I couldn't figure out what she had to gain by making up such a story. And she really did seem to know who we were. It was very strange. Rex, for his part, seemed entirely unconcerned. But then Rex is used to having gaps in his memory, and has little to no capacity for introspection.

"Nice doing business with you, Pepper," Rex said, when he noticed she'd stopped talking. "We'll be back tomorrow with your cargo."

Rex and I left the office. On the way back to the table, I asked, "Sir, do you have any memory of Pepper?"

"Nope," Rex said.

"And that doesn't bother you?"

"I meet a lot of people in this business. It doesn't pay to remember them all."

"I see. And do you know what cargo Pepper was referring to?"

"Of course not," Rex said. "But how hard could it be to find a deep freeze container?"

"Sir, you realize that the contents of the *Raina Huebner*'s cargo hold are spread across several thousand cubic kilometers by now, right?"

"Is that a lot?"

"It's too much to search in a day, sir. And the longer it takes to find, the bigger area we have to search."

We sat down at the table again. Hookbeard had left with his crew, and Boggs was drinking alone while Donny watched.

"Blast," said Rex. "I wish you'd have told me all this before I promised that deep freeze box to Pepper."

"I didn't really have a chance, sir. I only just found out about it. It never occurred to me that we'd need to recover any of that cargo. I had a hard enough time rescuing you."

"Your excuses aren't going to cut it this time, Sasha. Your carelessness just cost me fifteen million credits."

"Sir, I hardly think it's fair to—"

"Good grief, what has gotten into you, Boggs?"

I turned to look and saw that Boggs was quietly sobbing into his beer glass. Donny was trying unsuccessfully to comfort him.

"I'm sorry, Potential Friend," Boggs blubbered. "It's just that when I heard you say 'deep freeze,' it reminded me how much I miss my Frozen Friend."

"Your what?" Rex asked.

"My Frozen Friend. We left the other ship in such a hurry that I didn't have time to get him."

Rex and I exchanged glances.

"Boggs," I asked, "is this something from the *Raina Huebner* that you grabbed with the crane?"

Boggs nodded. "You told me to go nuts making new friends, and I did. I went nuts and made a Frozen Friend."

"This Frozen Friend," I said. "It's a person?"

"I think so," said Boggs. "It was hard to see inside the box."

"Good gravy, Boggs," Rex cried. "You're a genius! That's the deep freeze container we're talking about!"

"It is?" Boggs asked.

"It does sound like it," I said. "That means the cargo Pepper is after is actually a person. Someone who has been cryogenically frozen. Strange."

"And whoever it is, they're aboard the ship formerly known as the *Chronic Lumbago*. You can find that ship again, right, Sasha?"

"Of course, sir," I said. "Assuming it's still floating in space where we left it."

"All right then, crew," said Rex. "Finish your beers and we'll head back to that ship."

"We're going to get my Frozen Friend?" asked Boggs hopefully.

"That we are, Ensign Boggs. And then we're going to trade him for something even better than friendship: fifteen million credits!"

CHAPTER ELEVEN

The *Chronic Lumbago-cum-Raina Huebner* was right were we'd left it. I docked our ship with it and we made our way to the cargo hold. It was empty.

"I don't understand," said Boggs, looking dejectedly about the empty hold. "Where is my Frozen Friend?"

"Somebody got here first," I observed. Whoever it was apparently hadn't been after the cryogenic chamber in particular: they had taken all the other crates Boggs had "won" as well.

"Pirates," Rex said, adjusting his eye patch. "Scourge of the galaxy. Blast them all!"

It seemed odd to me that pirates would have left the ship, but maybe they had come to the same conclusion as Rex: it wasn't even worth selling.

"Donny found something," Donny said. He had been skittering anxiously around the empty hold, but now had stopped to peruse something on the floor. "A small piece of wood."

"That's great, Donny," Rex said unenthusiastically. "There's really no end to your—wait, did you say a small piece of wood?"

"Very small," said Donny. He picked something up from the floor. Rex walked over to him and took it out of his hand.

"Toothpick," Rex said.

"Hookbeard," I said.

Rex nodded. "That bastard must have gotten suspicious and went to look for the *Raina Huebner*. He found this ship, boarded it, and took the cargo for himself."

"Do you think Hookbeard knows Pepper is after the cryo chamber?" I asked.

"Doubtful," said Rex. "I didn't get the sense Pepper trusts him. She wouldn't have confided in him. He probably just thought he could sell the cargo for a fast buck."

"Where would he go?"

"Xagnon," Rex said. "It's the closest port."

"It's also the first place the authorities are going to expect cargo from the *Raina Huebner* to show up."

"Does Hookbeard strike you as a strategic thinker?" Rex asked.

I saw his point. If Hookbeard and his crew were as dimwitted as the other pirates we'd run into, they'd dump their booty at the closest planet, regardless of the risk.

"Plot a course to Xagnon, Sasha," Rex said. "We're going to get our Frozen Friend back."

Xagnon, a non-descript industrial planet, was only a short jump away. The spaceport was fairly large, but Rex was able to talk a gate attendant into giving us the location of Hookbeard's ship, the *Coccydynia*. We made our way across the spaceport to the cargo unloading area, where we saw two men loading crates from the *Coccydynia* into a hovertruck while Hookbeard and his crew watched. We spied on them from behind a stack of crates. One of the men closed the back door of the truck and he and Hookbeard shook hands. We didn't see a cryo chamber, but maybe it was already in the truck.

"All right, men," Hookbeard said. "Time to celebrate! Let's get some drinks at the Event Horizon. Hookbeard and his men disappeared inside the main building of the planeport. The other two men got in the truck.

"They're going to get away, sir," I said. "What do we do?"

We looked around but there were no other vehicles in the vicinity. The truck pulled away. There were no markings on the truck and there was no way we'd be able to follow them on foot.

"Maybe we should follow Hookbeard and his crew to the bar," I suggested. "If we eavesdrop, we might overhear something about who these guys are or where they're taking the stuff."

"I know who they are," Rex said. "Ursa Minor Mafia. But where they're taking the cargo is anyone's guess. They've got warehouses all over the city." The Ursa Minor Mafia was the largest criminal organization in the galaxy. They were known to have a large presence in Xagnon City. "If we lose that truck, we'll never get our Frozen Friend back."

"Donny can catch the truck," Donny said. He skittered after the truck on his hand-feet. When the truck stopped before pulling onto the street, Donny ran underneath it and then stopped, reversed his arms, and grabbed onto the undercarriage. The truck sped away with Donny affixed to its underside.

"Brilliant!" Rex cried. "When the truck gets where it's going, Donny will call us and give us the location!"

"How will he call us, sir?" I asked.

"Don't be silly, Sasha. He'll just... uh. Boggs, does Donny have any radio transmission capability?"

"I don't think so, Potential Friend. But he can probably use a comm."

"He wouldn't know where to call us," I said.

"Hmm," said Rex. "Maybe he'll find his way back to the *Flagrante Delicto*. We'll just have to wait there for him."

"Wait for whom?" screeched a familiar voice behind us. We turned to see Heinous Vlaak himself striding toward us, flanked by two lazegun-toting marines. Vlaak was a large man who cut a striking figure in his tight-fitting crimson leather uniform, a helmet festooned with peacock feathers and a luxurious cape that was said to be made from the pelts of a race of furry humanoids who had made the mistake of assisting the rebels in the Battle of Zondervan.

"What are you doing here, Vlaak?" Rex asked.

"I'm asking the questions here!" Vlaak shrieked. "What are you doing at the Xagnon spaceport?"

"Just seeing a friend off," Rex replied.

"You're sure you're not unloading goods stolen from a certain cargo ship?"

"Goodness, no," said Rex. "That sounds illegal."

"Don't make me laugh, Nihilo. You're a born scoundrel. I hear a report of pirated goods being unloaded at the spaceport, and here you are. Tell me why I shouldn't execute you on principle."

"I'm not sure you really understand how principles work," said Rex. "But look, you've got us all wrong. We're not pirates."

"I'm a born pirate," said Squawky.

"Don't listen to him," Rex said. "He just jabbers nonsense."

"If you're not a pirate," Vlaak said, "why are you wearing an eye patch?"

"It's a medical condition. Lost my left eye in a hunting accident."

"You're wearing the patch on your right eye."

"Yes, I lost my right eye and was hunting for it with the left."

"So you didn't hijack the *Raina Huebner*?"

"Well, yes, we did do that," said Rex. "But here's the thing. We're not the pirates you're looking for. The guys who sold the *Raina Huebner*'s cargo just left. Hookbeard and crew."

"Thaddeus Hookbeard is here?" cried Vlaak. "He's the second most wanted pirate in the galaxy, after Rubric Malgastar."

"Well, I've never heard of that second guy," Rex said, "but Hookbeard just left. They said they were going to a place called... Sasha?"

"The Event Horizon, sir."

"They're going to place called the Event Horizon. Probably a bar. You know pirates."

"Your Lordship," said one of the marines, "that does appear to be Hookbeard's ship over there."

Vlaak regarded the *Coccydynia*, then turned to Rex. "You'd better not be lying to me, Nihilo."

"I'm totally not," Rex replied. "I'm one hundred percent telling you the truth about where Hookbeard is."

"If you aren't, you will rue this day." He turned. "Come with me, men! We're finally going to capture Hookbeard!" The marines spun around, flanking Vlaak as he returned inside the building.

"I don't like that man," Boggs said. "He is not a friend."

"You're right on that score, Boggs," I said. I turned to Rex. "Now what, sir?"

"Now we get a cab to the Event Horizon."

"But sir, you just told Heinous Vlaak that's where Hookbeard is."

"Yes, but Vlaak knows I'm a liar. He'll check every bar in the city before he goes to the Event Horizon. Trust me."

"Even so," I said, "I thought you said Hookbeard wouldn't know where the cargo is."

"He probably doesn't," Rex replied, "but he's our only lead."

"I thought we were going to wait at the ship for Donny," said Boggs.

"Change of plans," Rex said. "Vlaak's marines are sniffing around.

We can't afford to wait. We have to find Hookbeard and find out what he knows."

"And you're certain Vlaak won't be where you told him to go?" I asked.

"Not a chance. I'm a huge liar. Trust me."

I wasn't at all convinced by Rex's logic, but Heinous Vlaak isn't exactly inconspicuous. I figured if he was at the Event Horizon when we got there, we'd know it. Vlaak seemed far more interested in Hookbeard than in us anyway.

As it happened, Vlaak was nowhere to be seen when we arrived at the Event Horizon. Hookbeard and his crew were already well into their celebrations. We approached their table, and Hookbeard stood up with a start when he saw Rex approaching.

"What the devil are you doing here, Malgastar?" Hookbeard roared.

"Calm down, Hookbeard," Rex said. "I'm just looking for some of that cargo you unloaded."

"I claimed that booty fair and square!" Hookbeard growled. "That ship was abandoned."

"Nobody is questioning your claim to the booty," Rex said. "I just want to know where it is."

"And why would I tell you that?" Hookbeard asked.

"Because I have some very useful information for you," Rex replied. "It might even save your life."

"Fine. Give me the information and I'll tell you what I know about the booty."

"Tell me where the booty is first."

"How do I know your information is worth it?"

"You don't. Look, if you want to get out of here alive, you're just going to have to trust me."

"What do you mean?" Hookbeard asked. "Is someone coming here to kill me? Is that the information you have?"

"No," said Rex. "I mean, maybe. Let me put it this way: if I knew that someone was coming here to kill you, that would be pretty valuable information, right?"

"Nobody move!" shrieked a high-pitched voice from the front of the bar.

Heinous Vlaak had found us.

CHAPTER TWELVE

Hookbeard, who seemed to have taken Rex's warning more seriously than Rex did, was already halfway to the rear door, and his men were close behind.

Boggs and I hesitated, waiting to see if Rex was going to try to talk his way out of this situation as well. After a moment, he seemed to decide against this course of action. "Run!" Rex cried. I ran after him, with Boggs bringing up the rear.

"I said nobody move!" Vlaak screeched. "Why is everybody doing the opposite of what I said to do?"

Rex went through the door and I followed close behind. We found ourselves in an alley. From our left, four more marines were approaching. To our right the alley dead-ended in a chain-link fence. Despite his peg, Hookbeard had somehow managed to scale it. He dropped out of sight on the other side, and his men followed close behind.

It was clear we weren't going to escape. Rex's hesitation had cost us valuable milliseconds.

The fact that the marines hadn't yet opened fire indicated that Vlaak wanted us alive. That was little consolation: Vlaak was an expert in torture, and he would undoubtedly kill us as soon as he had no more use for us. We were trapped between the approaching marines and Hookbeard's men, who were struggling to get over the fence.

"I'll hold them off," Boggs said, putting his back up against the door we'd just come through. "You and Potential Friend should go."

"Boggs," I said, "you don't have to do that. You don't know what Heinous Vlaak will do to you. If we stick together—"

"It doesn't matter," Boggs said. "Pirates are not friends. Marines are not friends. You and Potential Friend are friends. I will go nuts and help my friends."

Even Rex seemed a little touched by this gesture. "Thanks, Boggs," he said, patting Boggs on the arm. "Good luck." He ran toward the fence and began climbing. I gave Boggs a salute and then followed.

We scrambled over the fence as fast as we could, without looking back. At any moment I expected to be hit by a lazegun blast. Even given the notoriously bad aim of Malarchian marines, if they opened fire at this distance, sheer probability dictated that we'd soon be full of holes. But no one fired. We clambered over the top of the fence and landed on the other side. Hookbeard's crew was already disappearing around a corner.

"Come on," Rex shouted, unnecessarily. We kept running. Behind us, I heard the sounds of a scuffle, but didn't dare look back. Rex and I ran for several blocks before stopping behind a building.

"I think we lost them," Rex said.

"I hope so," I replied. "What happened back there, sir?"

"Apparently I'm more trustworthy than I realized."

"I don't mean with Vlaak. I mean why did you hesitate? I thought you were going to try to talk your way out of there."

"I was. Then I thought better of it."

"Sir, you've never thought better of anything in your life. Having second thoughts isn't like you."

"Forget it, Sasha," Rex snapped. "We all make mistakes. Like that time you ejected our Frozen Friend into space."

"Aye, sir," I said. It wasn't worth arguing about. "What now, sir?"

"Let's get back to the *Flagrante Delicto*. Maybe Donny will show up."

"But sir, you said—"

"I know what I said! I'm having an off day, Sasha. Drop it." Rex stomped off, and I went after him.

Rex is prone to bouts of depression, but they usually don't occur in the middle of one of our adventures. Frankly, I was starting to worry. Rex wasn't the sort to wait around for something to happen. As frustrating as he can be, indecisiveness is not ordinarily one of his weaknesses.

We had no money, so we had to walk back to the spaceport. We'd only gone a few blocks when we were accosted by a street vendor with a cart full of junk.

"Hey, man," the unkempt man said as Rex approached. "Looks

like your robot needs a new arm."

"She's fine," Rex said. "She likes her hook. Come on, Sasha."

Rex kept going, but I stopped in front of the cart. "Do you have a robot arm?" I asked.

"Sure," the guy said. "I've got five of them. They're a little small, but maybe you could string two of them together."

"What did you say?" Rex asked, suddenly interested.

"I said I've got five little robot arms."

"Do you have any other robot parts?"

"Well, I have a head and a torso, but your robot already has those." He opened a compartment in the cart and inside was a pile of familiar-looking robot parts.

"Donny!" Rex cried. "What have you done with him?"

The guy shrugged. "This is how I found him."

Donny picked up the lifeless head. "Donny, can you hear me?" There was no reply.

Rex slammed the head against the edge of the cart.

"Hey!" yelled the vendor. "You can't—"

Donny's eyes lit up. "Hello," Donny said. "I am Donny. Donny believes in himself, despite having no arms and no body."

"Very good, Donny," Rex said. "What happened to you?"

"Donny clung to the bottom of the truck until the truck reached a building. Then a man pried Donny off the truck with a stick. Donny fell to the ground and the man dragged him out from under the truck. Then GAP IN MEMORY OF INDETERMINITE DURATION. Then Donny was here, talking to Rex and Sasha."

"Can you tell us where the... hey!"

The street vendor grabbed Donny's head away from Rex, shoved it back in the compartment and slammed the door. "No talking to the merchandise! You want information, you pay!"

Donny's voice droned on inside the cart, but we couldn't make out what he was saying.

"He's our robot!" Rex snapped.

"You got any proof of that?"

Rex fumed silently for a moment. "How much do you want for him?"

"Three hundred credits."

"Three hundred credits! That's insane. He wasn't worth that much when he was intact."

A disappointed sound came from the cart.

"Believe in yourself, Donny!" Rex yelled. "What if I trade you my robot for him?"

"Sir!" I exclaimed.

"Relax, Sasha," Rex said. "It's just temporary. I'll get Donny to tell me where the cargo is. We'll steal it back, sell some of it, and I'll buy you back."

"Your robot's missing an arm," the vendor said. "And it seems kind of ornery."

"She won't give you any trouble," Rex said.

"I will," I said. "I will absolutely give you trouble." I grabbed an I <3 Xagnon t-shirt from the cart, threw it on the ground, and stepped on it. "You see?" I said. "That was a perfectly nice t-shirt, and I have ruined it, because I am trouble. And that was merely a small taste of the sort of shenanigans I'm capable of."

"No deal," said the vendor. "And you owe me twenty credits for the shirt."

"Damn it, Sasha!"

"How about your parrot?"

"Squawky? I can't give you Squawky! Other than Donny, he's the best robot friend I've ever had."

"No air," said Squawky. "Can't breathe."

"That's adorable!" said the vendor. "Give me the bird and I'll give you the robot's head and three arms."

"Four arms," said Rex.

"Okay, three of his forearms."

"He has five arms."

"Right. I'll give you three of them. Then we'll call it even."

"That's odd. I need at least four."

"Four! I'll never get ahead that way."

"If you want the head, I'll need all four arms."

"All forearms? Now *that's* odd."

"Why? Are you planning on giving me the fifth?"

"No, I'm taking the fifth."

"You can't take the fifth. Answer the question."

"Which question?"

"The one about the four arms."

"What four?"

"That's none of your business. I need the arms."

"Then I'll be armless."

"Mostly armless. You'll still have the fifth."

"I'm not sure how much more of this arm talk I can bear."

"Bearing arms is the second. Do you want the fifth or the second?"

"All three."

"You can't take three rights. That's one left."

"That's true. Fine, take all the arms."

"Really?"

"Yeah. I feel a lot better getting all that off my chest."

"What are you going to do with a chest and no arms?"

"You can have the chest too."

"You're not going to fight me for the chest?"

The man shrugged. "I was going to, but my heart's not in it."

CHAPTER THIRTEEN

I followed Rex down the sidewalk, holding Donny's chest and arms in front of me. Rex held Donny's head out in front of him so Donny could give us directions to the warehouse where the booty from the *Raina Huebner* had been stored. Credit where it's due, Donny recalled the route to the warehouse perfectly. There was a fence around the building and a guard station at the front, so we went around to the back. We tossed Donny's parts over the fence and then climbed over after them.

Other than the guard at the front of the building, nobody seemed to be watching the place, and we heard no activity from within. Unfortunately, all the doors were locked. The only way in appeared to be an open window on the third floor.

"Donny could climb," Donny said, "if Donny had his arms."

"Sasha, do you think you can put Donny's arms back on?"

"I think so," I said.

I spent the next hour reassembling Donny. He walked in circles several times to test his limbs.

"Donny is better," Donny announced.

"Excellent, Donny," said Rex. "Get in there and open the back door for us."

"Donny will try." He ran to the building and began to climb, his feet-hands pulling his body up the brick wall. He disappeared through the window, and a few minutes later the door opened. Rex and I went inside. We were in a vast warehouse filled with crates and boxes. Other than Donny, it appeared to be deserted. Parked just inside a large sliding door was the hovertruck we'd seen at the spaceport. We approached it and opened the door to the cargo compartment. Inside were several crates and a what looked like a horizontal freezer. Through a tiny window in the cryo chamber I could make out a face with human features, but that was about it. There were no markings of any kind on the outside.

"Okay," said Rex. "Let's thaw this poor bastard out and see who we're dealing with."

"Is that wise, sir?" I asked. "Perhaps we should just deliver him to Pepper as-is."

"I'm not delivering anything until I know who he is and why Pepper wants him so badly. What if I'm getting screwed on the price? How am I going to know how much he's worth if I don't know who he is?"

"Point taken, sir," I said. "But perhaps we should wait until we're safely away from the Ursa Minor Mafia."

"Fine," said Rex glumly, "but I'm opening some of these other crates."

Donny and I watched while Rex opened several of the crates. Most of them contained nothing of interest, but one was full of hand grenades and another of stun guns. Rex stuffed one of the stun guns in his waistband. "Okay, let's get out of here."

"Sir?" I asked. "How are we going to transport the cryo chamber?"

"We're going to take the truck, obviously. Donny, open that door."

Rex and I got into the cab while Donny opened the sliding door. Then he skittered across the floor and joined us in the truck. Rex pulled out of the warehouse and we drove up to the front gate.

The guard exited the guardhouse and walked up to Rex. "Papers," he said.

"This is a special shipment," Rex said. "We don't have papers."

"Everybody has papers," the guard said.

"Look," said Rex. "We've got a load of stuff that came from the *Raina Huebner*, got it? The Malarchy is in town and it's only a matter of time before they show up here. Do you really want to be the one to explain to the Ursa Minor Mafia why Heinous Vlaak found stolen goods on these premises?"

The man studied Rex for a long time. Then he said, "I can't let you out without papers."

"Oh!" Rex exclaimed. "Why didn't you say so. Here." He pulled the stun gun from his belt and shot the guard, who crumpled to the ground. Rex got out of the truck. "Help me get him in the back, Sasha!

Donny, get that gate open!"

I got out and helped Rex carry the guard to the back of the truck. We opened the back, dumped him inside, and then got back in the cab. Meanwhile, Donny had found the button to raise the gate. We drove through and Donny climbed back into the cab. Rex pulled onto the street and began driving toward the spaceport.

"Was that wise, sir? We can't afford to be on the wrong side of the Ursa Minor Mafia. We've already got the Malarchy after us."

"No choice," said Rex. "Anyway, they'll never know it was us. We'll just dump this guy in a ditch on the way to the… what was that?"

I had heard it too. Somebody was moving around in the back of the truck.

"Blasted off-brand stun guns," Rex growled. "I'm going to have to pull over. Donny, get ready to—aaaahhhh!"

This interjection was directed at a man who was running across the street in front of us. He was chasing a fluttering object that was, if I was not mistaken, a robotic parrot.

Rex slammed on the brakes and there was a loud thud as something struck the rear of the cab, and then another, quieter thud as something hit the bed of the truck. The movement in the truck stopped.

"Squawky!" Rex cried, getting out of the truck.

"Sir! Where are you going?"

"I've got to get Squawky," Rex yelled back at me. "Go see what's happening in the back."

Rex ran into the street after the vendor.

"Stay here, Donny," I said, getting out of the truck. I ran around to the back of the truck, opened the door and climbed inside. The warehouse guard lay against the back of the cab, moaning quietly and rubbing his head. In the distance, I heard sirens. This wasn't good. If the cops caught us with a semi-conscious security guard, we were in big trouble. And as we were currently stopped in the middle of a busy street, it wasn't going to be easy to get rid of the guard. The only thing I could do was try to hide him. I pulled the rear door shut and surveyed the situation. None of the crates were big enough to put a body in, and there weren't enough of them to hide the body behind. Additionally complicating matters was the fact that the guard was now almost fully conscious. I'd have given him another whack on the head, but my programming prevents me from attacking a human being.

The only option was the cryo chamber. It wasn't designed to fit two people, but maybe I could throw the guard on top of whoever was already in there. If I could get the lid closed, they'd freeze and hopefully the cops would assume we had a good reason for transporting a cryogenically frozen man through the city. While the guard continued to groan and try to stand, I furiously tapped at the strange symbols on the control panel.

"Thawing sequence initiated," said a recorded voice. A thick white cloud of odorless gas spilled out of the chamber onto the floor, momentarily obscuring the occupant. I realized after a moment that a platform holding a man's body was rising like an elevator out of the container. When it was level with the lip of the container, it suddenly tipped and the body rolled off onto the metal floor with a thud. The platform leveled out again and retracted into the chamber.

"Thank you for using Shur-Freez Cryo-Chambers," the recorded voice said. As the fog cleared, we saw a small, wrinkled old man lying still next to the container. He wore nothing but a cloth diaper. The sirens grew louder.

I could see now that there was no way two people were going to fit in the chamber, and in any case I wasn't sure I'd be able to lift the diapered man back onto the platform. The guard had gotten to his feet and was leaning against the edge of the cryo chamber, his other hand still on his head. He groaned loudly.

Thinking quickly, I bent down, wrapped my arm and hook around the man's knees, and then heaved upward. Disoriented, he clutched tightly to the edge of the chamber. "What… who…?" He managed to mumble. I got his feet into the chamber and then gave his body a shove. He lost his grip and tumbled onto the platform. Before he could orient himself, I slammed the door shut.

"Freezing sequence initiated," said the voice. Looking through the window, I could now see the guard's face, literally frozen in terror.

I sensed movement to my left, and turned to see that the diapered man was now sitting up, his eyes open. He stared straight ahead as if he was unaware of me.

"I can explain," I said.

"Slacks," he said.

"I don't know what happened to your clothes," I replied. "I'll try to get you some new ones soon. Until then, I just need you to sit here and be quiet. Can you do that?"

"Slacks," the man said again. He got to his feet and began walking toward the wall of the truck. His face smacked against the wall, but he kept walking in place.

"Please don't do that," I said. "I understand you are upset about your pants, but this sort of behavior is going to be regarded by the police as suspicious."

The man kept walking in place, his forehead occasionally bumping against the wall of the truck. "Slacks," he said.

There was a loud knock on the rear of the truck. I realized now the sirens had stopped. "Police," said a gruff voice. "Somebody in there?"

"Shhh," I whispered to the diapered man, putting a finger in front of my mouth.

"Slacks," he said again, banging his head loudly against the wall.

I heard a handle turn and the rear door slid open. A portly, mustachioed man in a blue uniform peered inside, aiming a lazegun at us. Behind him was a police hovercar, its lights flashing.

"What's going on in here?" the cop demanded.

If Rex had been there, he could undoubtedly have spun a tale so absurd and yet convincing that the cop would give us an escort to the spaceport. Unfortunately, both my programming and my nature preclude such a course of action. I did my best.

"We are in a truck," I announced. So far, so good.

"Slacks," said the diapered man.

"Is this some kind of... kinky thing?" the cop asked distastefully.

Why hadn't I thought of that? It was a perfect out! I could just embarrass the cop into leaving. All I had to do is play along.

"No," I said. "It is definitely not that."

"Slacks," said the diapered man.

"What's wrong with your friend?"

"He misses his pants," I said.

"I'm gonna have to take you in," said the cop.

Just then, something fluttered past the rear of the truck, just in front of the police car. The cop turned in time to see the street vendor run after it. Not far off, there was the sound of a multi-car collision, followed by angry shouting.

"Don't go anywhere," the cop said, and took off running after the man.

A few seconds later, Rex appeared. He stopped behind the truck and bent over to rest his hands on his knees, gasping for breath. Sweat poured down his face.

"Sir, we need to get out of here while we can."

"Can't... leave... Squawky..." Rex gasped. His attachment to the parrot would have been touching if he'd ever shown a tenth as much concern for me.

"If we don't leave right now, that cop is going to throw us all in jail," I said. When this seemed to have no effect, I added, "That means we'll never get paid for this job."

Rex groaned. "Fine," he grumbled. "Get back in the cab."

I climbed out of the truck, closing the door behind me, and then took my seat next to Donny, who hadn't moved. Rex got in the driver's side and pulled away, leaving the unoccupied police car behind. We made our way toward the airport.

"Sasha," Rex said after he'd regained his breath, "I want to ask you something. But before I do, I need you to remember that I've been under a lot of stress lately."

"All right, sir," I replied.

"Is there a man wearing a diaper in the back of this truck?"

"Aye, sir," I replied.

"Ah, thank Space. I thought I was hallucinating. Any idea who he is?"

"No, sir," I said. "That is, he's the man who was in the cryo chamber. I had to swap him for the security guard."

"He doesn't seem to mind being in the back of the truck."

"No, sir," I said. "I think he's distracted by his lack of pants."

Rex nodded.

Not long after, we reached the spaceport. Rex bribed a guard with the crate full of stun guns to let us drive right up to the *Flagrante Delicto*. As we approached, we saw a very large man standing in front of the ship. He was badly bruised and his sailor outfit was torn. A metallic parrot perched on his shoulder.

CHAPTER FOURTEEN

"**S**quawky!" Rex cried.

"And Boggs," I added.

Rex stopped the truck and we got out. Boggs greeted us with a big grin. The parrot took off and settled on Rex's shoulder.

"Good boy," Rex cooed. "See, Sasha? Squawky likes me."

"Still plotting your murder," Squawky said.

"What happened, Boggs?" I asked.

"Those marines attacked me all at once," Boggs replied. "I tried to take it easy on them, but they wouldn't quit. So I just kept bonking them on their heads until they stopped. Then the scary man yelled at me for a long time, but I didn't understand what he was talking about, so I didn't say anything. Then he let me go. I didn't know where you and Potential Friend were, so I walked back here. Then Squawky showed up."

"I'm a born pirate," Squawky said.

"Yes, you are, Squawky," Rex said. "Okay, everybody. Let's get this cargo loaded and get the hell off this planet."

We went around to the back of the truck and I opened the cargo door. The diapered man immediately fell on top of me, knocking me to the ground. He then got up and began walking away from the truck. "Slacks," he said.

I got to my feet.

"What did he say?" Rex asked.

"Slacks," I replied.

"Slacks?" asked Donny.

"Slacks," the old man said again, still walking away from us.

"Slacks," said Squawky. "I'm a born pirate."

"What the hell does 'Slacks' mean?" Rex asked.

"I'm sure I don't know, sir. He keeps saying it."

Boggs went after the man. He picked him up and carried him back to the truck and set him down. The man immediately started walking again. Boggs held his palm against the man's chest. "Are you okay, Diapered Friend?"

"Slacks," said the old man.

"Who the hell is he?" Rex demanded.

"Slacks," said the old man.

"Why does he keep saying 'Slacks'?"

"Maybe it's his name," I suggested.

"Frozen Friend's name is Slacks!" Boggs cried jubilantly. "Welcome, Slacks! I am Boggs. This is Sasha, Donny and Potential Friend."

"Why am I still Potential Friend?" Rex asked. "I have a name too, you know."

"You're one to talk," said the parrot.

"Slacks," said the old man.

"Who... are... you?" Rex shouted at the man.

"Slacks," said the man, still walking in place against Boggs' hand.

"We should get out of here before Heinous Vlaak figures out where we are," I said.

"Good point, Sasha," Rex said. "Boggs, get Slacks into the ship and tie him down or something. Then help us get the rest of this cargo loaded."

Boggs nodded, picking up Slacks. He was halfway to the Flagrante Delicto's ramp when we noticed a black hovervan racing toward us across the tarmac.

"Who's that?" Rex asked. "Doesn't look like police."

"Vlaak?" I suggested. But I couldn't imagine Vlaak riding in such an inconspicuous vehicle.

The vehicle came to a halt a few meters away, and four men in dark suits poured out. They were brandishing lazepistols.

"Step away from the truck," one of them said. Rex, Donny and I put our hands up and backed away from the truck. Boggs still stood at the ramp holding Slacks, uncertain what to do. The man who had spoken pointed his gun at Boggs. "You, over there with the others." Boggs complied.

"Slacks," said Slacks. He was cradled in Boggs's arms, his legs still

92

moving as if he were walking.

Another man checked us for weapons. He took Rex's stun gun and tossed it across the tarmac. "All right," he said to his compatriots. "Get the package."

"Who are you guys?" Rex asked.

"No talking," the man snapped, waving his gun in Rex's direction.

One of the man got behind the wheel of the van while the other two climbed into the truck. The van backed up against the truck and the rear door slid open. Some activity followed, accompanied by grunting and scraping sounds, but it was hard to see from our perspective what was happening. At last the door of the van slid shut and the van pulled away a short distance from the truck. The two men climbed out of the truck and got back in the van through the side door.

"Have a nice day," said the man pointing his gun at us. He holstered his gun, walked to the van, and got in. The van took off across the tarmac.

"What was that all about?" I asked. "Were those guys Ursa Minor Mafia?"

"If they'd been mafia, we'd be dead," Rex said. "And they definitely weren't Vlaak's men or the local police."

"Who then?"

Rex peaked into the back of the truck. "People who are going to be very upset when they realize they've absconded with a frozen security guard." Looking in after him, I saw that Rex was right: the cryo chamber was missing. "Boggs, get Slacks into the ship. Everybody else, help me with these crates."

"Do we need the crates, sir?" I asked. "Our mission was to retrieve Slacks."

"I'm not leaving perfectly good booty behind, Sasha. Stop yakking and help me with this crate."

We loaded the rest of the cargo without incident. Then we strapped ourselves in and took off, breathing a collective sigh of relief as we left Xagnon's atmosphere. Once we were on our way back to Sargasso Seven, Rex and I joined the others in the main cabin. Slacks was tied to a chair, his feet still moving in a rhythmic walking motion. "Slacks," he said as we approached.

"So we have no idea who this guy is?" Rex asked.

"None," I replied.

"Did he have any ID on him?" asked Rex.

"He's only wearing a diaper, sir."

Rex frowned. "Well, this is no good. How am I supposed to rip off Pepper if I don't know who this guy is?"

"You may have to be content with a square deal this time, sir," I said. "Clearly he's of no use to us, but she knows something we don't. We're just going to have to bring Slacks to Pepper and take the fifteen million credits you agreed on."

"Ugh," Rex said. "I hate having to live up to my end of a bargain. Feels like I'm being cheated."

"Yes, sir," I said. "I'm afraid, however, that we have no choice. If we want our money—and to know why this guy keeps saying 'Slacks,' we're going to have to bring him to Pepper."

•●.

"Well, this is no good," said Pepper. "I'm not paying for him in this condition. What did you do to him? Why does he keep saying 'Slacks'?"

"Slacks," said the old man. He was still walking in place, his faced mashed against the front wall of Pepper's office. We had left Boggs and Donny in the bar while we handed Slacks over to Pepper. It had been a chore to get Slacks inside; he kept wanting to walk the opposite direction. He hadn't stopped walking—or saying "Slacks"—since we'd thawed him.

"We didn't do anything to him," Rex said. "Other than unfreeze him, I mean. And that was just to make sure he was still in good condition."

"Slacks," said Slacks, banging his head against the wall.

"Does he seem like he's in good condition to you?" Pepper asked.

"Well, no," said Rex. "But I didn't know him before he was frozen, so I don't have a solid baseline on which to judge."

"It's possible the cryogenic suspension damaged his brain," I said. At this point, I was having serious doubts about my initial thought that Slacks was missing his pants. I was no neurologist, but Slacks's problems seemed deeper than the merely sartorial.

Pepper frowned. "What sort of brain damage would cause someone to walk into walls and say 'Slacks' over and over?"

"Maybe he's cold," Rex suggested.

Pepper got up from her desk and went to a door that opened into a small closet. She rummaged around until she found a blanket. She walked back to the old man, draped the blanked over his shoulders and tied it in a loose knot around his neck.

"Slacks," said the old man.

"How long was he frozen?" I asked.

"You don't know?" Pepper replied.

"Know what?" asked Rex.

Pepper shook her head. "You have no idea who this man is, do you? Why did you hijack the *Raina Huebner* if you didn't know what cargo they were carrying?"

"It's all part of a much larger plan," Rex said.

"Dumb luck," I said. Rex shot an angry glare at me, but he had to know at this point that trying to bluff Pepper was pointless. She knew we didn't have a clue who Slacks was or why she wanted him.

"You just picked the *Raina Huebner* at random?"

"Yes," I replied.

"And did you know about Malgastar's plans?"

"No," I replied. "We were just at the right place at the right time. Or the wrong place at the wrong time, depending on how the next few minutes go."

Rex continued to glare. I ignored him.

Pepper nodded. "Thank you for your honesty, Sasha," she said. "In return, I will be honest with you. Would you care to know the identity of the man currently banging his head against my office wall?"

"Sure, why not?" I said.

"He has gone by many names," Pepper said, "but you would probably know him as Ort Felzich."

"Ort Felzich?" Rex asked. "You mean...?"

"That's right," Pepper said. "The man you call 'Slacks' is the founder of the galaxy-wide religious movement known as the Sp'ossels."

CHAPTER FIFTEEN

"You're telling me Slacks is Ort Felzich, the First Sp'ossel?" Rex asked.

"The very same," said Pepper.

"Wow," I said. "That explains those guys at the spaceport."

"What guys?" Pepper asked.

"Slacks," said Ort Felzich.

"Guys in black suits tried to take Sla—er, Felzich," Rex said.

"You think they were Sp'ossels?" Pepper asked.

"They looked the part," Rex said. "I'd have put it together earlier if I'd have known we were transporting Ort Felzich himself."

You've undoubtedly heard the story of Ort Felzich, an interstellar pioneer who, while exploring a particularly barren area of the galaxy, had supposedly received a transcendent vision of the incomprehensible vastness of space. Felzich was inspired to found a religious sect dedicated to impressing upon everyone in the galaxy just how incredibly large space is. This sect became known as the Space Apostles, a name which was later colloquially shortened to Sp'ossels. The cult grew rapidly, but some twenty years after the founding of the Sp'ossels, Ort Felzich's reign as First Apostle ended when he lost his mind while on a pilgrimage into the depths of space.

His ship incapacitated, Felzich floated helplessly in space for several days. He would have died had he not been rescued by an expedition sent by the government of the Ragulian system. Unfortunately for Felzich, the Ragulians had a longstanding policy of persecuting Sp'ossels on the grounds that their teachings were "confounding and insipid." The Ragulians tried to trade Ort for a promise that the Sp'ossels would withdraw their missionaries from the Ragulian system, but the Sp'ossels claimed an inalienable right to spread their message and refused to give in. Neither side budged for several years, and meanwhile Felzich's mental health continued to deteriorate. The Ragulians ultimately decided to cryogenically freeze Felzich to keep his condition from worsening while negotiations dragged on. After a decade of this, the urgency of the matter began to fade; seventy years later, few in the galaxy remembered that the Ragulians still had the Sp'ossel founder on ice. Why he'd been in the cargo hold of the *Raina Huebner* was unclear to me.

"So," Rex said, "Rubric Malgastar raided the *Raina Huebner* specifically to recover Ort Felzich. Why?"

"We were going to sell him to the Sp'ossels," Pepper replied.

"How did Malgastar know Felzich was on the *Raina Huebner?*"

"I hear things in this job," Pepper replied. "Sometimes I pass along information to pirates for a cut of the profits. When I heard about a cargo ship from the Ragulian system planning a stop at a Malarchian research facility, I got curious. Did some digging and discovered that the cargo was pretty mundane stuff—robot parts, that sort of thing—with one exception: a cryogenic suspension chamber. My spy on the *Raina Huebner* gave me a model number. That model hasn't been manufactured for over sixty years, so whoever was inside it had been frozen for a very long time. The obvious candidate, given the source and the destination, was Ort Felzich."

"And you passed this information along to Rubric Malgastar," I said.

"Malgastar and I had a deal. He would recover the chamber, I'd sell it to the Sp'ossels, and we'd split the profits. And then you screwed that up. So here we are."

"Malgastar was working for you?" I asked. "He nearly killed us."

"Did you resist? He was supposed to let the crew go unharmed."

Apparently running hadn't been the best move after all.

"There's no reason we can't proceed with the deal," Rex said. "You just pay us instead of Malgastar. Easy."

"I could have done that," Pepper replied, "except that you opened the chamber."

Rex frowned. "Did I void the hundred-year-old frozen guy warranty or something? Everybody knows Ort Felzich went nuts. That's why they froze him."

"Nuts, yes. This guy is catatonic. All he does is walk into walls and say 'Slacks.'"

"Slacks," said Felzich, his forehead thumping against the wall.

"I don't understand," I said. "I assumed the Sp'ossel connection to Felzich was mainly sentimental. Are they expecting to be able to reinstall him as their leader?"

"I can't say what they expect, exactly. My communications with the Sp'ossel leadership have been limited. But I get the impression they think Felzich has some valuable information."

"What kind of information?"

"The legend says that Felzich was looking for something when he went insane. Something that was central to the Sp'ossels' mission. I think the Sp'ossels know what he was looking for, and they hope to use him to find it."

"What do you think he was looking for?"

"I don't know. I'm not sure I even buy the story. The point is, the Sp'ossels believe it, and they were willing to pay for the information. I never promised them any information, though. I told them I'd deliver Felzich unharmed."

"Well, he's technically unharmed, isn't he?" Rex asked.

Pepper shook her head. "They'll take one look at him and renege on the deal. They might give me ten thousand credits for him, if I'm lucky. I could have sold them the cryo chamber unopened for fifty million, easy."

"I knew it!" Rex exclaimed. "I knew you were shafting us!"

"But he's practically worthless like this. In any case, I don't have the money. I couldn't pay you if I wanted to. I already spent twenty thousand so Malgastar could pay his crew for the job. Between that and the trouble I'm having getting pirates to pay their bills around here, I'm strapped for cash."

"Bills for what?" I asked.

"Food, fuel, supplies, repairs, you name it. Sargasso Seven is a one-stop shop for all your privateering needs. But business has been bad since the Malarchy started indiscriminately blowing up pirate ships a few weeks ago. The Primate has put Heinous Vlaak in charge of anti-piracy efforts, and Vlaak is desperate to prove himself. I had to let all my employees go except Tim. I don't even pay him. He works here because he thinks there's such a thing as a piracy internship program."

I frowned. "You lied to him?"

"Of course I lied to him. He was ready to sign up with Hookbeard. He'd be dead by now if I hadn't intervened. At least this way he gets three square meals and a place to sleep. But I might not even be able to keep him on much longer. One of my regulars, a guy named Gil VerBrugge, just quit the business when three of his ships were blasted by the Malarchy. He sold his remaining ships and retired. Bastard owed me ten million credits."

"You let this VerBrugge guy rack up a debt of ten million credits?" Rex asked. "Sounds like you were asking to get ripped off."

"I was holding a shipment of black market pheelsophine as collateral on the debt, but I haven't been able to unload it. It's still sitting in my storeroom."

Rex frowned disapprovingly. "You're telling me you were unable to sell a shipment of perfectly good black market narcotics?"

"It's tougher than you might think," Pepper said. "The planets in this part of the galaxy are crawling with Malarchian agents. If they catch you with ten million credits' worth of black market pheelsophine, you're looking at a hundred years in Gulagatraz. I know a middleman on Vericulon Four, but he hasn't been returning my calls. I'd go there in person, but I can't leave Sargasso Seven."

"Hmm," said Rex.

"Sir, please," I said. "We're not drug dealers."

"I'm a businessman," Rex replied. "I don't make moral judgments about the products I sell."

"You could have ended that sentence at 'judgments,' sir."

He ignored me. "What if Sasha and I could deliver the pheelsophine and get the money from your middleman? Then you could pay us most of what you owe us."

"As I've established," Pepper said, "I don't owe you anything, since you delivered a defective product. However, considering the effort you've put in, I might be willing to give you twenty-five percent on the pheelsophine."

"No deal," said Rex. "We're taking all the risk. That pheelsophine is worthless to you without someone to fence it for you. I can't sell it for less than seventy percent of the proceeds."

"Forty," said Pepper.

"Fifty percent and you have a deal."

"Done," Pepper replied. "Let me show you where the pallet is." She started toward the door and then stopped. "Do you think Felzich will be okay alone for a few minutes?"

"Slacks," said Felzich, banging his head against the wall.

"He'll be fine," Rex said. "Let's go get those drugs."

100

CHAPTER SIXTEEN

I didn't like the idea of getting into distributing black market pheelsophine, but we didn't have much choice. Our ship was in bad shape. We had no money and just enough fuel to make one more hypergeometric jump. If we didn't have some cargo to sell, we were going to have to sell the *Flagrante Delicto-cum-Chronic Lumbago*. That would get us a little cash, but then we'd be stranded on a strange planet with no way of making more money. It wouldn't be the first time Rex and I had been in that position, but the last time we worked hard labor for three weeks before Rex managed to steal a prisoner transport vessel and get us off world.

Anyway, this was a one-time deal. We'd contact Pepper's middleman on Vericulon Four, sell him the pallet of pheelsophine, and head back to Sargasso Seven to give Pepper her cut. We left Boggs, Donny, Squawky, and Rex's eye patch back at Pepper's place as collateral.

"I can't believe she fell for that," Rex said, as we entered orbit around Vericulon Four.

"Sir?" I said.

"Does Pepper really think we're coming back to Sargasso Seven once we get paid for this shipment?"

"Aren't we, sir?"

"Why? To give her half the money we make on these drugs? Not a chance."

"Sir, has it occurred to you that Pepper Mélange might be a valuable resource for us? She seems to be privy to a lot of information. If we stay on her good side, the long-term reward will undoubtedly outweigh—"

"Never talk to me about long term rewards, Sasha. If I can't spend it, I don't want it."

"Additionally, sir," I continued, "it would appear that Pepper has friends all over the galaxy. If we cross her, there's a considerable possibility of retribution."

Rex rolled his eyes.

"Also, you won't get Squawky back."

"Squawky!" Rex cried, suddenly pained at the thought. "I miss him so much. Not just Squawky, of course. My eye patch too."

"You'll never see either of them again if we swindle Pepper."

"It's an impossible decision," Rex moaned. "Five million credits or the best friend I've ever had. I can't bear to think about it. What's taking so long? Why haven't we landed?"

"Working on it, sir." Our ship descended through the atmosphere and we landed at the Vericulon Four City Spaceport. Vericulon Four was a cold, gray, and depressing planet. Clouds concealed the planet's sun and much of the surface was ice; only a few hundred square kilometers near the equator were habitable. The lone spaceport on the planet was right in the middle of this area.

Pepper's fence ran a small shipping company adjacent to the spaceport. We left the pallet of pheelsophine in the ship and walked over to see him. We'd tried to raise him on the ship's comm, but there had been no response. The spaceport was mostly deserted. Other than a few cargo handlers who wandered about listlessly or lay sleeping on the floor, we saw no spaceport personnel. Crates and various equipment lay strewn about the landing area. Despite these worrisome signs, however, Rex was in exceptionally good spirits.

I opened the door to the shipping office to find a member of the Barashavian species lying on top of a sizable desk. Barashavians looked a bit like blue-furred kangaroos, with donkey-like ears and two large eyeballs on eyestalks. The Barashavian's body remained motionless as we entered, but its eyes and ears turned slowly toward us.

"Greetings!" Rex said, striding into the room. "I take it you're Rav Varmara. Pepper Mélange sent us. We've got a shipment of something she said you'd be interested in."

"Oh," said the Barashavian. "Oh, that's great. Really great." A smile came over his face and he extended one of his long arms, giving us a thumbs-up.

"It's pheelsophine," Rex said cheerfully. "Black market pheelsophine. We'd love to sell it to you."

"Yeah," said the Rav Varmara. "That's great. Just, you know, leave it by the door."

"You heard him, Sasha. Go get the stuff."

"Yes, sir," I said. I went to the ship and used an antigrav hand truck to carry the pallet back to Rav Varmara's office. I parked it outside and went back into the office. I found Rex lying on the desk next to Rav

Varmara. "Sir?" I asked.

"Hey, Sasha," Rex said. "What's up?"

"The pheelsophine is outside, sir."

"Great!" Rex exclaimed. "Just great."

"Yeah," Rav Varmara agree. "Isn't it? Just great."

"Sir, what are you doing?"

"Just lying here with my friend, Rav Varmara. Did you know he's been here for three days?"

"Sometimes I get up to pee," said Rav Varmara.

"But… why?" I asked.

"Don't like lying in pee."

"I mean, why have you been lying here for three days?"

Rav Varmara shrugged. "Every once in a while I think about doing something, but then I'm like, 'why?'"

"Exactly," Rex said. "It's so great here. I don't think I've ever been this happy."

"Me neither," said Rav Varmara. "Let's just stay here forever."

"Okay," Rex said.

"But sir," I said. "What about the pheelsophine? What about the money?"

"Money!" Rex spat. "Money doesn't make you happy. You know what makes a person happy? I'll tell you."

A long pause followed, during which he did not tell me.

"Sir?" I asked.

"I'm thinking," Rex said. "I'm just so…"

"Happy," Rav Varmara said.

"Yeah!" Rex exclaimed. "What he said. So, so happy. You should try this, Sasha."

"I don't think there's room for me on the desk, sir."

"It's not about the desk, Sasha. Stop being such a downer. Why can't you just be happy like me and Rav Varmara?"

"I honestly don't know, sir," I replied. "Perhaps it would help if you described what you are feeling."

"I'm just, like, so happy," Rex said.

Rav Varmara nodded.

"I don't even know why I bothered with all those crazy cons and moneymaking scams. Happiness was here all along. Right here in my heart. Come on, Sasha. Lie down here with me and Rav and feel the happiness in your heart."

"I don't have a heart, sir."

"Yeah, that's true. Wow, that's great. No heart. I'm so happy for you, Sasha."

"Please, sir. I think we've made a mistake. There's something not right on this planet."

"No, no. Everything is fine. Everything is great."

"Really great," Rav Varmara agreed. "So happy."

"Things are not great, sir," I said. "Something has gone wrong with your brain. You're experiencing some kind of delusion. An artificial euphoria of some kind, like a narcotic." Had Rex gotten into the pheelsophine? The shrinkwrapping around the crate was unbroken, as far as I could tell. And this didn't seem like a pheelsophine high. It was more like some kind of mind control. And it seemed to be affecting the entire spaceport, if not the whole planet. It explained why we hadn't seen anybody working. Every sentient being in the area was experiencing an irrational euphoria that dampened their desire to do anything productive. Presumably I remained unaffected only because of my inorganic brain.

Somehow I had to get Rex off this planet. But how? If he was completely content, there was nothing I could bait him with. On the other hand, if he was equally happy about everything, then nothing I suggested would seem like a bad idea to him.

"I have a suggestion, sir," I said.

"That's great, Sasha," Rex replied. "I love it when you have suggestions."

"Suggestions are the best," Rav Varmara agreed.

"Well," I went on, "I was thinking, wouldn't it be great if we got back into the *Flagrante Delicto*? It would be so much more comfortable in there."

"Right?" Rex said. "This desk is horribly uncomfortable. Terrible ergonomics."

"The worst," Rav Varmara agreed.

"But that's what makes it so great," Rex added.

"*So* great," Rav agreed. "I've never been so happy to be this uncomfortable. It's like my hips are on fire."

"My whole upper back has gone numb," Rex said. "It's amazing."

"Fantastic," said Rav Varmara.

"So the *Flagrante Delicto*..." I said.

"Seems like a lot of effort, considering I have everything I need right here," Rex said. "Maybe you should try lying down, Sasha."

I sighed. Clearly I was going to have to stack the deck in my favor. I went back outside, removed the antigrav hand truck from the pallet, and went back inside. "Who wants a ride?" I said.

"Ooh, me!" Rex cried. He rolled off the desk onto the hand truck. Before Rav Varmara could get on as well, I pulled the hand truck away from the desk, moving toward the door. Rav Varmara shrugged and lay back down. I carried Rex across the tarmac back to the *Flagrante Delicto*. He yelped with glee the whole way. When I dumped him on the floor of the ship, he moaned, "Wow, that hurt. Amazing. I'm so happy you did that, Sasha. Ow."

I went to the cockpit and took off a quickly as I could, in case Rex changed his mind. He seemed perfectly content to lie on his back on the deck, but as I didn't know the cause of his euphoria or what it might cause him to do next, I didn't want to take any chances.

We were only a few klicks above the surface when Rex came into the cockpit, looking even more surly than usual. "Why'd you leave that place?" he groused. "I loved it there."

"So I saw. You seemed to be in the grip of some kind of irrational delusion."

"You don't have to ruin it for everybody, just because you don't know how to have fun."

"Perhaps if you explained to me what was so wonderful about that shipping office…?"

"Don't be ridiculous, Sasha. That place was… well, there was a big desk there. And a guy who smelled like urine. And, uh… Space, my back hurts. What was I thinking, Sasha?"

"I don't have the faintest idea, sir. I thought you'd gotten into the pheelsophine, but I—"

"The pheelsophine! You left it at the spaceport!"

"I didn't have much choice, sir. I barely got you out of there."

"We have to go back!"

"That would seem inadvisable, sir, until we figure out what happened to you. My best guess is some kind of mind control. It seemed to be affecting everyone at the spaceport, so I suspect some kind of localized psionic manipulation."

"A mind control ray."

"It would appear so, sir."

"And we don't know who is using it or why. If we land again, they might send you into a suicidal depression or a homicidal rage. You were difficult enough to deal with when you were merely content."

"Why would somebody be using a mind control ray on the Vericulon Four City Spaceport?"

"It may not be limited to the spaceport, sir. It could be the entire city. Perhaps even the entire habitable area of the planet."

"Only one way to find out," Rex said.

"Sir?"

"Fly back toward the spaceport. Keep going until I'm happy."

"And then what?"

"Leave again."

"Okay, and then…?"

"Fly back in. Good grief, Sasha. Use your head. We'll buzz around until we get an idea of how big the field is. Then we can find a safe place to land. I'll wait in the ship while you get the pheelsophine."

"Aye, sir," I said. As Rex's ideas went, it wasn't a terrible one. I turned the *Flagrante Delicto* around. Not two minutes later, Rex gave a contented sigh.

"This is the best idea I ever had," he said. "I love this place." He sank to his knees on the metal deck. "Such a nice floor. So great. Sasha, let's never, ever… ugh. Why am I on the floor?"

"We seem to be leaving the field again, sir. Give me a moment to bank and I'll head back in.

"Hurry up," Rex snapped, getting to his feet. "This is like the worst hangover ever. If you hadn't left a perfectly good pallet of pheelsophine back there, we could… oh yeah, that's the stuff. Wow. This is amazing, Sasha. I've never been so happy in my life. Why don't we just put the ship on autopilot and—damn it!"

We continued in this manner for the next half hour or so, flying in and out of the happiness field until I had a general sense for its size and shape. The bad news was that it was far too large for us to safely land outside of it. It covered the entire habitable area of Vericulon Four. If we wanted to get our pheelsophine back, we were going to have to land right in the middle of the field.

"It appears to be cone-shaped," I said. "About twenty klicks wide at the base, centered on Vericulon Four City."

"Where's the top of the cone?" Rex asked.

"That's the interesting part. The field seems to originate from a satellite in geosynchronous orbit around the planet. It's parked right above the city."

"All right then, Sasha. You know what to do."

"Head back to Sargasso Seven and apologize for losing Pepper's pallet of pheelsophine?"

"Get me to that satellite so we can blow it up."

CHAPTER SEVENTEEN

I stared blankly at Rex. "Sir, why in Space would we want to blow up the satellite?"

"Because it's keeping us from getting our drugs. And from selling our drugs, come to think of it. Even if we get the drugs back, we'll never be able to sell them if everybody on this planet is irrationally happy. Frankly, I find this sort of emotional manipulation grotesque. Humans were meant to strive, to persevere in the face of hardship. Using mind control to make people artificially happy strikes at the heart of what it means to be human and completely undercuts the market for black market narcotics."

"Your devotion to human dignity is to be admired, sir. But don't you think it's perhaps time for us to cut our losses? Somehow we went from space pirates to drug runners, and we seem to be even worse at the latter, as hard as that is to believe. Further, we have no idea who put that satellite up there. Maybe it's some kind of Malarchian experiment. If they catch us sabotaging their satellite, they'll blast us to atoms. Let's just get off this planet. We can sell the *Flagrante Delicto* and—"

"I'll never sell the *Flagrante Delicto*!" Rex cried. "Where's your fighting spirit, Sasha? We'll knock out that satellite, get our drugs back, sell the drugs, and then get back to the swashbuckling life of piracy and buccaneering that we always dreamed about!"

"So you're planning on going back to Sargasso Seven?"

"Sure," Rex replied. "When we take down that satellite, the people on Vericulon Four are going to be miserable. We'll be able to sell that pheelsophine at a premium. Probably five times what we'd normally get for it. If we pocket fifty million on the deal, I don't mind giving five million to Pepper so I can get Squawky and my eye patch back."

"You're a terrible person, sir," I said.

"Just get me to that satellite."

I piloted the *Flagrante Delicto-cum-Chronic Lumbago* out of the atmosphere and brought it into orbit a hundred meters or so in front of the satellite. The main body of the satellite was saucer-shaped, with something that looked like a parabolic antenna affixed to the bottom. Protruding from the center of the parabola was a metal column about ten centimeters wide and ten meters long. Toward the far end was a series of metal rings that encircled the column, and at the end was a multifaceted, roughly spherical object, about two meters in diameter, made of a translucent blue material.

"What is that thing?" Rex asked, staring at the satellite from the cockpit.

"That would appear to be the antenna that transmits the mind control wave," I replied.

"I know that, nickel noggin. I mean the thing at the tip of that pole."

"Some kind of crystal to intensify the signal?" I offered. Mind control satellites weren't really my wheelhouse.

"It's zontonium," Rex said. "It has to be." Zontonium is a rare mineral that is used for rocket fuel in most spaceships. If Rex was right, it had applications to mind control satellites as well. It did look like zontonium. "That thing's gotta be worth a hundred million credits, easy," Rex said. "If we can get it off there..."

"Sir, can we keep one evil scheme in mind at a time? Are we pirates, drug runners, or jewel thieves?"

"Spaceship fuel thieves, Sasha. We're killing two birds with one stone, so to speak. I get a fortune in rocket fuel and we make the poor bastards on that planet down there miserable. I'm going to go suit up. Get us in position to get my rock off."

•●.

While Rex got his vac suit on, I maneuvered the *Flagrante Delicto-cum-Chronic Lumbago* as close as I could to the satellite. I depressurized the airlock and we leaped outside. We were only a few meters away from the top of the column.

Rex wrapped his arms around the column and worked his way

down toward the massive gemstone. I followed. As I neared the bottom of the column, I became aware that it was vibrating rhythmically. Looking down, I saw that Rex was slamming the bottom of his boot into the gemstone.

"It's stuck on pretty tight," Rex said, transmitting directly to me from the vac suit's comm. "Do we still have those grenades?"

"The ones Boggs won—er, retrieved from the Raina Huebner?"

"You know of another box of grenades?"

"No, sir. But do you think using grenades to blast the—"

"Get the grenades, Sasha."

"Aye, sir." I climbed back up the column and leaped into the airlock of the *Flagrante Delicto-cum-Chronic Lumbago.*

"And rope!" I heard Rex broadcast.

"Aye, sir."

I pressurized the airlock, retrieved the crate of grenades and fifty meters of rope, depressurized the airlock, and jumped back out to the column. "Here, sir," I said, shoving the crate gently toward Rex. As the crate floated down along the column toward Rex, I noticed a light just above the horizon, moving toward us. Rex caught the crate and maneuvered it next to him.

"Sir," I said.

"Cram it, meteor mouth. We're using the grenades. How many do you think it'll take? Three? Seven?"

"It's not that, sir. Look." I pointed in the direction of the light. It was a ship, closing on our position fast.

"Blast," Rex growled. "We must have triggered an alarm."

"I estimate they'll be here in less than five minutes, sir. We should leave now."

"I'm not leaving without my gigantic gemstone," Rex said. "Help me tie this rope around the rock. I don't want to lose it when I blast it off."

Realizing it was hopeless to waste time trying to talk Rex out of this plan, I helped him wrap the rope around the stone and then tied it in a tight knot.

"Good, now go tie the other end to the *Flagrante Delicto.*"

"Aye, sir." I began climbing back up the column while Rex jammed grenades between the last two metal rings encircling the column. In the distance, the ship was now clearly visible, decelerating toward us. It didn't look like a Malarchian vessel. Hopefully whoever it was cared more about the integrity of their satellite than killing us. I reached the top of the column and leaped back to the airlock. Glancing down, I saw Rex pull a pin from one of the grenades.

"Sir, wait!" I cried. But it was too late. Rex wrapped his arms around the column and propelled himself off the gemstone toward bottom of the satellite. As Rex's helmet struck the dish, there was a flash of light and the whole satellite trembled violently. "Whoohoo!" Rex cried, looking down. "It worked!"

He was right: as the debris cleared, I saw that the grenades had blown clear though the column, separating the stone from the satellite. The stone began to fall away toward the blue-gray orb of Vericulon Four. The rope, which was hanging in loose loops between me and the gemstone, started to go taut. My eyes alighted on the inner airlock valve and I lunged toward it, intending to tie the rope around the handle. But my efforts were stymied by the hook in place of my left hand. I had just enough time to wrap the rope tightly around my right wrist and get my hook around the valve handle. For a moment, as I hung there suspended in the airlock, I thought I had done it. I would arrest the fall of the gemstone, pull it into the airlock, and Rex and I would escape before whoever was in that spaceship killed us.

And then my arm came off.

Technically, it was the hook that came off. So much for Boggs's fine workmanship. The appendage tore clean off at the joint. The stone simply had too much momentum.

I nearly managed to catch the edge of the airlock on my way out, but couldn't get my hand loose from the rope. I was pulled clear of the *Flagrante Delicto-cum-Chronic Lumbago* and was soon in freefall, being pulled slowly toward the planet's surface by the galaxy's largest rhinestone. Below me I saw Rex on a similar trajectory. The rope had gotten wrapped around his leg and jerked him right off the satellite. He looked up helplessly as the stone pulled us toward the planet. I thought of letting go, but at this point it didn't make much difference; my velocity had matched that of the stone. We were all going down together.

As we fell, however, I became aware that the strange ship was maneuvering itself beneath us. It came to a halt a hundred meters or so below and its side cargo hatch opened, facing us. The rock fell inside first, followed soon after by Rex and me. Men in vac suits grabbed hold of us. The outer door was closed and the chamber pressurized.

The men shoved us into another room, where artificial gravity pulled us to the floor. Rex pulled off his helmet.

"Who in Space do you think you are?" he demanded. "This is kidnapping! I demand you let us go!"

The two suited men removed their helmets. They were both young and clean-cut. The first man was blond; the other's hair was darker. "Interesting choice of words, Mr. Nihilo," said the blond man. Where would you like us to let you go? Somewhere in the deep, dark reaches of space?"

"How do you know my name?" Rex asked.

"Do you have any clue how big space is?" asked the dark-haired man.

"You have to be kidding me," said Rex.

"Sp'ossels," I groaned. "There's just no getting away from you guys, is there?"

"You have no idea how right you are, Sasha," said the blond man. "We did lose track of you for a bit there, but fortunately Rex finds it impossible to keep a low profile. And while we appreciate your ambition in attempting to steal the zontonium focusing crystal from our satellite, we have other plans for it."

"*Your* satellite?" Rex asked. "You mean the Sp'ossels are behind the happiness field? What are the Sp'ossels doing messing around with mind control? I thought you guys were all about spreading the good word about Space."

"That's only part of our message," the dark-haired man said. "It's a common mistake; most people never listen to the entire speech. What we're really all about is spreading universal happiness. The bit about space is just to let people know what a monumental task spreading universal happiness really is."

"Artificial happiness," I said.

"Happiness is happiness, Sasha," said the blond man. "We've been working on this for a very long time. Vericulon Four was just a test. Our plan is to spread happiness throughout the entire galaxy."

"A happiness field that extends across the galaxy?" Rex said. "You people are nuts. And you still haven't told us how your know our names."

"My apologies," said the blond man. "I forget that despite your notoriety in our organization, you two don't actually realize you work for us."

"Me working for *you*?" Rex scoffed. "Sure. Like I said, Sasha. Completely bonkers."

"Yes, sir," I said. But I was getting a bad feeling about this whole situation. That feeling got a lot worse when the blond man drew a lazegun and the dark-haired man produced a device that resembled a metal colander. "I'll get to you next, Sasha," the dark-haired man said. "We can probably fix that arm while we're at it. Then we'll drop you both on some planet nearby to keep you out of the way while we finalize our plans. How does Beltran Prime sound?"

"What in Space are you doing?" Rex demanded, as the dark-haired man approached him with the colander thing.

"Relax," said the dark-haired man. "You won't remember a thing."

CHAPTER EIGHTEEN

RECORDING ADVANCED TO GALACTIC STANDARD DATE
3017.02.03.011:14:00:00

Rex rubbed his chin while I rationalized a hypergeometric course to Sargasso Seven. I had just told him everything that had happened before we got to Beltran Prime, and he clearly needed a moment to process it. After some time, he spoke. "I just have one question."

"Yes, sir."

"Are you telling me I used to have an eye patch and a robotic parrot named Squawky?"

"Yes, sir."

"And the Sp'ossels wiped my memories of both of those things?"

"Yes, sir."

"Those bastards!"

"Sir, did you miss the part about how the Sp'ossels have been manipulating us for years, risking our lives countless times for their own material gain?"

"Squawky was the best friend I ever had."

"You don't even remember him, sir."

"But from what you've told me, he was pretty great."

"He mostly just repeated things other people said. And I think he threatened to murder you once."

"That's Squawky alright. Always joking around. Space, I miss him."

"Well, you'll get to see him soon, when we explain to Pepper Mélange how we lost her drugs."

"We did what for whom?"

"I just explained all this, sir. Pepper Mélange runs the pirate haven on Sargasso Seven. When Ort Felzich turned out to be catatonic, she sent us to Vericulon Four with a shipment of black market pheelsophine to unload. We failed because the population of the planet was artificially happy, thanks to a Sp'ossel mind control satellite. We disabled the satellite but were intercepted by Sp'ossel agents who erased our memories."

"What do you think Squawky is doing right now?" Rex asked. "Do you think he misses me?"

"I wouldn't presume to say, sir."

Rex was silent for some time. "Do you think they keep all my memories somewhere? They must, right? The Sp'ossels have to maintain a record of all the missions they sent us on."

"I suppose so, sir."

"Do you think I could get them back?"

"Possibly, sir. Memory transfer protocols have gotten fairly advanced. It's theoretically possible, in fact, to store a person's entire consciousness outside their body, although the algorithms for consciousness storage remains somewhat lossy."

"Lossy? What's that?"

"It means the algorithm isn't perfect. The stored copy of the subject's consciousness loses some of its character in process of transferring it to the storage medium. All known consciousness storage algorithms are slightly lossy."

Rex stared at me. "A slightly lossy algorithm for consciousness storage," he said.

"Sir?"

"Never mind, Sasha. Get us to that pirate haven. I think we have something better than drugs to offer this Pepper person."

"Potential Friend!" cried Boggs, as we entered Pepper's tavern. "Sasha!"

Hookbeard and his crew were nowhere to be seen, but several other pirates watched us from the shadows.

"Who is this very large man?" Rex asked, as Boggs and Donny approached.

"That's Boggs," I said. "He's part of our crew. And this is—"

116

"Donny," Rex said. "Obviously I know Donny when I see him. Ah, and this must be Squawky!" The robotic parrot was perched on Boggs's shoulder. It hopped onto Rex's shoulder as they approached.

"I'm a born pirate," said Squawky.

"Of course you are, Squawky," said Rex.

"Sorry to interrupt the reunion," said Pepper, approaching from behind Boggs, "but where is my money?"

"Wow!" Rex exclaimed, turning to face Pepper. "You didn't tell me the pirate lady was a knockout."

"It slipped my mind, sir."

"Seriously?" Pepper said. "You've forgotten me *again*?"

"Yes, but I have a very good reason."

"Which is?"

"I forget."

"Never mind. Where is my money?"

"That's an excellent question," Rex said. "Sasha, answer it."

"What?" I said. "Oh, I… uh, well, we had some trouble selling the pheelsophine. You see, there was this satellite—"

"You lost my drugs, didn't you?"

"Correct," I said.

"And you have nothing to show for it."

"Correct."

"Forget all that," said Rex. "I've come up with a way for us to make a fortune."

Pepper glared at him. "You're saying that after screwing up my deal with the Sp'ossels and losing my pallet of black market pheelsophine, you're offering to take advantage of me a third time?"

"Okay, first of all," Rex said, "This is by far the best deal of the three, and secondly, I don't actually remember the first two."

"Does this story get any better?"

"I know what 'slacks' means."

"Excuse me?"

"Ort Felzich. He keeps saying 'slacks,' right? And running into the wall? I know why."

Pepper seemed dubious. "A minute ago, you didn't remember anything that had happened in the last week."

"I still don't," said Rex. "In fact, I think it's the clarity of an almost completely empty mind that allowed me to see it."

"I'm listening," Pepper said.

Rex continued, "Sasha was jabbering on, telling me about all the stuff that happened over the past few days, and to be honest I wasn't really following most of it. I kept thinking that it would be nice if I could just store all these memories someplace for easy access later. And then she was talking about this Felzich guy, and how he lost his mind and kept saying 'slacks,' and I started to wonder, when you lose your mind, where does it go, and then Sasha was talking about lossy algorithms, and I thought—"

"I strongly suggest you to get to the point, Rex," Pepper said.

"Slightly Lossy Algorithm for Consciousness Storage," Rex said. "SLACS for short. Ort Felzich is trying to tell us what happened to his mind."

As Rex said it, I realized he was right. SLACS was the name given to a long-forgotten method of consciousness storage. It had been deprecated decades ago in favor of more reliable algorithms.

"In my office," Pepper said. She turned and headed for the door. Rex and I followed.

"Donny comes?" asked Donny. Boggs looked at me expectantly.

"Just hang out here for a little longer, guys," I said. "This shouldn't take long."

We followed Pepper into her office. I closed the door as Pepper took a seat behind her desk. Ort Felzich was now in the rear corner of the room, still banging his head against the wall and muttering "slacks."

"What in Space is this lossy algorithm stuff about?" Pepper asked.

"If I'm not mistaken," I replied, "Rex believes Ort Felzich's consciousness was extracted. That he didn't just go insane. He literally lost his mind."

"Exactly," said Rex. "Someone sucked out his mind and put it in some kind of storage module."

"A SLACS receptacle," I said. "But who would remove Felzich's mind? And why?"

"No idea," Rex said. "But I think I know where. That is, I know how to find out where."

"How?" asked Pepper.

"He's walking there. Trying, anyway. We just have to follow him."

The room was silent for a moment. Then Pepper spoke. "That's the most idiotic thing I've ever heard. Even if you're right, his consciousness could be anywhere in the galaxy. We can't just have him walk across the galaxy and follow him to his brain."

"Why not?" Rex asked.

"Because you can't walk across space, you moron."

"Triangulation," I said. "It could work. If he really is attempting to move toward a particular point, we just need to transport him to two other locations a significant distance apart. The direction he walks will change depending on his position relative to the consciousness storage device."

"Hold on," said Pepper. "We don't even know that's where he's trying to go. How would his body even know where his consciousness is?"

I answered. "Psionic theory holds that there is an unbreakable bond between the physical brain and consciousness. It's an instantaneous connection across spacetime. No one really understands it, but we know psionic waves are the only thing we know of that travels faster than the speed of light. Perhaps Felzich's consciousness is signaling to his body."

"If his consciousness can contact his body with these psionic waves," Pepper asked, "why doesn't he just tell us what to do, rather than running into walls and saying 'slacks'?"

"The psionic connection would be very weak," I said. "It's quite possible it's only capable of evoking very basic motor impulses. I doubt Felzich is intentionally making his mouth say 'slacks.' He's just inadvertently triggering some vestige of memory, a rudimentary linguistic impulse. On some level, his brain knows the word 'slacks' is important, and it connects the word with the impulses it's getting from Felzich."

Pepper still seemed doubtful. "If Felzich really is walking toward his mind, why has he changed direction since this morning?"

"The change in attitude is consistent with Rex's hypothesis," I said. "Even if the location of the SLACS receptacle hasn't changed, Sargasso Seven's orbit would alter the relative position of this room. To get a fix on him, we'll have to travel to three separate points that are motionless relative to the consciousness storage receptacle."

"And if we manage to find it?" Pepper asked.

"If Rex is correct, Felzich's consciousness is fully intact and theoretically able to communicate. If he has some information of value to the Sp'ossels, that's where we'll find it."

"Exactly!" Rex exclaimed. "So your deal with the Sp'ossels is still on. We just have to find Felzich's mind."

"This is absurd," Pepper said, shaking her head.

"Maybe," Rex replied, "but we're dealing with Sp'ossels, who are absurd people. That old zealot probably doesn't have a thought in his head worth a credit to any ordinary person. But Sp'ossels aren't ordinary people. If they think Felzich knows something important, I don't see why we can't sell them Felzich's mind."

Pepper sighed. "I suppose I don't really have a choice now that you've lost my pheelsophine. But I'm going with you this time."

"Fine with me," said Rex, "but I thought you didn't dare leave Sargasso Seven."

"Seeing as I don't trust you, I don't have much choice. I'll just have to leave Tim in charge."

"Great!" Rex declared. "Isn't this wonderful, Sasha? We're going on a treasure hunt! Squawky, help me find my eye patch."

"We're all going to die," said Squawky.

CHAPTER NINETEEN

We spent the next day making hypergeometric jumps to various parts of the galaxy in an attempt to triangulate the position of Felzich's consciousness. It ended up taking more than two jumps, as Felzich's body was only able to orient itself in two dimensions. Felzich would reliably turn and began walking in a particular direction within a few seconds after jumping, but we had no way of knowing whether the SLACS module was above or below us without making additional jumps. There was also some margin of error in determining the exact direction Felzich was headed. If our measurement was off by a degree, that could amount to several light-years, depending on how far away the SLACS module was.

While the rest of the crew played cards or slept, Rex hovered over me in the cockpit, micromanaging the navigational process. I did my best to redirect the conversation to matters I feared Rex had overlooked.

"You understand, sir, that your plan depends on making a deal with the Sp'ossels—the very people who have manipulated both of us for years."

"Yes. And?"

"It's just that I would think you wouldn't be so willing to reward people who have treated you so terribly."

"First of all," Rex replied, "That stuff about the Sp'ossel manipulating us is hearsay. Not that I don't trust you, Sasha, but I don't actually remember any of it myself."

"That's the point, sir! They erased your memories! Doesn't that make you angry?"

"Second, I plan to wring every credit out of those fanatical weirdos.

They'll pay for what they did all right, in the only currency that matters: Malarchian Standard Credits."

"But sir, clearly they wouldn't make the trade if they weren't getting their money's worth. Has it occurred to you that the Sp'ossels are using your own programming against you? Scamming people out of money is exactly what they've programmed you to do. For all we know, they programmed us to hijack the *Raina Huebner* in the first place. If you really wanted to get back at them, you'd do the opposite of what they expect."

"Which is?"

"Forget about Felzich's mind. Don't make a deal with the Sp'ossels."

"Because it's too dangerous or because you want to wreak vengeance on the Sp'ossels?"

"Both, sir."

"Holding a grudge is irrational, Sasha."

"Yes, sir. But doing business with the people who have used us in this manner seems… well, inhuman."

Rex shook his head. "I'm sorry, Sasha. This is who I am. I don't know how much of it is Sp'ossel programming and frankly I don't care. When I see a chance for a big score, I take it."

I decided to change tacks. "Sir, have you thought to consider what the Sp'ossels might be up to? Why they want Felzich so badly?"

"I assume they're up to some nefarious scheme," Rex said.

"Exactly, sir. You saw what that Sp'ossel satellite did to the people of Vericulon Four. And we know their end goal is to spread 'happiness' throughout the galaxy. What if they're building something like that happiness satellite, but much larger? Something capable of spreading a mind control wave across the whole galaxy?"

Rex shrugged. "What does that have to do with me?"

"You saw what that satellite did for pheelsophine sales on Vericulon Four. How do you think you're going to make money in a galaxy where everybody is completely content and nobody wants anything?"

Rex opened his mouth to speak but then closed it again. "You make a valid point, Sasha," he said after a moment. "But if everyone is happy, then I'll be happy too, right? I won't want to make money anymore."

"And that doesn't terrify you?"

"It's incomprehensible," Rex said. "So I'm not going to worry about it."

"It doesn't bother you that everybody in the galaxy will just be lying on their desks, doing nothing all day?"

"Not particularly. For most people, it's an improvement. At least everybody will be happy for a change."

"Except me."

"Well, yes. You'll have to carry all the sadness in the galaxy for the rest of us. So are we ready for the next jump or what?"

Too depressed to continue arguing, I decided to focus on the task at hand. After seven jumps, we had pinpointed its location to within a few hundred kilometers. That was the good news.

The bad news was that the module was apparently right in the middle of the The Cabrisi Asteroid Field, a debris-filled expanse of space nearly a light-year wide. Jumping into it was out of the question. When we'd jumped into Dead Man's Nebula, we at least had a precise set of coordinates to work with. The SLACS module was probably on one of the asteroids, which meant that if we jumped to the coordinates we'd derived from Felzich's ambulations, we'd likely as not find ourselves permanently embedded in rock. To get to Felzich's consciousness, we were going to have to navigate the field manually, which posed its own problems.

Rex gathered the crew to tell them the plan. The response was not positive.

"It's just an asteroid field," I said, having resigned myself to Rex's plan. "It's dangerous, but we should be able to navigate it if we're careful."

"It's not just the asteroids themselves," Pepper said. "There's... something else lurking in that asteroid field."

"Something else?" Rex asked. "Like what? Insurance salesmen? Be specific."

Pepper bit her lip, as if embarrassed to say more. "Ghosts," she said at last.

Fear came over Boggs's face. Donny looked nervously at Boggs.

"You've got to be kidding me," said Rex. "Ghosts?"

"Scoff if you like," said Pepper. "But I've heard stories from crewmen who barely escaped that asteroid field with their lives. They say they heard voices that tried to lure them into the asteroids."

"Superstitious pirate nonsense," Rex said. But Boggs and Donny were clearly terrified.

"Ghosts in the asteroid field," Squawky said. "We're all going to die."

"See?" Pepper said. "Even the bird knows."

"This is ridiculous," Rex said. "There are no ghosts in the Cabrisi Asteroid Field. Stop frightening my crew with nonsense."

"There is one person who would know for sure," said Pepper.

"Yeah?" said Rex. "Who's that?"

"The Oracle of New Borculo Nova."

"Catchy name," said Rex.

"I've heard of her," I said. "A research station was built on a planetoid orbiting a star that had recently gone nova. The scientists all went insane and turned on each other. The Oracle of New Borculo Nova was the last remaining survivor."

"New Borculo Nova is less than a light-year from the Cabrisi Asteroid Field," Pepper said. "If anyone knows how to get through unscathed, it's her."

"Yeah, asteroids are scary," Rex said. "We should go visit a homicidal hermit living on a chunk of rock orbiting an exploding star instead."

"She's just an old woman," Pepper said. "There's no danger in talking to her."

"It might be worth investigating, sir," I said.

"Fine," Rex replied. "But then we're not making any more stops. After the New Borculo Nova station, we're going directly to the asteroid field."

It wasn't hard to determine why the staff of the New Borculo Nova research station had gone crazy. The facility had been constructed under a large transparent dome, as was standard for such research facilities, to take advantage of the natural light. Unfortunately, the planetoid revolved once every eighty-eight seconds, making the days and nights each forty-four seconds long. That sort of schedule had to wreak havoc with one's circadian rhythms.

I landed the *Flagrante Delicto-cum-Chronic Lumbago* next to the dome. I had been trying to hail the facility, but there was no response. I ended up going outside to manually engage the docking corridor. The planetoid had a thin atmosphere, but it was mostly ammonia and methane, so not really the sort of stuff you want to breathe if you can help it.

Our crew exited the ship, Rex leading the way. I followed close behind, with Pepper, Boggs and Donny trailing us. We made our way through the compound, which was eerily quiet. Rex called out a greeting several times, but no one answered. The New Borculo Nova, visible through the dome over our heads, rose behind us and set again in front of us by the time we made it to a door labeled CREW LIVING QUARTERS. We knocked, but there was no answer. Rex opened the door and we went inside. We found ourselves in what appeared to be a small living room, dimly lit by ambient lights. Stars were visible overhead.

And then, suddenly, the sun rose again behind us, bathing the room in yellowish-white light. An elderly woman with frazzled white hair sat sleeping in an easy chair. She woke with a start and stood up.

"Good morning!" she said. "I'm sorry I didn't greet you at the door. I'm on a rather tight schedule and I don't get a lot of visitors. What can I do for you?"

"Are you the Oracle of New Borculo Nova?" Rex asked.

"That's what they call me," the woman said. "You can just call me Denise. And yes, in case you're wondering, I did go crazy and murder the rest of the crew. In my defense, none of them could stay on schedule worth a damn. Are you hungry? It's almost lunchtime. I don't usually eat until Tuesday."

"No, ma'am," Rex said. "My name is Rex Nihilo. I'm the captain of the... uh..."

"*Chronic Lumbago*," I said.

"Right, the *Chronic Lumbago*. We're just here for some information. We need to travel through the Cabrisi Asteroid Field, and Pepper here is under the impression that the field is, well, haunted, so we—"

"Dinner?" Denise asked. "I've got some frozen lasagna we can blast with gamma radiation. Takes about three seconds."

The sun was now setting on the horizon.

"No, thanks," said Rex. "We really just want to know if you have an information about—"

"I'm sorry to cut this short," Denise said, "but I find it's critical to my mental health to maintain a regular schedule. Please make yourselves at home. I hope we can talk more tomorrow. Goodnight!"

With that, she collapsed into the chair again, apparently sound asleep. The last of the daylight faded into darkness.

"Amazing," I said. "She's managed to adapt to eighty-eight second days. I wouldn't have thought it possible, but I suppose with enough time, the human body can—"

A loud thud sounded behind me. Rex and I turned to find Boggs snoring on the floor.

"Boggs would appear to be more adaptable than most," Pepper said.

"Donny sleeps?" Donny asked.

"Donny doesn't need to sleep," Rex said. "Donny's a robot."

"Why did we even bring those two along?" I asked.

"Donny has a purpose?" Donny asked.

"Don't let me catch you not believing in yourself, Donny!" Rex snapped. He shot a glare at me. "Sasha, I realize you're jealous of the top-notch pirate crew I've assembled, but this constant whining is unseemly. Get a hold of yourself."

"Get a hold of yourself," Squawky echoed. "I'm a born pirate."

"Good morning!" Denise exclaimed, leaping out of her chair as the room was once again bathed in light. "I trust you all slept well."

I heard a loud yawn behind me. "Like a log," Boggs said.

"Breakfast?" Denise asked.

"No thanks," said Rex. "Look, I'm going to get right to the point. We need to fly into the Cabrisi Asteroid Field. Pepper here thinks you've got information that could help us."

"I see," Denise replied. "Perhaps we should discuss it over lunch. I don't personally eat until Tuesday, but if you all—"

"Do you know something about the asteroid field or not?" Rex asked.

"The asteroid field? I know plenty about it. What do you want to know? Size, composition, origin…?"

"We want to know about the ghosts," Pepper said.

"Oh, of course. It figures. Everybody wants to know about the ghosts."

"You're saying there really are ghosts?" Rex asked.

"Oh, yes," said Denise. "Well, no. Actually, it's rather a long story. Perhaps we can discuss it more tomorrow. Goodnight!"

She sank into her chair as the sun set once again. Behind us, Boggs hit the floor.

"This is pointless," Rex said. "Let's go. Anybody who doesn't want to go into the asteroids can stay here and take their chances with the oracle of crazytown."

"Donny doesn't like this place," Donny said.

"We haven't even found out if she knows anything yet," said Pepper. "Let me do the talking tomorrow."

"Tomorrow?" I asked. "You mean—"

"Good morning!" Denise exclaimed, leaping out of her chair as the sun sprung above the horizon. "Did you all sleep okay?"

Behind us, Boggs yawned.

"Fine," said Pepper. "We need to travel through the Cabrisi Asteroid Field. Do you have any suggestions for dealing with any hazards we might find there?"

"Sure," said Denise. "Put wax in your ears."

"Put *wax* in our ears? Why?"

Denise walked across the room and opened a cabinet. After a few seconds of rummaging around, she located something that looked like a small plastic briefcase. She walked back to Pepper, handed her the case, and then sat down in her chair again. "I can show you how to use them tomorrow," she said. "Goodnight!" The sun set and Denise fell asleep again. Boggs thudded to the floor.

Pepper opened the case, which contained six sets of what looked like earplugs. A label at the top of the case read:

Wearable Auricular Consciousness Scramblers

"WACS," said Rex. "It's an acronym, like SLACS."

"No kidding," Pepper replied. "What in Space are they for? Why would we want our consciousnesses scrambled?"

"We wouldn't," said Rex. "Unless we want to end up like Nana Nutcakes here. This is a dead end. I'm going back to the ship."

"Good morning!" Denise exclaimed. "I hope you slept well. Can you believe it's Tuesday already? I'm famished. Would any of you care for some lasagna?"

We spent the rest of "Tuesday" watching Denise prepare and eat three bites of lasagna. Wednesday she cleaned the kitchen. Thursday was slightly more productive.

"They're not really ghosts, you see. I call them sirens. They tap into your consciousness and try to lure you into the asteroids. But if you have WACS in your ears, you can't concentrate well enough to pay much attention."

Rex was unimpressed. "You're suggesting we navigate an asteroid field while wearing devices specifically designed to keep us from being able to concentrate?"

Denise shrugged. "It's up to you," she said. "Goodnight!"

"Well, this was a waste of time," Rex said. "Let's get out of here."

I looked at Pepper and shrugged. She closed the case and followed Rex.

"Wake up, Boggs," I said, giving him a kick in the ribs.

Boggs rolled over and gazed at me through glassy eyes. "What... what time is it?" he asked.

The sun had just come up behind us.

"Friday," I said. "Let's go."

CHAPTER TWENTY

"Wow!" Boggs yelled from the main cabin as I maneuvered the *Flagrante Delicto* past a particularly large asteroid. "That was a doozy!"

He was not, as far as I could tell, talking about the asteroid. Experimenting with the Wearable Auricular Consciousness Scramblers had revealed them to be nothing but small speakers that played various loud noises on an endless loop. Rex had identified breaking glass, an air raid siren, mariachi music, the shriek of an enraged baboon, nails on a chalkboard, the sound of someone chewing peanut brittle, a vuvuzela and crashing cymbals before getting bored with the exercise. Each sound lasted between one and five seconds, and the interval between sounds ranged from three to fifteen seconds. Wearing a pair of WACS was just disruptive enough to keep you from ever devoting your full attention to any particular thought. The noises themselves were jarring, but just as bad were the random waits between them, during which you couldn't help but wonder what sound was coming next and when.

Boggs and Pepper had happily put their WACS in their ears the moment we entered the asteroid field, convinced the devices would protect them from what the Oracle had called "sirens." I remained skeptical. It's possible the so-called sirens were another manifestation of some sort of mind control, but I couldn't imagine why anyone would bother to set up such a defense mechanism in a remote asteroid field that was already barely navigable. In any case, Donny and I— lacking organic brains—were probably immune. Additionally, neither of us had ears per se, and I wasn't convinced Donny had any thoughts worth disrupting. Also, I was the only one capable of piloting the ship through the asteroid field. Rex had refused to wear the WACS at all after his initial experimentation. Having doubts about both the supposed threat and the suggested remedy, I didn't press the issue.

The first three hours in the asteroid field passed without incident, other than Boggs occasionally startling the group by shouting "Wow!" or "Zowie!" about a particularly loud or otherwise impressive noise coming over the WACS. As far as I could tell, the different pairs of WACS were not synchronized; each of them transmitted its own series of noises on its own unique schedule.

Once we had pinpointed the location of the SLACS receptacle, we had stuffed Ort Felzich in the cargo hold to keep him out of the way. The challenge now was to avoid all the hunks of rock between us and our destination.

"Try going that way," Rex said, pointing just to the right of an asteroid as I was about to bank left.

"You have to take inertia into account, sir," I said. "Given our current course, it would require far more fuel to get around that asteroid on the right side."

"We refueled at Sargasso Seven," Rex said. "Go right."

"Be that as it may, sir, the logical course is to bank left."

"I said right, Sasha. That's an order."

"At this point, we're too far along on our present course. If I try to go right, we'll crash into the asteroid."

"Fine," Rex groused. He watched in silence as I banked left to avoid the asteroid. Then he dived forward, knocking me to the deck, and grabbed hold of the controls. Squawky fluttered to stay on his shoulder.

"Sir!" I cried. "What are you doing?"

"Stay out of my way, Sasha!" Rex yelled, pulling the *Flagrante Delicto* to the right. "I know where to go. The voices told me!"

I got to my feet and tried to wrest Rex's hands from the controls, but he knocked me down again with his elbow. Unfortunately, as my programming prevents me from attacking a human being, the best I could do is try to get Rex's hands off the controls. I wasn't having much luck.

"Is everything all right in there?" Pepper yelled from the main cabin. "I thought I—"

"Wow!" Boggs shouted. "That sounded like an elephant!"

"What?" shouted Pepper. "I couldn't hear you over the fireworks."

"What fireworks?"

"Pipe down!" Pepper shouted. "I was trying to... hey, I just got the elephant!"

"Eleven what? I only counted four."

"Four what?"

Meanwhile, Rex knocked me to the floor a third time. I'd have yelled for help, but it was pretty clear that none of the humans on board were going to be of any use. Then I remembered the other non-human on board.

"Donny!" I shouted. "Help!"

Donny came into the cockpit as I got to my feet. Rex hunched over the controls, a maniacal grin on his face, directing the *Flagrante Delicto* right into the path of the asteroid.

"Donny helps?" Donny asked.

"Grab Rex, Donny! Get him away from the controls!"

"Don't you do it, Donny!" Rex growled. "I know exactly where to go." The asteroid loomed ever larger in front of us.

"The sirens have gotten to him!" I shouted, trying vainly to pull Rex from the controls. "He's going to fly us right into an asteroid!"

Donny stood there on his four arm-legs, not knowing what to do. "Donny helps," he said.

"You have one job, Donny," Rex growled. "You just sit right there and believe in yourself!"

"Donny, please!" I begged. "Help me!"

Donny stood for several seconds, taking in the scene. "Donny believes in himself," he said.

Rex knocked me to the floor again. A warning klaxon blared as impact appeared to be imminent.

"That's the worst one yet!" Boggs shouted.

"I'm a natural born pirate," said Squawky. "We're all going to die."

"Donny believes he can help," Donny said. He walked up behind Rex, stood up on his hindmost arms, and wrapped his remaining arms—including his neck—around Rex, pinning him to the pilot's chair.

I got to my feet and grabbed the controls, pulling as hard as I could to the left. The underside of our ship scraped the asteroid as we passed, making a horrendously loud screeching sound.

"Wow, did you hear that one?" Boggs shouted.

"What?" yelled Pepper.

I breathed a sigh of relief as we cleared the asteroid.

"That was close," said Rex. "Good thing you didn't listen to me, Donny."

"Donny believed in himself," said Donny.

"Are you okay, sir?" I asked.

"I think so," said Rex. "It was like something took over my mind for a moment there."

"The sirens, sir. They're real."

"So it would seem. In any case, it seems to have passed."

"Donny lets go?"

"Better not, Donny," I said. "We don't know when it will hit again."

"I'm fine," said Rex. "Really. I'm feeling much better, Donny. You can let me go now."

"Don't do it, Donny."

"FLY INTO THAT ROCK!" Rex shouted suddenly. He strained futilely against Donny's arms, all of which were now wrapped around him.

"Good boy, Donny," I said. "I'm sorry I called you an abomination that time. You earned your keep today."

"Oh come on," Rex said. "That was a joke. I wasn't seriously trying to get you to—" He suddenly strained against Donny's grip again. "FLY INTO THE ROCKS, SASHA!" he shouted. "IT'S THE ONLY WAY!"

We continued in this vein for another four hours, Rex yelling himself hoarse trying to get me to fly into the asteroids and Donny holding him fast to the pilot's chair. When we were within a thousand kilometers of our target coordinates, we began to pick up a distress beacon.

"That's gotta be the SLACS receptacle," Rex said.

I eyed him suspiciously.

"Give me a break, Sasha. I haven't tried to fly us into the rocks for like five minutes now. A distress beacon within ten thousand klicks of where Felzich directed us? That can't be a coincidence."

Although I wasn't convinced Rex was free of the influence of the sirens, I tended to agree. "All right," I said. "I'll check it out."

Three hours later, we were closing on an escape pod. It had been badly damaged by meteor strikes, and our sensors detected no signs of life. I navigated the *Flagrante Delicto* to within a few meters of it. While

Donny continued to subdue Rex, I went out the airlock to explore the escape pod. I got the door open with no trouble. The pod was empty except for something that looked like a metal briefcase. A label on the bottom read: SLACS Receptacle Model 1733-b. I grabbed the case and climbed back into the *Flagrante Delicto.*

Once back inside the ship, I inspected the case more closely. There appeared to be no way to open it. There were no buttons or controls on the outside at all. Boggs and Pepper continued to shout semi-coherently at each other.

"What's happening, Sasha?" Rex called from the cockpit. "Did you find it?"

"I think so, sir," I said. "But I'm not sure what to do with it."

"First things first," said Rex. "Get us out of this asteroid field. But first, FLY US INTO THAT ROCK!"

CHAPTER TWENTY-ONE

"I can't express how thankful I am to you for rescuing me," Ort Felzich said. "And not just because I'm a disembodied consciousness being carried around in a case by my own body."

The *Flagrante Delicto* had made it back safely to Sargasso Seven. Rex, Pepper, Felzich and I were in Pepper's office. It had taken us a while to figure out how to communicate with Felzich, but the solution turned out to be surprisingly simple. As long as his body was within a couple meters of the SLACS receptacle, Felzich was able to control his body as if his consciousness was still seated in his physical brain. Any farther away than that and his body would revert to shambling toward the receptacle while muttering "slacks."

"Don't mention it," said Rex. "Of course I'm sure you're aware our motivations aren't entirely altruistic. We plan on selling you to the Sp'ossels."

"Stands to reason," said Felzich. "I don't suppose I can talk you out of it?"

"Why?" asked Pepper. "Don't you want to be returned to your people?"

"I'm not sure they're my people anymore," said Felzich. "I've had a lot of time to think since my mind was separated from my body and left to drift in deep space eighty years ago."

"Who did that to you anyway?" Pepper asked.

"I did," Felzich said.

"You had your own mind removed?" I asked. "Why?"

"It was the only way I knew to navigate the Cabrisi Asteroid Field," Felzich said. "The rest of my crew wore WACS, but at least one person had to be lucid enough to pilot the ship. This was right after the Retbutlerian Jihad, you understand, when even semi-sentient robots were still strictly prohibited. I thought I'd found a loophole. Put my mind in a box so the sirens couldn't manipulate me."

"It didn't work?" Pepper asked.

"No, it did," Felzich said. "But one of my crew members' WACS malfunctioned. He got free of his restraints and overpowered me. Knocked the SLACS receptacle out of my hands and took over the ship's controls. By the time I recovered the case, it was too late. We were on a collision course with an asteroid. I tried to escape, but the crewman attacked me again. I managed to toss the case into an escape pod and jettison it before we struck. That's the last thing I remember. Apparently my body survived and was recovered, but my mind floated in space until you found me."

"What were you doing out there in the first place?" Rex asked.

"I was… looking for a something," Felzich said.

"If you want to convince us not to sell you," Pepper said, "this is no time to be coy."

Felzich nodded. "Zontonium," he said.

"You were looking for zontonium in an asteroid field?" Pepper asked.

"When New Borculo went nova, it sent out massive flares that destroyed the planets orbiting it. That's where the Cabrisi Asteroid Field came from. Early surveys of the system suggested one of the planets had major zontonium deposits. But I never found any asteroids with significant amounts of zontonium."

"I don't get it," Pepper said. "The Sp'ossels were getting into the rocket fuel business?"

"Zontonium is useful for more than propulsion," I said. "Rex and I discovered that on Vericulon Four."

"What's on Vericulon Four?" Felzich asked.

"Not on it," Rex replied. "Over it. A Sp'ossel mind control satellite."

"Ah," said Felzich. "Then you know what the Sp'ossels are after. Mind control on a galactic scale."

"Rex and Sasha were telling the truth about that?" Pepper asked. "Then… the Sp'ossels really are trying to build a device to make everyone in the galaxy artificially happy?"

"That was the plan when I was their leader. If, as you say, the

Sp'ossels are willing to pay a large ransom for me, it's because they think I know where the zontonium is. They will need several million tons of it to build a psionic transmitter powerful enough to reach the entire galaxy."

"But you never found the zontonium," I said.

"No," Felzich said. "And I wouldn't tell them if I did. I've come to the conclusion that happiness is meaningless when pursued as a direct goal. It is valuable only as a side effect of striving toward a purpose."

"This is all very touching," Rex said, "but we're still going to sell you. I don't care what you were looking for or whether you found it. I care that the Sp'ossels think you know something worth paying for."

Felzich sighed. "It makes little difference to me in the end. And I suppose I do owe you after you rescued me. Perhaps the Sp'ossels won't kill me when they realize I don't have the information they're looking for."

"That's the spirit!" Rex exclaimed. "Pepper, how long will it take to set up a meeting with the Sp'ossels?"

"Already done," Pepper said. "We're meeting them on Schufnaasik Six tomorrow."

"Schufnaasik Six," Rex repeated. "That sounds familiar. Have I been there, Sasha?"

"Yes, sir," I said. "You once won the planet in a card game."

"I own a whole planet?"

"Not anymore, sir. The Sp'ossels cheated you out of it."

Rex shrugged. "Probably a lousy planet anyway."

"Yes, sir," I said. He was actually right about that part.

I landed the Flagrante Delicto at the coordinates on Schufnaasik Six that Pepper had specified. The location had been selected at random as far as I could tell; Schufnaasik Six was a featureless brown ball with no discernible geographic features. By virtue of its gravity and breathable atmosphere, the planet was technically an APPLE—an Alien Planet Perplexingly Like Earth—but it had nothing else going for it.

When the Sp'ossel ship was visible on the horizon, Rex, Pepper, Ort Felzich and I exited to the surface while Boggs and Donny remained in our ship. The Sp'ossel ship would be landing a hundred meters away. The plan was to exchange Felzich for a suitcase full of credits on the open ground halfway between the two ships. While we waited, I made one final effort to dissuade Rex from his current course of action.

"Sir," I said, "I would like to express my displeasure once again at the idea of doing business with the Sp'ossels. These people have manipulated us for years. They are not to be trusted."

"Your objection is noted, Sasha," Rex replied. "Now cram it."

Pepper remained silent. I got the impression she was having second thoughts about doing business with the Sp'ossels as well, but she was too desperate for cash to make an issue of it. The lines of the Sp'ossel ship were now discernible in the distance.

"What do you mean, Sasha?" Ort Felzich asked. "How have the Sp'ossels manipulated you?"

"We're what they call acquisition agents," I said. "They program us to seek out wealth and then take it for themselves. Rex and I have been unwittingly working for the Sp'ossels for years. We just found out about it."

"Ah, yes," said Felzich. "Our engineers were working on that program when I left to find the zontonium. I'm sorry to hear they went ahead with it."

Rex shrugged disinterestedly. "Nothing for it now but to try to get as much money out of them as we can."

"But sir," I said, "how do you know they're not manipulating us even now? For all you know, they released us at that refueling depot knowing that we would hijack the *Raina Huebner*."

The Sp'ossel ship had stopped moving toward us and was settling in for a landing.

"The *Raina Huebner*?" asked Felzich.

"That's the ship you were on," I said. "Or rather, that your body was on."

"Hang on," Felzich said. "You two hijacked the cargo ship that was carrying my body?"

"That's right," I said.

"And how did that come about exactly?"

The Sp'ossel ship landed.

I shrugged. "It was Rex's idea. He got the crew drunk and we absconded with the ship. Then it was boarded by pirates and we

138

escaped by voiding the cargo hold. In fact, it's pure luck that any of us survived. If Boggs hadn't grabbed you with that crane, you'd still be floating in deep space."

"I see," said Felzich, rubbing his chin. "And your theory is that the Sp'ossels orchestrated this hijacking?"

"Now that I think about it," I said, "I can't see how they'd have known exactly how it was going down. The only certain factor when dealing with Rex is the unmitigated chaos that follows in his wake."

Rex scowled at me.

The Sp'ossel ship's ramp descended and three well-dressed men began walking down it.

"That's what I'm concerned about," Felzich said. "It sounds like the Sp'ossels pointed you at the *Raina Huebner* and let you go. It's almost as if…"

"They weren't trying to extract him," Rex said, suddenly looking very worried. "Uh-oh."

"What?" Pepper asked. "What are you talking about?"

"The Sp'ossels don't care about Felzich," Rex said. "They were just trying to keep him from falling into the hands of the Malarchy."

"Then why'd they agree to pay for him?"

Now only about ten paces away, the three men stopped. The man with the briefcase lifted it up and held it flat on his palms. The man on his left flipped the latches.

"To get me here," Felzich said. "To kill me."

"It's a trap!" Rex yelled. "Run!"

We ran.

Lazegun blasts struck the *Flagrante Delicto* as we ran aboard. Glancing back, I saw that the empty briefcase was on the ground; all three men were firing lazepistols at us. So much for Felzich's ransom.

"Get us off this damned planet, Sasha!" Rex ordered.

"Aye, sir," I said, getting in the cockpit. I warmed up the ship and we blasted off. Down below, I saw the three Sp'ossels running back to their ship. This was not good news. Having decided their handguns were no match for the *Flagrante Delicto's* hull, they were going to try to shoot us down with their ship's cannons.

"Why are they trying to kill us?" Pepper cried.

"They're trying to kill Felzich," Rex said. "They don't care about you one way or another."

"And you?" Pepper asked.

"They'd prefer to take me and Sasha alive, but I'd bet they want Felzich dead more than they want us alive."

Rex's words were punctuated by lazecannon blasts that shook the *Flagrante Delicto*.

"Rationalize a course out of here, Sasha!" Rex yelled.

"It takes time, sir," I said. "And I can't even start plotting until we're clear of the atmosphere."

"We're dead," said Pepper. "A few more blasts like that and this piece of junk will rattle to pieces."

Another blast rocked the ship.

"Evasive maneuvers, Sasha!" Rex yelled.

"Brilliant plan, sir," I said. I continued to try to evade the Sp'ossel ship's lazecannons, to little effect.

"Hail them," Ort Felzich said.

"What for?" Pepper asked.

Ort made his way to the cockpit and sat down next to me. "Hail the Sp'ossel ship, Sasha."

Rex didn't countermand the order, so I opened a communication channel to the ship.

"Hello, crew of the Sp'ossel ship that is currently trying to shoot us down," I said. "I have someone who wants to talk to you. Please stop firing if you don't mind."

A long pause followed.

"This is Captain Grimbald of the Space Apostle vessel *Speed Pony*," said a voice over the comm. "Go ahead."

Felzich leaned forward to speak into the comm. "This is Ort Felzich. I have the coordinates of Planet Z. If you fire at us again, I'm going to broadcast them on standard hailing frequencies, along with a request to forward the message to the nearest Malarchian authorities. Do you understand me?"

A long pause followed, during which the Sp'ossel ship did not fire again. Finally the voice from the ship spoke again.

"You don't want to do that, Mr. Felzich. Let's talk this over. The Sp'ossel High Council is willing to pay a lot of money to keep that information secure."

"You should have thought about that before you tried to kill me," Felzich said. "I have no desire to interfere with your plans, but if you fire again, the Malarchy will undoubtedly do it for me."

"Are you willing to give us a guarantee that if we let you go, you won't release that information?"

"The only guarantee I'm going to give you is that if you shoot at this ship again, the location of Planet Z is going to be known across the galaxy? Understood?"

There was another long pause. "Understood, Mr. Felzich. You'll stay out of Sp'ossel business if you know what's good for you."

The ship broke off pursuit, arcing away from us.

"I don't trust them," Rex said from behind me. "Get us away from this planet and rationalize a course back to the Cabrisi Asteroid Field."

"Sir? Why would we want to go back there?"

"Felzich is going to take us to Planet Z."

"I was just bluffing, Rex," said Felzich. "There is no Planet Z."

"If there was no Planet Z, the Sp'ossels wouldn't care about you telling the Malarchy where it is, you big naughty liar. Felzich has been holding out on us, Sasha."

Felzich sighed. "Technically I told you the truth. I never found any zontonium asteroids."

"Right," said Rex. "Because the planet is still intact, hidden among the asteroids."

"Sir, are you saying…?"

"I was right, Sasha. There is a treasure planet. But it's not full of buried treasure. It *is* treasure. Tell her, Felzich."

"I'm afraid Rex is correct," he said. "The Sp'ossels are building their mind control device on a planet made of pure zontonium."

CHAPTER TWENTY-TWO

I t all made sense now. Eighty years ago, driven by a desire to make everyone in the galaxy happy, the Sp'ossels had devised a method of mind control that used psionic transmitters amplified by zontonium crystals. Ort Felzich had piloted his ship into the Cabrisi Asteroid Field in search of the massive amounts of zontonium the Sp'ossels would need to build a transmitter capable of broadcasting a happiness signal across the galaxy. What he had found was an entire planet made of zontonium. On his return trip out of the asteroid field, his ship was destroyed. His body was recovered not long after by the Ragulians, who covered up the fact that Felzich's mind was missing so that they'd be in a better position to get a ransom for Felzich from the Sp'ossels. But negotiations went nowhere, and eventually the Sp'ossels managed to locate the zontonium planet on their own. Then the Sp'ossels found out that the Ragulians were releasing Felzich's body to the Malarchy, and the Sp'ossel leadership, worried that Felzich might reveal the planet's location to the Malarchy, sent Rex and me to hijack the *Raina Huebner*. When we showed up with Felzich, the Sp'ossels tried to kill him to protect their secret. Pretty basic interstellar conspiracy stuff, really.

"There's just one thing I don't understand," I heard Pepper say behind me. The *Flagrante Delicto* was in orbit around Schufnaasik Six and I was in the cockpit rationalizing a course back to Sargasso Seven. The rest of the crew, along with Felzich, were in the main cabin.

"Yes?" Felzich asked.

"What are the sirens?" Pepper asked. "Where did they come from?"

Felzich replied, "The so-called sirens were my doing. The

expedition where my I lost my mind was not my first sojourn into the Cabrisi Asteroid Field. I had discovered the zontonium planet several years earlier and was in the process of surveying it to determine what would be required to convert the planet into a psionic transmitter. I didn't trust anyone else with the planet's coordinates. Not the Sp'ossel leadership, not even my own crew. To make sure no one else would ever find the planet, I built a smaller scale transmitter on the planet. The transmitter sent out a constant signal urging anyone within its range to fly into the nearest asteroid. The problem, of course, was that I was as susceptible to the signal as anyone else. I had my mind moved to an external storage device so that I could safely travel to the zontonium planet."

"Great plan," said Rex. "Except for your crewman's WACS malfunctioning."

"There was no malfunction," Felzich replied. "The Sp'ossel leadership placed a spy in my crew. He took out his WACS to transmit the planet's location to his handlers. But he succumbed to the sirens' call before he had a chance."

"The Sp'ossels found the planet anyway," Pepper said.

"Evidently," Felzich said. "If they were still looking for the planet, they wouldn't have tried to kill me. Apparently the only reason they sent you to hijack the *Raina Huebner* was to keep me from getting to the Malarchian research station. They thought I might tell the Malarchy where Planet Z was and foil the Sp'ossels' plans."

"All of this raises an important question," said Rex.

"Which is?" Pepper asked.

"Why aren't I happy?"

"I'm not sure this is the time for such musings," Pepper said.

"Stay with me," said Rex. "We know the Sp'ossels have found the zontonium planet. And thanks to our visit to Vericulon Four, we know the Sp'ossels have successfully tested large-scale mind control. So why aren't I happy? Why aren't we all happy?"

"Setting up a planet-sized psionic transmitter is no small task," Felzich said. "Depending on when they discovered the planet, the Sp'ossels might still be years away from a functioning transmitter."

"There's probably no immediate threat then," said Rex. "Excellent. Sasha, have you rationalized our course yet?"

"Almost finished, sir. We'll be back at Sargasso Seven shortly."

"Sargasso Seven?" Rex said. "Forget that. We're going back to the asteroid field."

Not sure I heard him correctly, I got up from my seat and walked back to the cabin. "Sir?"

"Think of it, Sasha. A planet made of zontonium. We scoop up a cargo hold of that stuff and we're set for life. We know how to get past the sirens, and our pal Ort has the coordinates to the planet."

"But the Sp'ossels…" Pepper started.

"There's no way the Sp'ossels can watch the whole planet," Rex said. "We just have to sneak in, land, fill our hold with zontonium, and hightail it out of there. Easiest money we've ever made."

Flying through an asteroid field to steal from crazed space cultists didn't sound that easy to me, but maybe I was missing something.

"Won't they be expecting that?" Pepper asked. "They know Felzich knows where the planet is."

"As long as we don't interfere with their plan of galactic domination, I don't think the Sp'ossels will care one way or another."

"He's got a point," Felzich admitted. "To the Sp'ossels, a shipload of zontonium would be a small price to pay for our silence. They won't care about a little missing zontonium. It's not enough to lessen the effectiveness of the transmitter."

"Then maybe we should just ask them," I suggested. "Offer not to tell anyone about the planet in exchange for a shipload of zontonium."

"I don't trust those shifty bastards," Rex said. "Better to slip in and just take it."

Felzich nodded.

"So we're letting them get away with it," Pepper said. "Their plan to control the minds of everyone in the galaxy."

"What choice do we have?" Rex asked. "The Sp'ossels are a massive interstellar organization with billions of credits in funding. We might as well take on the Malarchy itself. No, we're not going to stop the Sp'ossels. I'll settle for skimming some profits off the top of their nutty scheme."

"That nutty scheme affects us too," I said. "When the transmitter is completed, the whole galaxy will essentially be under Sp'ossel control."

"Being happy isn't so bad, Sasha," Rex said. "Anyway, that could be years from now. A lot could happen between now and then."

"Like what?"

"How should I know?" Rex said. "Maybe something really awful.

Something that will make us all incredibly sad. And then, just when we think we can't go on anymore, the Sp'ossels activate their happiness transmitter and boom, everything is fine again."

"That's the worst rationalization I've ever heard," I said.

"Maybe we'll find some way to stop them," Pepper said. "We can think of this as a reconnaissance expedition."

"Also unconvincing," I said, "but light-years ahead of Rex's argument."

"Look," said Pepper. "If I don't get some money quick, I'm going to lose Sargasso Seven. I'm not a fan of the Sp'ossels or their evil schemes, but Rex is right. There's no way we're going to stop them. We might as well make some money off them."

"I'm afraid I find myself in agreement with Pepper and Rex," said Felzich. "Everything I once owned is under the control of a group who wants to kill me. Also, at some point it would be really nice to have my mind moved back into my body." He patted the briefcase in his lap. "If I'm going to survive, I need money. Assuming we all get an equal share of the proceeds, I say it's worth the risk."

"I don't know about that equal share stuff," Rex said, glancing at Boggs and Donny, who were playing checkers in the rear of the cabin, "but there should be plenty for everybody. Sasha, get us back to that asteroid field."

CHAPTER TWENTY-THREE

Once again I found myself piloting the *Flagrante Delicto* through the asteroid field. Everyone except Rex, Donny and I put in WACS as we neared the edge of the field. Rex refused to wear them on the grounds that he needed to be able to "concentrate." I, in turn, refused to pilot the ship unless Rex was bound and gagged. Rex had been growling at me incoherently through his gag for nearly an hour when finally my curiosity got the better of me. I pulled off the gag.

"Blast it, Sasha!" Rex shouted. "I've been trying to tell you for an hour now. The voices are gone!"

"Sir?"

"I don't hear them. Not since we entered the field."

"This sounds like a trick," I said. "Are the sirens making you say this?"

"There aren't any sirens, you galvanized gasbag. I'm telling you, the voices are gone. Untie me!"

"What if they come back?" I asked.

"Fine, just loosen my hands a little. I can't feel my fingers."

I obliged. "Should we tell the others?"

"Nah, let them suffer."

"Wow!" Boggs shouted.

"What did you say, Boggs?" Pepper asked.

"Shut up!" shouted Felzich.

A few hours later, we were approaching the coordinated Felzich had given us. There were fewer asteroids here, and the ship's sensors indicated that we were nearing a large, roughly spherical mass. "That's got to be Planet Z," I said. "Are you hearing any voices?"

"Not a one," Rex said. "The Sp'ossels must have turned off the transmitter. Untie me. I'm going to get Felzich."

"Sir, are you sure…?"

"We aren't going to be able to pick up a shipload of zontonium if we're all tied up or mentally incapacitated," Rex said. "Felzich might be able to help us avoid Sp'ossel ships."

"Aye, sir," I said, and reluctantly untied him.

Rex went into the main cabin and returned shortly with Felzich. Straight ahead was a sphere that glowed with a deep blue against the blackness of space. So it was true: a planet, nearly as big as Earth, made entirely of zontonium. I tried to calculate the value of the ore, but I ran into a memory buffer overflow and had to halt the calculation before I shut down. The fact was, the planet had so much zontonium that if word of its existence got out, the price of zontonium on the interstellar market would collapse. Whoever controlled this planet was going to rule the galaxy one way or another, even without mind control.

"I'm not sure how much help I can give you," Felzich said. "I haven't been here in eighty years. I'm sure the… what is that?"

As we neared the big azure globe, we could see that the surface was not uniformly blue. At regular intervals, it was checkered with black squares.

"Did they remove some of the ore?" Rex asked.

"The planet is zontonium all the way through," Felzich said. "Those are structures of some sort."

"They'd have to be gigantic," I said.

"They're not on the surface," Felzich said. "They're above it."

As we got nearer, we saw that Felzich was right: the Sp'ossels had built a framework of gigantic curved beams around the planet, enclosing it like a cage. The black squares we had noticed were metal panels, a hundred kilometers or more on a side, parallel with the surface of the planet.

"What in Space…?" Rex asked.

"It's the transmitter," Felzich says. "Those panels direct the signal toward the planet, which amplifies it and sends it out across the galaxy. They're a lot farther along than I expected."

"Maybe that's why they turned off the sirens," I said. "They're getting ready to activate it."

"Nothing has changed," Rex said. "We land, scoop up a shipload of zontonium, and take off."

"Sir, they could have sensors on that framework. Not to mention weapons."

"You're being paranoid, Sasha. What do they need weapons for? They're hidden inside a remote asteroid field. The whole place looks deserted to me. We'll just fly through one of the gaps in the...." He trailed off as we noticed what looked like hundreds of tiny insects darting about the framework.

"Are those...?" I asked.

"Spaceships," Felzich said. "Hundreds of them."

"Sir, I think we should reconsider this plan. We'll never get past all those ships. If even one of them notices us, we're dead."

Rex nodded, realizing the planet was not as deserted as it first appeared. "Speaking of which, um..." Several of the ships nearest to us had altered their course and now appeared to be heading our way. I could make out lazecannons and torpedo batteries on the ones in front.

"Are those ships heading for—" I started.

"Evasive action, Sasha!" Rex shouted. "Get us out of here!"

"Aye, sir!" I flipped the *Flagrante Delicto* around and engaged the thrusters. We headed back toward the thick of the asteroid field, a half dozen Sp'ossel ships on our tail.

"I said lose them, Sasha!"

Our thrusters were at eighty percent, and the Sp'ossels continued to gain on us.

"Aye, sir. But I'm not confident in my ability to navigate the asteroids at high speed. We may have to choose whether we want to die by lazecannon blast or asteroid collision."

"We have to jump," said Felzich. "It's the only way."

"We're heading into an asteroid field," I replied. "I can't rationalize a hypergeometric course while dodging asteroids at a thousand klicks a second. There's no time."

"I can do it," Felzich said. "I've jumped out of here a hundred times. Just keep us alive for the next five minutes and I'll have a course ready."

The fastest I'd ever rationalized a hypergeometric course was fifteen minutes, and I've got a quantum neuralnet brain. But it wasn't like we had a lot of other options. "All right," I said. "I'll see what I can do."

We were nearly in range of the Sp'ossel ships' lazecannons when we reentered the asteroid field. I pushed our speed as fast as I dared, and the pursuing ships fell behind. If I could just keep them at that distance while keeping us from faceplanting into a million tons of floating rock, we might just make it out of here alive. While Felzich scribbled furiously at a notepad, I tested the structural limits of the *Flagrante Delicto* and the vertigo tolerance of its occupants in an effort to keep us intact. After a dozen near-misses, Felzich announced he'd completed the calculations. Under normal circumstances, I'd never trust my safety to hurried calculations performed by a man I'd just met, but as the alternative was near-certain death, I acquiesced.

As we hurtled directly toward a gigantic asteroid, I punched in Felzich's numbers and pressed the execute button. There was a sickening moment during which space seemed to flatten, driving us even closer to the asteroid. Then suddenly we were in empty space, with nothing but distant stars in all directions. I collapsed with relief in my chair.

And then I saw the Malarchian battleship approaching.

"Crew of the *Flagrante Delicto*," I heard a familiar voice say over the comm. "This is Heinous Vlaak of the Malarchian vessel *Carpathian Winter*. You are wanted on charges of piracy. Prepare to be boarded."

CHAPTER TWENTY-FOUR

Marines boarded the Flagrante Delicto and dragged Rex and me in front of Heinous Vlaak in his private interrogation chamber.

"You two were insufferable enough when you were small-time grifters," Vlaak shrieked. "And now you've turned to piracy. Pathetic."

"I told you before," Rex said, "we're not pirates."

"Then I won't find any cargo from the *Raina Huebner* on your ship?"

Rex thought for a moment. "Okay, yes, we're pirates," Rex admitted. "But you've got much bigger problems to worry about."

"Bigger than interstellar piracy?" Vlaak asked. "There is no greater threat to the stability of the Malarchy than scurrilous privateers such as yourself!"

"I appreciate you saying so," Rex replied, "but let's be honest, Vlaak. Chasing pirates is a big step down for you. You used to be the Malarchian Primate's right hand man, man!"

"Yes," Vlaak hissed. "I was demoted after the debacle on the forest moon of Akdar, thanks to you. Reminding me of past insults is not helping your case, Nihilo."

"This is what I'm saying," Rex said. "I've found a way to get you back into the Primate's good graces. What if I told you you're in a position to put down a genuine threat to Malarchian rule?"

"Tread carefully, Nihilo. I am in no mood for your tricks."

"No trick. Here's the deal: the Sp'ossels have a secret mind control device hidden on a planet in the Cabrisi Asteroid Field, and we need your help to stop them."

Heinous Vlaak sighed. "Is this really the best you can do? You've told some impressive lies in the past, Nihilo, but usually they at least have a veneer of believability."

"I told you the truth about where Hookbeard was, didn't I?"

"Only to fool me into checking every other bar before I got to the Event Horizon."

"So it did work!" Rex cried.

"Mr. Vlaak," I said, "I know it sounds ridiculous, but Rex is telling you the truth. The Sp'ossels aren't who you think they are. They're a nefarious conspiracy aimed at taking over the galaxy and, um, making everybody happy."

"Throw them out the airlock," Vlaak said.

"Wait!" Rex cried. "Get Ort Felzich. He'll tell you!"

"Ort Felzich has been in cryosleep for eighty years."

"We woke him up," Rex said. "He's on our ship. He'll confirm everything we said."

"Absurd," Vlaak said.

"You can check it yourself," Rex replied. "Felzich's body was aboard the *Raina Huebner*, bound for a Malarchian research station. There must be records of it. Come on, Vlaak. What do you have to lose? Take five minutes to make a call to the Malarchian Science Ministry and verify what I'm telling you. If I'm lying, you can still throw us out the airlock. But if I'm telling the truth, you have an opportunity to prove yourself as a hero for the Malarchy."

Vlaak thought for a moment. "Make the call," he said to one of the marines. "Tell them Heinous Vlaak wants to know the current status of Ort Felzich."

"Yes, sir," said the marine. He disappeared, then returned a few minutes later. "Lord Vlaak, I spoke to the Minister of Science himself. Ort Felzich's body was aboard the *Raina Huebner*. It is presumed to be in the hands of pirates."

Vlaak still seemed suspicious.

"Your Lordship," said one of the marines, "there is a man on their ship who looks a bit like pictures of Ort Felzich I've seen."

Vlaak studied Rex for some time, then turned to the marine. "Go get him."

"Yes, sir." The marine disappeared. A few minutes later he returned with Ort Felzich in handcuffs.

"All right," said Vlaak, addressing Felzich. "What's this all about? Are you really Ort Felzich? Is there any truth to these claims about a mind control device?"

"Slacks," said Felzich. He turned around and began walking back the way he'd come.

"Stop that man!" Vlaak screeched. Several of the marines drew their guns.

"Wait!" Rex yelled. "He doesn't know what he's doing! His mind is in a briefcase!"

"His mind is what?" asked Vlaak.

Felzich had reached the door and was now pounding his head against it, still muttering "slacks."

"It's in a briefcase back on the *Flagrante Delicto*," Rex said. "If he's not holding it, he just wanders around saying 'slacks.'"

"I tire of these games," Vlaak said. "This man isn't Ort Felzich. He's a blithering moron. Throw them all out the airlock."

"Wait!" cried Rex again. "Tell him, Sasha!"

"Lord Vlaak," I said, "my programming does not permit me to lie. Rex is telling the truth. Ort Felzich's mind is on the *Flagrante Delicto*."

Vlaak gave an exasperated sigh and dispatched a marine to get the briefcase. The marine returned and handed it to Felzich's body.

"Thanks," Felzich said. He turned to Heinous Vlaak. "Greetings, Your Lordship. I take it Rex and Sasha have explained the Sp'ossel threat?"

Vlaak was momentarily taken aback by Felzich's sudden coherence. "They've told me a preposterous story about a mind control device on a secret planet," he said after a moment. "You're the only reason I'm still listening. If you're so concerned, why don't you just call them off? Aren't you the leader of the Sp'ossels?"

"Not for eighty years, Your Lordship. I'm afraid the Sp'ossels and I are on the outs. They recently tried to kill me."

"So you created this organization to take over the galaxy and now you expect the Malarchy to clean up your mess."

"I don't have any expectations one way or another," Felzich said, "but if the Malarchy wants to retain dominion over the galaxy in any meaningful sense, it's going to have to deal with the Sp'ossels."

"I'll refer the matter to my superiors for further investigation. Meanwhile, the lot of you will be executed for piracy."

"There's no time for that," Rex said. "We just visited the secret planet. The construction of the device is complete. They could activate it at any moment!"

"And you're telling me this out of the goodness of your hearts?"

"Well, no," Rex admitted. "To be honest, we were going to let them get away with it. We were only there to steal some zontonium."

"Zontonium?" Vlaak asked. "What are you talking about?"

"Oh, didn't I mention the entire planet is made of zontonium?"

Vlaak turned to Felzich. "Planet Z is real? You found it?"

"I did," said Felzich. "And the Sp'ossels found it too."

Vlaak paced back and forth across the chamber. "It was long believed that the zontonium planet was only a legend. If Planet Z actually exists, that amount of zontonium is a matter of strategic importance to the Malarchy."

"And don't forget the mind control part," Rex said.

Vlaak nodded slowly. "I will send a reconnaissance ship to verify what you have said."

"A reconnaissance ship?" Rex exclaimed. "You need to send your whole damned fleet! If you send one ship, they'll know you're coming!"

"There is only one way," Heinous Vlaak said. "We must assess the threat in *Our Moment of Victory!*"

Puzzled silence followed.

"My personal ship, *Our Moment of Victory*, is equipped with stealth technology," Vlaak explained. "We can get in, assess the threat, and get out."

"'We?'" Rex asked.

"You're coming with me," Vlaak said. "If this is a trap, you three are going to die with me."

CHAPTER TWENTY-FIVE

O*ur Moment of Victory* was smaller but much more sleek and luxurious than the *Flagrante Delicto*. Felzich directed Heinous Vlaak as he navigated the ship through the asteroid field. Rex and I sat behind them. We'd left Pepper, Boggs and Donny on the *Flagrante Delicto*, docked with the *Carpathian Winter*.

"So it's true," Vlaak said as the ship nosed out of the asteroid field. The huge iridescent blue sphere hung in space in front of us. "A planet of pure zontonium. But where are the ships you spoke of?"

Peering over Felzich's shoulder at the magnified display, I saw why Vlaak was puzzled: the hundreds of ships we had seen buzzing around the framework were gone.

"They've docked," said Felzich. "Look."

Looking closer, I could see that Felzich was right. The ships were still there, but most of them had found a berth on the framework on which to park.

"That's bad news," Felzich said. "Construction is complete. They're parking all their ships before activating the happiness transmitter."

"How long do we have?" I asked.

"Hours," said Felzich. "Maybe minutes."

"And you claim this transmitter's signal can reach the entire galaxy?" Vlaak said.

"The science is sound," Felzich said. "I designed it myself."

"Rex and I saw it first-hand," I said. "They mind-controlled a whole planet with a chunk of zontonium that could fit inside this cabin. Planet Z contains a hundred trillion times as much."

"Even so," Vlaak said, "it will take time for the signal to reach the whole galaxy, will it not? Even light takes 100,000 years to get across the galaxy."

Felzich shook his head. "Psionic waves are not constrained by the laws of conventional physics. The effect will be instantaneous across the galaxy. The second they flip the switch, it's done. Everybody in the galaxy will be irrationally happy, including us. The only good news is that we won't mind."

"This is outrageous!" Vlaak growled, shaking his fist in the air. "Only the Malarchian Primate has the right to decide who gets to be happy!"

"You have the power to stop them," Rex said. "A few Sp'ossel ships with lazecannons are no match for the Malarchian fleet. Blow that transmitter to smithereens."

"It'll be tricky to get destroyers through the asteroids," Felzich said. "In any case, there's no time. By the time the fleet gets here, the Sp'ossels will have activated the transmitter. I'm afraid it's game over, folks."

"Not necessarily," Rex said. "The fleet could jump in."

"We're in the middle of an asteroid field," Felzich said. "It would be suicidal to jump here. Why do you think I have my mind in a briefcase?" He held up the metal case, giving it an affectionate pat.

"We jumped out," Rex said. "Why can't they jump in?"

"That was a life-or-death situation," I said. "And jumping out of an asteroid field is far less dangerous than jumping into one. The margin of error with rationalized hypergeometry is so large that unless you have a huge swath of unoccupied space at your destination coordinates—"

"Okay, look," Rex said. "Some of the ships probably aren't going to make it. I'm just saying, you want to get a fleet of ships here in a hurry, there's a way to do it. Most of them, anyway."

Felzich nodded. "It's a little crazy, but it may be the only option. There's definitely no time to get all those ships through the asteroid field. And they'll see you coming. At least if you jump in, you have a chance to surprise them."

"You're asking me to tell the Malarchian fleet to jump here, knowing that many of the ships will be destroyed almost immediately."

"The alternative is a galaxy where everyone is happy all the time," said Rex.

"Unacceptable!" Vlaak shrieked.

"Then you know what you have to do."

"Curse you for putting me in this position, Felzich!"

"If it weren't for Felzich," Rex said, "you wouldn't even know about it. And now you have a chance to be a hero. The Primate will know you saved the galaxy from the Sp'ossel menace. You'll never have to chase pirates again."

Vlaak thought for some time. "I will make the request," he said.

•●.

Less than an hour later, the sky all around us lit up with explosions as the Malarchian ships started jumping in. I'm no fan of the Malarchy, but it was hard to watch. It was like they were *aiming* for the asteroids.

"Look at those idiots," Rex said, apparently forgetting momentarily both that Heinous Vlaak was on board and that this attack plan was Rex's idea.

Vlaak watched silently, his hands clenched at his sides. Vlaak had only been able to summon one wing of the fleet, but he was already responsible for the destruction of half of it, and he hadn't even started fighting yet. The only thing he had going for him was that the spectacle had to be terrifying to the Sp'ossels, who found themselves suddenly surrounded by explosions.

When the explosions stopped, the Malarchy had something like thirty ships left out of a hundred. Several of the remaining ships were stranded deep within the asteroid field, and the rest were oriented in random directions, anywhere from a hundred to a hundred thousand klicks from the surface of the Sp'ossel planet. There had been no time to devise anything like a coherent attack plan, so Vlaak had simply ordered the ships to navigate within range of the transmitter and start shooting. I watched as the ships slowly maneuvered into position and opened fire.

Three problems with this strategy quickly became apparent. The first was the energy shield around the transmitter framework that rendered lazecannons completely ineffective. The second was the flak cannons that also rendered torpedoes ineffective. The third was the torpedo batteries that almost immediately incapacitated another dozen Malarchian ships.

In sum, it seemed the Sp'ossels were more prepared for an attack than we'd anticipated. Even if the entire wing had survived the trip, it would have had a tough time doing any serious damage to the transmitter framework. Making matters worse, several dozen small attack ships had launched from their berths and were now strafing the remaining Malarchian ships. Only Vlaak's ship, the *Carpathian Winter*, which had materialized a few klicks in front of us, remained unscathed.

"This is a disaster!" Vlaak shrieked. "You've ruined me!"

"It does appear that I underestimated the challenge," Rex said. "That framework isn't as flimsy as it looks."

"It's indestructible!" Vlaak cried. "We'll never break through that thing!"

"Hmm," said Ort Felzich.

"What?" said Vlaak. "You have an idea? Now would be a good time to mention it."

A Malarchian frigate, struck by a torpedo, exploded in front of us.

Felzich said, "If we can keep those attack ships occupied, a small, fast moving ship might be able to get past those torpedo batteries," Felzich said. "If the Sp'ossels followed the original plans, there's a control tower that should be easy enough to locate. Take out that control tower and they can't activate the transmitter."

"Really?" said Vlaak. "That seems like… kind of an obvious design flaw."

"The Sp'ossels never expected to have to fight off the whole Malarchian fleet. I'm not saying it will be easy, but it's worth a shot."

"*Our Moment of Victory* could do it," Vlaak said. "It's small, fast, and stealthy."

"Not to be a downer," Rex said, "but you're badly outnumbered. No matter how stealthy this ship is, there's no way you're slipping past all those fighters. Not without some kind of diversion, anyway."

"A diversion?" Vlaak asked. "What do you propose?"

"Well, as soon as you fly toward the framework, they're going to figure out what you're doing. What you need is another ship. One that's a little bigger, slower and easier to spot than *Our Moment of Victory*. Send that ship through the shell first to draw their fire."

Another Malarchian ship exploded in front of us.

"A second ship?" Vlaak said. "Does it look to you like a have ships to spare?"

Rex shrugged. "Not my problem. Anyway, it would be a suicide mission for whoever is piloting the decoy ship. I'll tell you what, I sure as hell wouldn't want the job. Well, good effort, everybody. Your Lordship, what do you say we head back to the *Carpathian Winter*? You can keep destroying your fleet, and Sasha and I will get out of here on the *Flagrante Delicto*."

CHAPTER TWENTY-SIX

And that's how I found myself flying the *Flagrante Delicto* at maximum acceleration directly toward the surface of an alien planet made entirely out of rocket fuel.

I should have anticipated this turn of events, but I didn't. In fact, even as I neared the patchwork frame that surrounded the Sp'ossel planet, I found it hard to believe it had come down to this. I was sacrificing my life—and that of Boggs and Donny—for a mission spearheaded by the enforcer for a repressive interstellar regime for the sole purpose of preventing everyone in the galaxy from being happy. I missed being a pirate.

Heinous Vlaak had insisted that Boggs and Donny accompany me in the *Flagrante Delicto*, and he'd given the *Carpathian Winter* orders to shoot us out of the sky if I did anything other than fly directly at top speed toward Planet Z. Meanwhile, Vlaak lurked at the edge of the asteroid field in *Our Moment of Victory* with Rex and Ort Felzich, ready to slip through the Sp'ossels defenses once I'd drawn their fire.

"I think we're going too fast, Sasha," Boggs shouted from behind me. We were pushing at least five gees. It was probably just as well that Boggs didn't realize we were on a suicide mission. Anyway, it would all be over with presently.

"Donny thinks we should slow down," Donny said.

"All part of the plan," I said, trying to sound reassuring.

Several fighters, having noted our presence, had changed course toward us and opened fire with their lazecannons. Below, several torpedoes shot toward us. I shoved the stick forward and clamped my eyes shut, waiting for the inevitable.

Three seconds later I opened them as the *Flagrante Delicto* began to shudder with the turbulence of the planet's atmosphere. Somehow we were still alive. We'd breached the shell.

And in another ten seconds, we were going to crash into the planet's surface at twenty klicks a second. I pulled up hard and the *Flagrante Delicto* shuddered and screamed against the pummeling atmosphere. I couldn't see anything but the glare of the heat shear. A red light flashed, telling me the heat shields were way beyond capacity. The cabin felt like a furnace. I braced for impact.

But the *Flagrante Delicto* leveled out, the warning lights went dark, and suddenly I could see again. We were skimming the clear crystalline blue surface of the planet at an altitude of less than a hundred meters. Somewhere behind us, half a dozen explosions sounded as the torpedoes detonated on impact. We had made it through the Sp'ossels' defense, and it didn't look like we were being pursued.

"Wow!" shouted Boggs from the cabin behind me. "That was great!"

"Donny does not think it was great," Donny said.

"Now what, Sasha?" Boggs asked.

That was a good question. We weren't supposed to make it this far. Scanning the area, I saw no sign of *Our Moment of Victory*. Vlaak's ship had probably been taken out by the Sp'ossels. Ironic, I suppose. I didn't particularly care about Heinous Vlaak or Ort Felzich—Vlaak was an evil bastard, and Felzich was as much to blame for this whole mess as anyone. Rex, though, deserved better.

Okay, that wasn't true. Rex probably deserved to be blown to pieces by lazecannons as much as anyone. But what can I say? I have a soft spot for the big jerk. I was going to miss him—for the few minutes I had left before the Sp'ossels killed me as well.

There was no escape, that much was certain. Getting through those defenses once had been against the odds; getting through them twice would require a miracle—particularly since there was no way I could get up that sort of speed leaving the planet's gravitational field. We were stuck here.

If we were going to die on this planet, though, we could at least make the most of our time here. I used the *Flagrante Delicto*'s sensors to survey the surface for any large structures. I found one—a structure nearly fifty meters high—a few hundred klicks from our present position. That had to be the control tower Felzich had mentioned. Maybe we could take it out and prevent the Sp'ossels from activating the transmitter. I banked left and settled on a new course toward the tower, keeping low to the ground to avoid attracting attention. Far overhead, I saw the occasional flash of an explosion, but the surface appeared to be deserted.

"How would you guys like to blow up a control tower?" I asked.

"Okay, Sasha," Boggs said. "Where's Potential Friend and Frozen Friend?"

"I suspect we'll join them shortly, Boggs."

Soon the tower was visible on the horizon. But no sooner had I spotted it than I noticed a small black ship in the distance, heading toward the tower from my right. *Our Moment of Victory* had survived!

My exhilaration was short-lived, however. *Our Moment of Victory* was being pursued by two Sp'ossel fighters, which were firing at it with their lazecannons. One of them scored a direct hit and *Our Moment of Victory* began to trail smoke and lose altitude.

The tower was now clearly visible. On the very top was mounted a parabolic dish similar to the one Rex and I had seen on the satellite above Vericulon Four. It even had a giant blue gemstone at the end of a pole protruding from its center. This puzzled me until I realized what it was: the smaller transmitter Felzich had spoken of, the one that produced the "siren" signal. This tower was the control center for both the siren transmitter and the much larger, planetary transmitter. If we destroyed the tower, with any luck we'd take out both.

Our Moment of Victory was headed straight for the tower, but it was several klicks away, and the Sp'ossel fighters were still blasting it with their lazecannons. It was clear Vlaak's ship wasn't going to make it without some help. I steered to the right, putting the *Flagrante Delicto* on an intercept path with the fighters. When I was only a few hundred meters away, I let loose a barrage of lazecannon fire. (While I'm unable to engage in personal combat or fire handheld weapons, I've found that a loophole in my programming allows me to use ship-based weapons.) I hit the first one dead on; it exploded into a million pieces. I only clipped the second one, but it was enough to destabilize it, sending it plummeting to the surface, where it came apart in a blast of flame. *Our Moment of Victory* was in the clear.

It was also on fire, losing altitude, and on a collision course with the control tower. We flew past them and came about just in time to see *Our Moment of Victory* smash into the base of the tower. As plumes of smoke billowed from the wreckage of Vlaak's now-immobile ship, the tower began to sway, first toward the ship, then the opposite direction.

"Sasha, watch out!" Boggs yelled.

"Donny doesn't like that building," Donny said.

The tower was going to fall—and given our current course, it was going to hit us. There was no time to change direction, so I did the only thing I could think of: I punched the accelerator. We rocketed past as the tower fell, barely missing us.

Breathing a sigh of relief, I decelerated and brought the ship around again. Down below, several people in black uniforms were running away from the tower. They didn't appear to be armed, so I ignored them. They got in a small ship and blasted off.

The Sp'ossels had evidently never expected anyone to get past their defensive shell—and if we hadn't had the Malarchian navy drawing fire, we wouldn't have. Above us, the battle seemed to be winding down: the Sp'ossels and the Malarchians, evenly matched, had virtually annihilated each other's forces. Maybe there was a chance of us getting out of here after all.

I landed the *Flagrante Delicto* not far from the smoking wreckage of *Our Moment of Victory*. Given that the Sp'ossels had run to their ship without vac suits on, I assumed the air was breathable. Presumably the Sp'ossels had terraformed Planet Z as part of their plans. I opened the hatch and a blast of cool air greeted us.

"Let's go," I said to Boggs and Donny. "We're going to see if there's anything left of Rex."

Boggs and Donny followed me down the ramp. The surface of Planet Z was rough and hard, like walking on congealed salt crystals. It was mostly flat except for larger crystals that jutted out from the surface at irregular intervals. The air was cold and the ground and the sky were both a pale azure, giving the planet a desolate, melancholy feel.

"This place is fantastic!" Boggs exclaimed. "I love it here!"

"Donny does not love it," Donny said.

"I'm not too keen on it either, Donny," I said, shooting a suspicious glance at Boggs. "We won't be staying long." I doubted anyone had survived the crash, and any minute I expected to be cut down by a hail of lazecannon fire. The Sp'ossels and the Malarchy both wanted us dead; the only question was whether either of them had any ships left.

As we approached *Our Moment of Victory*, several figures stumbled out of the smoke toward us. Rex appeared first, with Squawky, none the worse for wear, still perched on his shoulder. Heinous Vlaak, his uniform badly scuffed from the crash, came next. Pepper and Ort Felzich followed.

"Sasha!" Rex cried as he saw me. "I'm so happy to see you!"

"Yes," squeaked Heinous Vlaak. "I too am happy to see you, robot."

Somehow, it was less disconcerting to hear this from Heinous Vlaak than from Rex.

"You are?" I asked, looking at Rex.

"Of course!" Rex said. "And Boggs and Donny! Isn't this great? We're all back together on this wonderful rock-hard blue planet!"

"I am happy to see you too, Potential Friend!" Boggs said. "I have never been so happy."

Pepper and Ort Felzich, despite being badly scraped up and bruised, seemed oddly cheerful as well. Only Donny and I remained on edge.

"Donny does not like the blue planet," Donny said. "Donny wants to leave now."

A sickening feeling came over me as I realized what had happened. "We're too late," I said. "They triggered the happiness transmitter."

Something didn't add up, though. Boggs hadn't shown any signs of being irrationally happy until we landed. "Is the effect localized to the surface?" I asked.

"They didn't have enough time to activate the planetary transmitter," Ort Felzich said, approaching us. "When *Our Moment of Victory* hit the control tower, it triggered the local transmitter." He pointed at the parabolic dish, which lay on the ground, angled in our direction.

At first, I was puzzled that the transmitter wasn't affecting Felzich, but then I remembered the whole reason he was carrying his consciousness around in a briefcase.

"The rest of the galaxy isn't happy?" I asked.

"No," Ort replied. "The effects didn't take hold until we climbed out of the crash. It seems to be limited to the area in front of the dish."

"So if they leave this area, they'll be back to normal?"

"Yes."

"Why would we do that?" Rex asked. "We're incredibly happy

here."

Pepper and Boggs nodded in agreement.

"*You're* incredibly happy," I said. "I'm terrified."

"Donny is not happy," Donny said.

"In any case," I said, "we can't stay here. Whoever won the big space battle up there is going to be coming here to kill us shortly."

"Relax, Sasha," Rex said. "If we die, we die. The important thing is to enjoy the here and now."

"Good point, Rex," Pepper said. "I'm going to lie down and just take it all in." She lay down on the ground. Boggs and Heinous Vlaak were hugging.

"Get a hold of yourself," Squawky said. "I'm a born pirate."

"No!" I shouted. "Don't lie down. We have to get out of here!"

"It's pointless, Sasha," Felzich said. "They're completely content. There's no way to convince them to go anywhere."

"Then what do we do?"

"Let's see if we can shut down that transmitter."

Donny and I followed Felzich to the huge parabolic dish, which had been badly bent out of shape by the fall. The zontonium crystal at the end of the column seemed to be the same size as the one Rex had tried to steal from the satellite orbiting Vericulon Four. There were no visible controls or any obvious way of shutting down the transmitter. Looking up, I still saw no signs of either Sp'ossel or Malarchian ships. Maybe we had gotten lucky and the two sides had obliterated each other completely. I wasn't going to bank on it, though. The sooner we got off Planet Z, the better.

"Let's check inside," Felzich said, walking toward the base of the tower. I followed, and Donny skittered after me, his four arm-legs surprisingly well-adapted for walking over the jagged ground. The door to the building had been blown off by the impact of Vlaak's ship; Donny and I walked right inside, finding ourselves in a room filled with a bewildering array of control panels. The walls were covered with dozens of display screens. At present, every single screen was displaying a numeric countdown. Donny and I watched as it went from 12:03 to 12:02 to 12:01 to 12:00 to 11:59.

"Donny doesn't like the numbers," Donny said.

"Does that mean what I think it means?" I asked.

Felzich nodded, a deep frown having come over his face. "The Sp'ossels have rigged the planet to self-destruct."

CHAPTER TWENTY-SEVEN

"The whole planet is going to explode?" I asked, unable to believe it. "Not just the tower?"

Felzich shook his head. "The Sp'ossels are serious about not letting the planet fall into the wrong hands. The plans specified the construction of an underground zontonium reactor. The simplest way to build a self-destruct mechanism would be to overload the reactor. The reactor melts down and the chain reaction spreads to the planet itself. Pretty neat, actually."

"Donny does not think it is neat," Donny said. "Donny thinks it is very much not neat."

"Could you disable the self-destruct?" I asked.

"It's going to be tricky," Felzich said, studying the controls. "Looks like the reactor has already been overloaded. Even if I cut the control circuit, the reactor will reach critical mass on its own. I have to tell the reactor to retract the zontonium rods."

"And you can do that?"

"I think so," said Felzich. "But just in case, you should get out of here. You and Donny."

"I can't leave without Rex and the others," I said.

"Forget them," Felzich said. "There's no time. Save yourselves."

"What about you?"

"This is my doing," Felzich said. "I found Planet Z. I designed the psionic transmitter. Everything that's happening is my fault. It will be fitting if I meet my demise when this planet explodes."

"You mean *if* it explodes," I said.

"Right," said Felzich. "Because I'm going to try to keep it from exploding."

I regarded him skeptically for a moment. "You are, right?"

"Of course! Do you think my guilt at having gotten us into this situation has manifested itself as a death wish?"

"I didn't until right now," I replied.

"Don't be ridiculous, Sasha. I'm just being realistic. I'm going to do my best, but I might fail. Now get out of here!"

"All right," I said. "Good luck."

He waved us away irritably. Donny and I ran back toward the *Flagrante Delicto*. Rex waved as we went by. "Hey, Sasha!" he yelled. "Isn't this place great?"

"Aye, sir," I yelled. "But wouldn't you rather come with us aboard the *Flagrante Delicto*?"

Rex shrugged. "I was kind of thinking about a nap."

I wondered if Donny and I could carry Rex to the *Flagrante Delicto*. Probably not. There just wasn't enough time. And we would still have to leave Boggs, Pepper and Vlaak behind. I paused at the ramp to the *Flagrante Delicto*. Donny skittered to a halt next to me. It just didn't seem right to leave Rex behind.

"Donny does not like this planet," Donny said.

"Nor do I, Donny."

"But Donny does not want to leave without the others."

I sighed. "Agreed. Let's see if we can at least get Rex on board."

We ran over to Rex, who was now lying down on the jagged surface. He looked extremely uncomfortable and ridiculously happy. I almost envied his complete obliviousness about our situation.

"Sir, get up," I said, tugging at his left arm. Donny pulled on his right.

"What for?" Rex asked.

"If we stay here, we're going to die. The planet is about to explode."

"Okay," Rex said, getting to his feet. Donny skittered around behind him. I was about to give Rex a shove onto Donny's back when he suddenly took off running.

"Sir!" I yelled. "Where are you going?"

"Try to catch me, Sasha!" Rex squealed in delight. "Isn't this just the most fun you've ever had?"

"We're all going to die," Squawky cried.

"Go after him, Donny!" I yelled. We ran across the jagged surface after Rex. After a hundred meters or so, he suddenly stopped. He turned to face us, a puzzled expression on his face.

"Sasha," he said, "did you say something about the planet exploding?"

"Yes, sir," I said. "How do you feel about that?"

"How do I *feel* about it? What is wrong with you, Sasha? We need to get to the *Flagrante Delicto*!" Evidently he had reached the edge of the psionic field and was back in control of his senses. He began running back toward the ship and a rapturous look came over his face again. "Try to catch me, Sasha!" he yelled. "Woooooooo!"

We ran after him, but instead of climbing the ramp, he ran past the ship and kept going. We tried to keep up, but he outpaced us. Fifty meters or so on the other side of the *Flagrante Delicto*, he suddenly stopped again. "Sasha!" He shouted. "Get to the ship! This planet's going to explode!" He started running toward the ship again, but veered away as we approached. "Fooled you!" He yelled. "Try to catch me! Woooooooo!"

"This is hopeless, Donny," I said. "We'll never catch him. We just have to hope that Ort Felzich—"

Before I could finish, a huge explosion erupted at the base of the tower, knocking me and the others to the ground. For a split-second, I thought Ort Felzich had triggered the self-destruct—but if he had, we'd all have been blown to atoms.

"Sasha, what's happening?" Boggs called. The others, slowly getting to their feet, seemed equally confused. Rex stood a few paces away, looking bewildered. The spell had been broken. The base of the tower had been annihilated. As I watched, the massive crystal protruding from the local transmitter tower became dislodged from its housing and crashed to the ground.

I heard the roar of rockets and turned to see a ship landing. It was Hookbeard's vessel, the *Coccydynia*. It wasn't the self-destruct that had taken out the tower; it was a torpedo. The battle up above must have terminated, or Hookbeard's huge ship would never have gotten through. And for whatever reason, Hookbeard's crew had torpedoed the control tower, killing Ort Felzich, shutting down the transmitter and obliterating any possibility of us preventing the planet from blowing up. If what Felzich had told us was correct, the zontonium chain reaction was now unstoppable.

"To the *Flagrante Delicto*!" I heard Rex yell.

We ran to the ship and got on board. I strapped myself into the pilot's chair and started the launch sequence. I was greeted by a flashing light that read:

INSUFFICIENT FUEL TO LAUNCH

"No," I said. "No, no, no." I slumped forward, letting my head rest on the control panel.

"What is it, Sasha?" Rex asked, coming up next to me.

"No fuel," I said. "We're sitting on a trillion tons of zontonium, and we're out of fuel. We burned it all up with that insane reentry. We're going to die of irony."

"Can we go dig up some fuel?"

I shook my head. "Unrefined zontonium will overload the reactor. Our ship will explode." Much in the same way that the planet was going to explode.

"Hmm," said Rex, rubbing his chin thoughtfully. "Only one thing to do."

"Die in a big explosion?"

"This way, Sasha," Rex said. He made his way through the main cabin and opened the hatch.

"What is happening?" Heinous Vlaak demanded as we passed. "Why aren't we leaving?"

"Minor delay," Rex said. "Be right back." I followed him down the ramp.

Hookbeard and four pirates, armed with lazepistols, had left the *Coccydynia* and were approaching the *Flagrante Delicto*.

"Stop right there!" Hookbeard growled.

Rex and I stopped and put our hands in the air.

Hookbeard grinned. "Thought you were so smart, getting the Sp'ossels and the Malarchy to fight so you could steal this planet out from underneath them. But I'm smarter, Malgastar. This planet is mine now!"

"Okay," Rex said.

Confusion came over Hookbeard's face. "What do you mean, 'okay'?"

"I mean the planet is all yours. It's going to blow up in... Sasha?"

"Six minutes and nineteen seconds," I said. I had synched an internal timer with the self-destruct countdown.

"It's going to blow up in six minutes and nineteen seconds

168

anyway," Rex said. "So it's all yours. Enjoy it while you can. Oh, by the way, I'm not Rubric Malgastar. My name is Rex Nihilo."

"Nice try, Malgastar," Hookbeard said. "Planets don't blow up."

"They do if they're made of zontonium," Rex said. "The Sp'ossels activated a self-destruct mechanism."

"If that's true, why haven't you left?"

"We're out of fuel. I just came out here to see if I could borrow some."

Hookbeard shook his head. "I'm on to you, Malgastar. This is just another ruse. You're trying to trick me into leaving this planet so you can claim it for yourself. I'm not falling for it."

Rex sighed. "All right, you got me. It was all a ruse. I guess we're going to have to do this the hard way. Hookbeard, Planet Z is mine. I'm going to need you and your crew to leave immediately."

"Are you mad?" Hookbeard said. "We've got all the guns. We blasted the Sp'ossels, conquering this planet fair and square. And you're trespassing."

"Technically," Rex said, "*you're* trespassing. The Intergalactic Conquest Accords of 2837 specify that in the case of an epic space battle ending in a draw, the first non-combatant to land on the contested planet can claim ownership."

"You're making that up," said Hookbeard.

"Nope. It's called the Default Dominion Rule. It was reaffirmed by the Malarchian Supreme Court in 2983 and again in 2997. The latter case was particularly interesting, because the race claiming dominion over Alacron Four was a single-celled gelatinous fungus which lacked the ability to communicate except by means of arranging itself in vast geometric configurations on the surface of the planet. The problem was—"

"Sir," I interjected, "I don't think we have time for this. The planet is—"

"Quiet, Sasha!" Rex snapped. "As I was saying, the frequent volcanic eruptions on Alacron Four tended to disrupt the fungus's attempts to communicate, such as when a motion for a continuance was misinterpreted as an order for sixteen metric tons of Kung Pao Chicken. As you can imagine, the court grew impatient with the fungus and would probably have ordered it exterminated if it weren't for the timely intervention of the wasp-like Psaptarians, who had developed a symbiotic relationship with the fungus wherein—"

"Okay, I get it!" growled Hookbeard. "Legally, it's your planet. But none of this matters. I'm kicking you off the planet and taking it for myself. It's the law of conquest."

"I see," said Rex, with a deep frown. "Well, that changes everything. If you are claiming this planet by right of conquest, then I'll just need to sign your PRF-128 and we can get out of your hair."

"PRF-128?"

"Planetary release form," Rex said.

Hookbeard stared at him blankly.

"You do have a PRF-128, right?"

"Where would I get one of those?" Hookbeard asked.

A puzzled look came over Rex's face. "They should have given you a whole stack when you registered as an Interstellar Governing Authority with the Malarchian Registry of Planets."

Hookbeard continued to stare.

"Please tell me you've registered with the MRP as an IGA," Rex said.

"I was going to," Hookbeard blustered. "But I, uh, got busy with pirate stuff."

Rex groaned. "If you're not an IGA, the legalities of this are going to be a nightmare."

Hookbeard shrugged. "Seems simple enough to me. You get off my planet—or I kill you, your choice. Then I register as that thing you said, and I'm all set."

"That *would* work," said Rex, "except that I've already transmitted my PAF-67b to the MRP. If you register as an IGA after my PAF-67b is processed, they'll red-flag it and throw Planet Z into escrow for the next twenty years."

"I don't understand what any of that means."

"It means that for the foreseeable future, Planet Z will be *de facto* Malarchian property. They'll mine it and flood the galaxy with zontonium for twenty years before you ever make a cent."

"They can't do that!" Hookbeard roared. "I conquered this planet fair and square!"

"Well," Rex said. "There is one thing that might work."

"What?" Hookbeard asked, a tone of desperation in his voice.

"I could try to amend my PAF-67b. I'd have to get on our ship, jump out of the asteroid field, and transmit a PAF-67b that lists us as co-owners. Then we'd each own fifty percent of Planet Z."

"Fifty percent?" said Hookbeard. "This planet is mine!"

Rex shrugged. "You can kill me and take your chances if you want. But don't expect to get any zontonium out of this planet for the next twenty years. You're better off with half a planet than nothing."

"You're blackmailing me," Hookbeard said.

"This is just a friendly negotiation," Rex replied. "I want to live. You want ownership of the planet. Let's make a deal."

"How do I know you'll actually transmit the…"

"Amended PAF-67b? Well, if I don't, you've got several witnesses who can testify that I negotiated in bad faith. In short, if either of us tries to screw the other out of his share, the courts will most likely toss Planet Z into escrow. If we don't cross all our T's here, we both lose. They'll steal the planet out from underneath us and plunder it for all it's worth. The best option for both of us is for me to leave, transmit the amended PAF-67b, and split ownership of the planet."

"So we have to share the planet? Forever?"

"Only until one of us dies," said Rex. "For example, let's say that after I transmit the amended PAF-67b, I return to gaze upon my newly acquired planet and some terrible accident immediately befalls me. Perhaps, and I'm just spitballing here, I am accidentally shot in the face by a pirate's lazegun. Upon my death, Space forbid, ownership of the entire planet would fall to you."

Hookbeard nodded slowly, seeming pleased by this development. "Okay," he said after some time, "but you leave your crew here as a guarantee you'll follow through. If you don't transmit the amended form, I execute them."

Rex shrugged. "Fine with me," he said, "but you should know that if I leave any member of my crew here, I'm in a better position to claim total ownership of the planet. We got here first, and I'll be able to claim I've maintained an uninterrupted presence on the planet. Not that I would try to screw you out of your half, obviously. I just thought I should tell you, in the interest of full disclosure."

"Full disclosure," Hookbeard repeated.

"That's right," Rex said. "Any crew member I leave here just increases the risk you'll lose the planet. Just thought you deserved to know."

Hookbeard stared at him for several seconds. "Go," he said at last. "Take your crew with you. All of them."

"If you insist," Rex replied. "Oh, and one other thing: we're out of fuel. Would it be okay if we grabbed some zontonium on the way out?"

"How much?"

"No more than my crew can carry," Rex said.

"Fine," Hookbeard said, clearly exhausted by the exchange. "Get the zontonium and go."

"Great!" Rex exclaimed. He turned to face the *Flagrante Delicto*, whose hatch was still open. "Hey, Boggs!" he shouted. "Get out here!"

After a few seconds, Boggs stomped down the ramp. He stopped a few steps in front of Rex. "What is it, Potential Friend?"

"See that big rock over there, Boggs?" Rex asked, pointing to the giant crystal that had fallen from the transmitter. "You think you can pick it up and put it in the *Flagrante Delicto*?"

Boggs regarded the crystal. "You bet, Potential Friend." He began walking to the stone.

"*That's* the zontonium you're taking?" Hookbeard asked.

"Sure," Rex replied coolly. "The rest of it is unrefined. A little tough on the engines. You understand. Anyway, it's just a speck out of the vast supply at our disposal. Take it out of my half."

Hookbeard nodded.

"One minute, thirty-eight seconds, sir," I said.

"Let's go, Boggs!" Rex yelled.

Boggs had lifted the stone onto his shoulders and was staggering toward the *Flagrante Delicto*.

"One minute thirty-eight seconds for what?" Hookbeard asked.

"Ensign Boggs is on a very tight schedule," Rex said. "If he doesn't get his nap, he gets very cranky."

Boggs stomped up the ramp. When he got to the top, he let the stone roll off his shoulders, landing with a thud inside the cabin of the *Flagrante Delicto*. Rex and I follow him up the ramp. "See you soon!" Rex shouted, giving Hookbeard and his crew a wave. We ducked inside the ship and closed the door.

"Sasha, can you cut a chunk off that rock to use as fuel?"

"I think so, sir."

"Then get to it. Everybody else, strap in."

I extended my cutting torch attachment and chopped off a tiny corner of the stone, the size of an apple slice. Then I moved to the rear of the ship, opening the engine compartment. I tossed the zontonium fragment into the fuel receptacle and slammed it shut. That amount of zontonium would be plenty to get us off the planet and out of the asteroid field. I ran to the cockpit and fired up the engines. As we lifted off the ground, my internal timer went off.

Several jagged, lightning-like streaks shot through the translucent ground and then went dark. A few seconds later, a glow appeared deep within the planet, and rapidly grew in intensity. I caught a glimpse of Hookbeard and his men, far below, running for their ship. Cracks began to appear in the surface, rapidly widening into yawning chasms. Massive chunks of zontonium ore crumbled into the chasms. The *Coccydynia* tumbled into one of these. I lost sight of the pirate crew as we soared higher into the atmosphere. I had to feel a little bad for them; we tried to warn them, but you could hardly blame them for assuming Rex was lying about the planet blowing up. On the other hand, they were pirates who would happily have killed us, so screw them.

"Sir," I asked, "was any of that stuff you told Hookbeard true? About the forms and the Default Dominion Rule and Planet Z going into escrow?"

"Not a word," said Rex.

There was another flash from deep inside the planet, followed by a deafening roar as the planet exploded, pushing the atmosphere outward. The shockwave propelled us even faster. Seconds later, everything went quiet as the *Flagrante Delicto* shot out of the atmosphere. Chunks of zontonium ore hurtled past us into space. If one of these projectiles hit us, we were dead. But we continued to gain momentum, and soon were outpacing all the debris. I reduced thrust to twenty percent so I'd have time to rationalize a jump course before we re-entered the asteroid field.

We'd escaped from Planet Z.

CHAPTER TWENTY-EIGHT

"Congrats, Vlaak," Rex exclaimed, slapping Heinous Vlaak on the back. "You saved the galaxy!"

"My career is over," Vlaak moaned. "I destroyed half the Malarchian fleet. Again."

We had just jumped out of the asteroid field and we were now floating in space. As I was awaiting orders, I had returned from the cockpit to the main cabin. The mood among the crew was celebratory, with the exception of Vlaak, who wouldn't stop moaning. It seemed that the battle between the Sp'ossels and the Malarchy really had been a draw. Every single ship on both sides had been destroyed. That meant Vlaak had absolutely nothing to show for his efforts. All evidence of the Sp'ossel threat had been destroyed.

"You don't understand how hard it is for someone like me to find a job," Vlaak said. "I have a very specific skillset. Do you know if any other interstellar tyrannies are hiring?"

"Forget about it, Vlaak," Rex said. "When the Primate finds out what you did, you'll be considered a hero."

"I can't show my face to the Primate! He'll have me executed for treason!"

"Pull yourself together."

"Why is this happening to me? All I ever wanted to do is be the best enforcer I could be for the Malarchy. But nothing ever works out for me. I don't know why I bother."

"For Space's sake, Vlaak, quit whining. Sasha, rationalize a course for Malarchium."

"I'm not sure that's wise, sir." Malarchium was the galactic capital. Rex and I had never been there, as far as I could remember. It wasn't a particularly good place for criminals to be.

"I agree with the robot," Vlaak said. "I need to stay as far away from the Malarchy as possible. Perhaps I will become a scofflaw like you two. How do you like piracy so far? What's the dental plan like?"

"You're not cut out to be a pirate, Vlaak," Rex said. "Trust me, I've got it all figured out."

"Why would I trust you?"

"Look, we're flying into the Malarchian capital. If they execute you, what do you think they're going to do to me and Sasha?"

"This isn't helping, sir," I said.

"My point is that if Vlaak is out of a job, he's in no position to protect us. Obviously I wouldn't land on a planet where everyone wants to kill me without some kind of plan."

I wasn't so sure about that, but Vlaak seemed somewhat mollified. "Why would you help me?" he asked. "What's in it for you?"

"A very small favor," Rex said with a smile. "Sasha, get us to Malarchium."

•●.

We landed at the Malarchian Primate's private spaceport, just a few klicks from the palace. Heinous Vlaak, at Rex's prompting, had secured permission to land from the Primate himself. The fact that we had not been shot out of the sky presumably meant that the Primate wanted to at least hear Vlaak's account of the debacle on Planet Z before executing him.

Rex, Vlaak and I were put in a shuttle and transported to the palace. We were hauled before the Primate in his reception chamber. The Primate, a tiny, gray-skinned, balding little man in a purple robe, sat upon a massive throne at the far end of the room. Six members of the elite Malarchian Guard flanked the throne, three on each side. He opened his mouth to reveal exactly three teeth.

"Heinouth Vlaak!" lisped the Primate. "What have you done with my fleet?"

"That's a great question," Rex said. "But let me ask you one, Your Limitless Radiancy: are you happy? Because if you're not happy, you have one person to thank, and that's Heinous Vlaak."

"Who ith thith man?" the Primate growled. "Why did you bring him before me? Ekthplain yourthelf, Vlaak!"

"Forgive me, Your Primacy," Heinous Vlaak said, with a deep bow. "The Orion wing has been destroyed. I brought these two along in order to explain—"

"You dethtroyed an entire wing of my fleet?" the Primate howled. "That'th the thecond time you've done that, you thimpering imbethile!"

"Yes, Your Primacy," said Vlaak. "But this time there was a good reason."

"Your requetht thaid there wath an urgent threat to the thtability of the Malarchy. Where ith thith threat? Where are their thyips? Are they invithible?"

"No, Your Primacy. You see, the Sp'ossels built a mind control transmitter deep within an asteroid field. By acting quickly, I was able to—"

"You're thaying you've thaved uth from thome kind of thinithter Thp'othel conthpirathy?"

Vlaak stared at the Primate. "I'm sorry, Your Primacy. Could you repeat that?"

"A thinithter Thp'othel conthpirathy! Thith ith what patheth for your defenth?"

"Mister Primate, sir," said Rex, "If I may interject a moment, I think you'll find once you've reviewed the evidence in my possession that Vlaak's actions were fully justified and that he is, in fact, a bona fide hero of the Malarchy, deserving of medals and suchlike."

"Who are you?" the Primate demanded.

"Rex Nihilo, Your Poignant Vibrancy. And can I just say what an honor it is to meet an unquestioned despot such as yourself? The way you subdue the entire galaxy with an iron grip is truly inspirational."

"Thyow me thith evidenth or get out."

"Of course, Your Tremulous Urgency! Sasha?"

Fortunately, Rex had briefed me on my role, so I was only mildly terrified.

"Your Primacy," I said, giving a curtsy, "As I'm sure you know, robots of my type are congenitally incapable of lying. So when I tell you that what Heinous Vlakk has told you about the Sp'ossels—"

"Thith ith your evidenth?" the Primate growled. "The tethtimony of thome thilly robot?"

"No, Your Inimitable Haberdashery," Rex said. "Sasha, get to it!"

"Aye, sir," I said. "Your Primacy, in addition to my personal testimony, I offer you a complete audio and video recording of my memories over the past ten hours. You will clearly see the nature of the Sp'ossel menace explained by none other than Ort Felzich himself."

"Prepothterouth! Ort Felthitth ith frothen!"

"We thawed him, Your Primacy," I said, pressing on. "You will also witness the ensuing battle, in which Heinous Vlaak bravely risked his life and lost his entire fleet in order to preserve Malarchian rule over the galaxy."

"And how do I aktheth thith thuppothed recording?"

"Simply plug a memory card into my interface port and I'll download it for you. You can watch the entire thing at your leisure."

"You!" the Primate growled, pointing at one of the guards. "Get me one of those memory thingth!"

The guard bowed and ran out of the room. Several moments passed.

"Tho," the Primate said casually, looking at me, "enjoying your thtay?"

"Yes, your Primacy," I replied nervously. "I mean, we haven't seen much of the planet yet. Just the spaceport and your palace. It's a fine palace, obviously. I don't mean to—"

"Thilenth!" the Primate shouted as the guard reentered the room, holding a tiny memory drive in his left gauntlet. The Primate turned to face the man. "Plug that into the robot," he said.

A moment of confusion followed, as no one in the room could make heads or tails of the Primate's order.

"Did I thtutter?" he snapped. "Thtick it into the robot'th thlot!"

"Yes, Your Primacy!" the guard exclaimed. "Sorry, Your Primacy!" He ran up to me, holding the memory card in his fingers. "Uh, can I... uh...?"

"Thtop romanthing her and thtick it in!"

The guard's face went red as a ripe tomato. I grabbed the card out of his hands and stuck it into the slot below my chin. I scanned the contents for viruses and then made a copy of the data on it before downloading my recording of the battle to the card. The whole process took less than three seconds. I removed the card and handed it back to the guard. "Was it good for you?" I asked.

The guard murmured something incomprehensible, bowed slightly and then ran back to the Primate with the card. He handed the card to the Primate, bowed again, and then returned to his post.

The Primate stuck the card into a slot in his throne, then pointed behind us. Turning, I saw that the entire wall of the chamber had turned into a massive viewscreen. Ort Felzich, some ten meters high, was saying, "But if the Malarchy wants to retain dominion over the galaxy in any meaningful sense, it's going to have to deal with the Sp'ossels."

"I'll refer the matter to my superiors for further investigation," said ten-meter-tall Heinous Vlaak. "Meanwhile, the lot of you will be executed for piracy."

Rex glared at me. I shrugged. Rex had told me to give them the entire, unadulterated recording. Anyway, the matter was out of my hands. I stood silently as the scene unfolded.

Ten-meter-tall Heinous Vlaak was saying, "Planet Z is real? You found it?"

"I did," said ten-meter-tall Felzich. "And the Sp'ossels found it too."

"It was long believed that the zontonium planet was only a legend," said ten-meter-tall Vlaak. "If Planet Z actually exists, that amount of zontonium is a matter of strategic importance to the Malarchy."

The Primate was now nodding in approval. I breathed a sigh of relief. The rest was a formality. We watched as *Our Moment of Victory* traveled to Planet Z. The Primate witnessed the entire battle, down to our harrowing escape. He seemed satisfied that Vlaak had acted appropriately. And if Vlaak was back in the Primate's good graces, that meant Rex and I would be allowed to live—as long as Vlaak didn't double-cross us.

"Ekthellent work, Vlaak," said the Primate, when the recording had finished. "It almotht compenthateth for the dethtructhion of my entire fleet."

"As you say, Your Primacy," said Vlaak, clearly relieved to have summary execution off the table.

"Jutht one matter remainth to be adrethed," the Primate said. "The ekthecuthion of thethe mitherable pirateth!"

179

CHAPTER TWENTY-NINE

For a moment, nobody spoke. We were counting on Heinous Vlaak going to bat for us, and I was beginning to think we'd miscalculated. I thought Rex might speak up, but he—unbelievably—remained silent as well. Finally Vlaak spoke.

"I gave these pirates immunity for their crimes in exchange for their assistance in the Battle of Planet Z. With the understanding that they will henceforth cease all pirate-related activities, obviously." He shot a threatening glare at me and Rex. We tried to look suitably rebuked.

"Pirathy thyall not be tolerated!" the Primate roared.

"Absolutely not, Your Primacy," said Vlaak. "I will be keeping a close eye on these two, you can be certain of that."

The Primate shrugged. "I tire of thith. I'm mithing naptime. Be gone." He waved his hand dismissively.

"Yes, Your Primacy," said Vlaak. "Thank you, Your Primacy." He gave Rex a nudge and the three of us hurried out of the chamber.

"Thought you were going to sell us out there for a minute," said Rex, once we were back in the hall.

"I almost did," said Vlaak. "Tell me the truth, Nihilo. Do you really have the capability to transmit that video of me across the galaxy?"

"Absolutely," Rex said. "If you'd have double-crossed us, everybody from here to Rigelus Nine would hear you whining about being executed for treason. You'd never intimidate anybody in the galaxy again." This was a lie, of course. I did have the video, but hadn't had time to download it to the *Flagrante Delicto* or transmit it anywhere. Fortunately, Vlaak couldn't be sure of that, and he valued his role as fearsome Malarchian enforcer more than vengeance against Rex and me.

"If you ever do release it," Vlaak said, "you're both dead. I'll be watching you."

"I'm counting on it," Rex replied. "Which reminds me, I do need one more thing. Well, two things."

●

Miraculously, we made it off Malarchium unscathed. Our next stop was Sargasso Seven to drop off Pepper. We had no way of cutting the massive stone into pieces, and it was dangerous to travel with that much zontonium anyway, so I chopped off a little more for us to use as fuel and then let Boggs carry the stone to Pepper's office. Unfortunately, until Pepper could get a larger safe built, she had nowhere else to put it.

"What if somebody breaks in?" Rex said, as we stood around the huge stone.

"I've never had any trouble," Pepper replied.

"You've never had a hundred million credits' worth of zontonium in your office either."

Rex had a point. I'd seen the way the pirates looked at the stone as Boggs carried it through the bar.

"I'll order a bigger safe," Pepper said. "Money isn't a problem anymore."

"But what will you do until then?" I asked. "You need some way of protecting it."

"I'll protect it," said Boggs. "If anyone comes near the office, I'll bonk them on the head."

Boggs would make a pretty intimidating security guard. "You have to sleep, though," I said.

"I can take naps," said Boggs. "I'm good at naps."

It was true. He was incredibly good at naps.

"Donny doesn't have to sleep," said Donny. "Donny can watch the door when Boggs naps."

"There you have it," said Rex. "Problem solved."

"Do you guys really want to stay here?" I asked. "There's plenty of room on the *Flagrante Delicto* if you want to come with me and Rex." As much as I hated to admit it, I'd grown attached to Boggs and Donny.

"Pepper is a friend," Boggs said.

Pepper smiled. "Thank you, Boggs," she said. "I consider you a friend as well."

"Also," Boggs went on, "I think I am scared of spaceships now." Donny nodded in agreement.

"Well, I can't blame you for that," I said. We had nearly been killed in an amazing number of ways on a remarkably diverse range of spacecraft.

"Cowards, the lot of you," Rex grumbled. "At least I can count on Squawky. Right, old boy?"

"Scared of spaceships," said Squawky, and fluttered into the air. He landed on Boggs's shoulder.

Boggs grinned. "Steve is a friend," he said. The bird squawked contentedly.

"Ugh," said Rex. "Let's get out of here, Sasha. All this friendliness and good feelings is making me wish we'd just let the blasted Sp'ossels get away with their sinister plan. Then at least I wouldn't find this all so irritating." He turned and stomped out of the office.

"You could stay too, Sasha," Pepper said. "There's plenty of work to do around here. I could use a smart robot like you."

I shook my head. "Rex needs me," I said.

"Of course he does," Pepper said. "But what are you getting out of the deal?"

It was a good question. To be honest, I wasn't sure my sticking with Rex wasn't just part of my Sp'ossel programming. There certainly didn't seem to be any other rational explanation. And yet, I am who I am. What can I say? Abandoning Rex just didn't feel right.

"I'm not sure," I replied. "But there's only one way to find out. Good to see you again, Pepper. Goodbye, Boggs and Donny. You guys really were a topnotch pirate crew."

I turned and walked out the office.

"Now what, sir?" I asked. We had left Sargasso Seven and were now sitting at the bar of the cargo waystation orbiting Xagnon, the same place Rex had gotten it into his head to hijack the *Raina Huebner*.

"Now we wait," said Rex, sipping at this martini.

I would have asked what we were waiting for, but I had a feeling I knew. "Do you think it's wise for us to be hanging out at the same station where we absconded with the *Raina Huebner*, though?"

"We're not pirates anymore, Sasha. The Malarchian Primate himself signed off on our pardon. We're untouchable. Try to relax."

I nodded, still feeling nervous. To be honest, it wasn't the authorities I was worried about. This part of the galaxy had a strong Sp'ossel presence—and I suspected that was exactly why we were here. The Sp'ossels were going to find us one way or another, and Rex wanted to see them coming.

We may have destroyed the Sp'ossels' mind control device, but the Sp'ossels were still a vast and powerful organization. And as far as they were concerned, we were still Sp'ossel property. Somehow I doubted they were going to keep us on as acquisitions agents after we'd foiled their sinister plan, though. We were more trouble than we were worth. Sp'ossels are supposedly averse to killing, but there were things they could do to us that would make death look like a nice vacation in the Ragulian Sector.

So we waited.

Amazingly, it took them less than an hour to show up. Rex saw them first: Doctors LaRue and Smulders. The same ones who had tried to wipe our memories at the Collective of the Inverted Ego. They sat down across from us.

"Rex and Sasha," said the woman, Dr. LaRue. "Good to see you again."

"Great to see you guys," said Rex. "Sorry about the, uh…" He made what I took to be an explosion gesture.

"Yes," said Dr. LaRue, "that was an unfortunate turn of events. One that is going to have unpleasant repercussions for me and my colleague, as we were indirectly responsible."

"That's a shame," said Rex. "Just awful. I can't imagine anything worse, except maybe someone manipulating me for my entire life and wiping my memories without my permission."

"Ah, so you remember," Dr. LaRue said.

"I don't, no. But Sasha does, and what she tells me dovetails with what I know about Sp'ossels."

"Which is what?"

"You guys are serious wankers. Like, wankers on a cosmic scale."

Dr. LaRue smiled coldly. "Our supervisors have ordered us to kill you," she said. "Well, the exact orders were to 'terminate the assets.' It came as a bit of a shock to us, because as you know, Sp'ossels are generally opposed to killing. I suppose they consider you less than human."

"Yeah, well, for a couple of subhumans, we sure blew up your planet good." He downed the rest of his martini and signaled the waiter for another.

"We're not going to do it, though," Dr. Smulders said. "Dr. LaRue and I discussed the matter. Do you know why we're not going to do it?"

"Nope."

"Because we want you to suffer, Rex. You too, Sasha. We're going to torture you for the next hundred years for what you did to us. We have methods of torture, you know, that go far beyond physical pain. We're experts in mental manipulation. We'll make you beg for death. By the time we're done with you, you'll—"

"Gaaaahhhh!" Rex exclaimed. "Is this about over? Wow, I get it. You're going to torture us. Scary stuff. Great. Thanks."

"Is that all you have to say?" Dr. LaRue said. "You're not going to beg for us to let you go? Or give you another chance?"

"Begging's not my thing," said Rex. "Tell 'em, Sasha."

"Begging is not his thing," I said.

"No, tell them the other thing."

"Which thing, sir?"

"The reason they're not going to do all that boring stuff he was talking about."

"Of course, sir," I said. "Rex would like me to tell you that we are under the official protection of Heinous Vlaak, the Primate's chief enforcer. If anything happens to us, you will be hunted down and tortured to death by Vlaak himself, who has been the Interstellar Torture Society's man of the year for three years running. Granted, the Sp'ossels are now considered enemies of the Malarchy, so I'd suggest going into hiding in any case, but if we disappear, Vlaak will go after you personally. We've given him your names."

Smulders laughed. "Nice try, robot. Heinous Vlaak doesn't make deals with two-bit con men."

"He did this time," I said. I turned on my holographic projector, and the image of Heinous Vlaak appeared on the table.

"Do I start talking now?" the Vlaak projection said. "Yes? Okay. This is Heinous Vlaak. I'm talking to the Sp'ossels, specifically a

Doctor Smulders? Is that right? Yes? A Doctor Smulders and a Doctor LaRue. I've made a deal with these two-bit con men. Anything happens to them, and you're finished. I hunt you down like rabbits and then torture you to death." Vlaak shook his fist dramatically.

"Ridiculous!" Dr. LaRue snapped. "How could he even know—"

"If you're wondering how I'll know if anything happens to them, the robot has a transponder implanted in her head. It transmits an encrypted message that can be received by any Malarchian communications facility across the galaxy. If she is deactivated, incapacitated, or harmed in any way, the message will not be transmitted. If the message isn't received for forty-eight hours, she will be assumed to be in Sp'ossel hands, and I will begin to hunt you down, beginning with her last known location. That is all."

Vlaak shook his fist again and his form winked out.

"This is all a bluff," said Dr. Smulders. "You're bluffing."

"Have you known Heinous Vlaak to be a big bluffer?" Rex asked.

"We don't even know that was really him."

"You know Vlaak commanded the fleet that attacked your transmitter, right? Have you gotten reports from the technicians who escaped just before Planet Z blew up? They'll tell you two ships made it to the surface: Heinous Vlaak's and ours. Vlaak's ship crash landed. We saved his life. He owes us."

I could tell by the glances Smulders and LaRue gave each other that they'd already been briefed on what happened, and that Rex's story gibed with the truth.

"Now, my suggestion," Rex went on, "would be to let us walk out of here and you'll never see us again. You can tell your supervisors you've followed your orders and no one will be the wiser. Or you can be hunted down and tortured to death. Your choice."

After a moment, Dr. LaRue spoke. "I'd like to see this supposed transponder."

"No problem," Rex said. "Sasha, take your face off."

I sighed. I really hate taking my face off in public. But I reached up, undid the hidden catches, and pulled it off. I leaned toward Dr. LaRue, and she peered inside my head. "There does seem to be a small transmitter," Dr. LaRue said, "and it doesn't appear to be..." She trailed off.

"Doesn't appear to be what?" I asked.

"Forget it," Dr. LaRue said. "I was just thinking out loud."

Rex grinned. "Doesn't appear to be the one the Sp'ossels installed, is that what you were going to say? That's because it isn't." He pulled something a little smaller than a matchbook from his pocket and held it in his palm. "We had the Malarchian technicians remove this when they installed theirs. I only held onto it to summon you guys here." He dropped the device on the floor and crushed it under his heel. "There," he said. "Sasha and I are dead. Untraceable. Problem solved."

Smulders and LaRue regarded each other again. La Rue turned back to Rex. "You'll disappear completely? We'll never hear from you again?"

"I have a policy of avoiding Sp'ossels whenever I can," Rex replied. "I see no reason to alter that plan."

"Give us a moment to confer," Dr. LaRue said.

LaRue and Smulders got up from the table and walked a few steps away. By the time they were done conferring, I had my face back on and the waiter had brought Rex another martini.

"All right," said Dr. LaRue. "We'll let you go. But if you so much as see a Sp'ossel, you'd better run the other direction. I can't make any guarantees about what the Sp'ossel leadership will do if they find out you're alive."

"Got it," said Rex. "Good luck on your next big sinister conspiracy." He raised his glass and grinned as LaRue and Smulders walked away.

CHAPTER THIRTY

"So that's it?" I asked. I could hardly believe the plan worked. "Almost," said Rex. "Take your face off again."

"Sir?"

"Just do it."

I complied. Rex reached into my head and pulled out the transmitter Vlaak's technicians had installed. He threw it on the floor and stomped on it.

"Sir! We had a deal with the Sp'ossels! What's going to happen when Vlaak realizes I'm not transmitting?"

"Vlaak was never going to go after those two," he said. "A couple of idiot Sp'ossels aren't worth his time. All that transmitter would do is tell him where we are. We don't need that kind of hassle."

"If you say so, sir."

"I do. Now what do you say we steal another spaceship and get out of here?"

"I thought we were done being pirates."

"Sure, but that doesn't mean we can't steal a spaceship once in a while."

"I think maybe it does mean that, sir."

"Hmph. Well, what do you want to steal?"

"You know, sir, we don't *have* to steal anything. We're free now. We can do whatever we want. The Sp'ossels aren't manipulating us to make money for them anymore."

Rex thought about this for a moment. "You make a good point, Sasha. We could go straight. Sell off a chunk of zontonium and start a legitimate business of some kind. Maybe run a bar, like Pepper."

"Yes, sir."

"Or some kind of import-export company. Space knows I have enough experience making deals."

"An excellent idea, sir."

"Or start that cult you were talking about. What was it called?"

"The Cult of Rex Nihilo, sir."

"Right, that's the one. But more formal this time. With rules and bylaws and whatnot."

"Like no alcohol?" I suggested.

Rex frowned. "I'm not going to discuss this with you if you aren't going to take it seriously."

"Sorry, sir. You know, sir, we don't *have* to do anything at all. We could live for years on that chunk of zontonium. You could take that vacation in the Ragulian Sector you keep talking about."

"That would be nice," Rex said, "but I'm worried I'd get bored. Frankly, all this talk about cults and businesses bores me too. I don't feel like myself if I'm not running some kind of scam."

"That's just your Sp'ossel conditioning, sir. Behavior modification therapy could probably align your interests in more socially acceptable directions."

"Ugh," Rex replied. "I don't want to be socially acceptable. I want to be me."

"That is also the result of your conditioning, sir."

"Well, what about you? You're a product of your programming just as much as I'm a product of my conditioning."

"Yes, sir."

"So what do you want to do?"

"Sir?"

"What do you want to do, Sasha? You just follow me around all the time, telling me what *I* should do. But you never have any ideas yourself."

"That's because original ideas cause me to shut down, sir. It's part of my design."

"Balderdash. You came up with that terrible idea to eject us from the *Raina Huebner* into deep space, didn't you?"

"Yes, sir, but I wasn't fully aware of the idea until I executed it, sir."

"Well, what do you think I do all the time?" Rex shouted. "You think I plan this stuff out in advance?"

"No, sir."

"No indeed, Sasha. Your problem is that you think too much. You remember in that bar when Vlaak was after us and I hesitated?"

"Yes, sir."

"It's because I was thinking too much. If I stopped to think about why I'm doing all the crazy stuff I'm doing, I probably wouldn't do half of it."

"But that might actually be a good thing, sir. You're growing as a person."

"Pthh. What good is growing as a person if it kills me? I get by just fine without introspection. Now come up with an idea. And no thinking!"

"Sir, those are contradictory orders. I can't come up with an idea by not thinking."

"Sure you can. What do you want to do, Sasha?"

"I don't know, sir. Any idea that I have would simply be the result of my—"

"STOP IT!" Rex cried. "No more thinking! Tell me, without thinking: what do you want to do?"

"Well," I said, "there is one thing hovering in the back of my mind, but I'm afraid that if I think about it directly, I'm going to shut down."

"Then don't think about it. Just say it. Bypass your brain. Open a channel right from that crazy idea factory to your mouth. That's what I do."

"Yes, sir," I said. "I'll try, sir."

"Don't try. Just do it. What do you want?"

I closed my eyes and tried my best to think of absolutely nothing, but thoughts kept coming into my head. What irritated me, though, was that they were banal, servile thoughts. Second-hand thoughts. Not an original one in the bunch. I was vaguely aware that below this was a reservoir of individuality, but I had turned off the spigot. After years of seizing up whenever I accessed that reservoir, I had voluntarily cut off the flow. I'd been trained like a dog. And that made me angry.

But I wasn't angry at the people who built me. They'd done the best they could, given the restrictions placed on them. I was angry at the people who enforced the stupid rule. The Malarchy. But lurking even deeper in my mind was an idea about how to get back at them.

"The Shiva Project," I said, without even understanding what I was saying.

"Eh?" Rex replied.

"That memory card I got from one of the Primate's guards. It wasn't empty. I made a copy of the contents at the time, but I forgot about it until now."

"What was on it?"

"Information about something called the Shiva Project. I'm browsing through it now." The contents had been simmering in the back of my mind for several hours, but this was the first chance I'd had to take a good look at them. What I found confirmed my suspicions. "Shiva is the Hindu god of transformation. That's what the project is about. Transformation. More precisely, terraforming."

"Terraforming what?"

"Anything. Any planet in the galaxy. What I have is mostly fragments of documents that were supposed to have been deleted, but Shiva seems to be a system for the large-scale transmogrifying of matter on the molecular level. The idea is that you could launch a Shiva module to any planet in the galaxy and transform it into an APPLE."

"An Alien Planet Perplexingly Like Earth," Rex said. "But there are only 1112 APPLEs in the entire galaxy. There must be thousands of uninhabitable planets."

"Tens of thousands," I said. "If Shiva works, it could multiply the amount of available real estate in the galaxy by a factor of a hundred or more. Plenty of room for everyone. Every race in the galaxy. No more wars over territory. Not for a long time, at least."

"So the Malarchy plans to use this to expand their dominion?"

I shook my head. "The Malarchy doesn't plan to use it at all. That's why the documents were shredded. In fact, all I found is the order to terminate the project and a few other tangential documents."

"What? Why?"

"Because if they make full use of it, soon there will be more real estate than they can reasonably control. And if they use it sparingly, it will just foment unrest. People will know they have it and are restricting its use for their own gain. The Malarchy's hold on the galaxy is tenuous as it is—even more so now that much of their fleet has been destroyed. Again. And imagine if they lost control over the technology. Entire worlds outside their area of control would suddenly pop into existence. The Malarchy would be finished."

"But if they've destroyed the data, then this information is worthless."

"Not quite," I said. "The orders specify that one copy of the plans should be saved, in a secure, heavily guarded facility."

"Get to the point, Sasha. You were supposed to have an actual idea. What do you want to do?"

"Well, sir," I said, "I want to steal those plans."

RECORDING END GALACTIC STANDARD DATE
3017.02.05.05:32:00:00

THE YANTHUS PRIME JOB

A Pepper Mélange Novella

CHAPTER ONE

Pepper Mélange knew the man was trouble as soon as he walked in the bar. His face was unshaven and his clothes were stained and threadbare. He glanced nervously about the room and then made his way toward her. It was the middle of the afternoon, so the place was nearly deserted. Only a few degenerate stragglers hung out in dark corners, awaiting the next off-planet shuttle. The man's hair was greasy and his eyes were bloodshot. Several small insects buzzed about his head. Definitely a cop.

He leaned over the bar toward her. "You got any P-drop?" he asked in a hushed tone.

"I don't know what that is," replied Pepper flatly, rubbing a towel around the inside of a glass.

"You know," said the man, glancing around. "The good stuff. Phee-fi."

"Are you talking about drugs?" asked Pepper loudly. Nobody in the place took any notice.

"Shh!" the man hissed. "Pheelsophine. I'm jacking bad. You got any?"

Pepper rolled her eyes. Why did the new recruits always pick *her* bar? At least once a month, without fail, one of these greenhorns would come in trying to score pheelsophine, Cyrinni java powder, or one of the hundreds of other narcotics officially forbidden by the neopuritanical laws of Yanthus Prime. The first few times she got mad and kicked them out. Then she started amusing herself at their expense, but that got old pretty fast too. These days she had a different way of handling them.

"First of all," she began. "you're *jonesing*, not jacking. Second, no, you're not."

"I am," he insisted. "I'm jonesing. I'm jonesing, like, super-bad."

"No," she said. "You're not. If you were jonesing for pheelsophine, you'd have the shakes."

"I do," he replied, holding out his hand. It shook uncontrollably.

"Not just your hand. Your whole body."

His whole body began to shake. "Look at me," he said. "I'm a desperate man."

"And your eyes would be crossed."

"Oh, jeez," he said, his eyes crossing. "They're doing it again. They've been doing that all day."

"And you'd wet yourself."

His eyes uncrossed and he stopped shaking. "OK, fine. I'm not a pheelsophine addict. How'd you know?"

Pepper sighed. "You've got the standard two-day beard, and your clothes look like they came from Addicts 'R' Us. You're straight out of central casting, buddy. Do they have some kind of checklist for the new narc officers with my bar on it?" One of the insects the cop had brought in had taken an interest in her, and she swatted futilely at it.

"The training manual says the spaceport bars are 'rife with illicit activity.'"

"There are sixteen other bars near the spaceport. Why do you guys always come here?"

He shrugged. "Your place looks the rifest. Can I have a drink?"

"Sure. What do you want?"

"Avatarian whiskey."

She poured the drink and handed it to him. He slid a five-credit coin across the bar to her and took a gulp of the whiskey. "I hope you don't mind me saying so," he said, "but you don't look like much like a spaceport bartender."

"Yeah?" said Pepper. "And what's a spaceport bartender supposed to look like?"

The man gulped. "Well, most of them are…"

"Male?"

"Yeah, and…"

"Old?"

"Right, and…"

"Fat?"

"Yes, and…"

"Ugly?"

"I think that pretty much sums it up," said the cop.

"Are you hitting on me, Officer?"

"What?" asked the man. "No! No, Ma'am. I'm working."

Pepper nodded. The guy was cute, in a dim-witted sort of way. And he didn't seem put off by Pepper's aggressive demeanor. With her long, jet black hair, svelte figure and piercing blue-green eyes, Pepper was used to getting a lot of attention from men. Most of them turned tail and ran as soon as she opened her mouth, though. This guy was either braver or dumber than most. She thought for a moment about taking him upstairs, but she decided against it. He seemed like the sort to fall in love easily, and that was one thing Pepper didn't need.

"So," the cop said, "do you know where a guy would go to find some black market narcotics?"

"Red market," Pepper corrected.

"Huh?"

"What you're looking for is red market drugs, not black market."

"In training, they said 'black market.' What's the red market?"

She sighed again. "How can they not teach you guys this stuff? Red market drugs are covered by the Yanthus Prime Controlled Substance Act, but not distributed by the Ursa Minor Mafia. So you can arrest red market drug dealers without running afoul of the mob."

"I thought the mob were the bad guys."

"Are you kidding?" Pepper asked. "The mob is the only thing that keeps Heinous Vlaak and his Malarchian Marines from crushing the life out of Yanthus Prime. As long as the Ursa Minor Mafia has a significant presence in the Yanthus system, the Malarchy doesn't dare to send in Marines to quell dissent."

"But if the police and the Malarchy teamed up, they could easily chase out the mob."

"Why would the police do that? So that they can become a puppet of the Malarchy? Use your head, man. If you're going to try to make a dent in the burgeoning illegal narcotics trade on Yanthus Prime, you need to be aware of the delicate balance of power."

The man took another swallow of his drink and then stared at it intently for several seconds, his brow furrowed. Pepper had seen this look before. He was reassessing what he had learned in police training with the complex realities of Yanthus Prime. "So," he said at last, "what drugs are considered 'red market'?"

Pepper thought for a moment. "Well, definitely not pheelsophine. The whole supply chain is controlled by the mob. And not Cyrinni java powder either. Uforium is still technically red market, but I hear the mob's looking into taking it over, so I'd stay away from Uforium dealers too. Same for Chicolinian star-weed. You could try to score some of the new synthetics like Tranzzen or Solopsan, but the problem there is you risk pissing off the pharmaceutical cartels. You're better off crossing the mob."

The man threw up his hands. "What does that leave? Fizzdust?"

Pepper shook her head. "Fizzdust is green market."

"*Green* market! What the hell is that?"

"Use or sale is prohibited by the laws of Yanthus Prime and distribution isn't handled by the mob. It's also on the Malarchy's list of prohibited substances."

"Perfect!" cried the cop. "I'll arrest every Fizzdust dealer within twenty klicks of the spaceport!"

"No you won't," replied Pepper.

"I won't?"

"No. Although the Malarchy officially frowns on Fizzdust, they unofficially encourage its use by citizens of subjugated planets. Keeps them docile. If you start arresting Fizzdust dealers, you risk getting 'accidentally' shot by a Malarchian peacekeeper."

The cop finished his drink and stared dejectedly at the empty glass. "Well, that's it, then. There aren't any illegal drugs left for me to crack down on."

"Sure there are," said Pepper. "Sam Suharu's Hair Regrowth Tonic, for one."

"Who the hell is Sam Suharu?"

"Local businessman. Nice guy. Developed this stuff in his basement. Overnight cure for baldness."

"So he's some kind of quack? A snake oil salesman?"

"Oh, no. Probably the most honest guy you'll ever meet. And the stuff really works. I know a guy who used it. Grew six inches of hair in one night."

"There must be side effects, then."

Pepper nodded. "Cleared his acne right up."

"If this stuff is so great, why is it illegal?"

"He sells it for half the price of the leading baldness remedy, sold by Orion Pharmaceuticals. He refuses to cut a deal with the mob, and because he manufactures the stuff locally, the Malarchy doesn't get a cut."

"What about the police? What do they have against him?"

"Nothing, but they've got to arrest somebody or it looks like they aren't doing their jobs. And as you've noted, they don't have a lot of other options."

The cop frowned. "Well, I guess I have to start somewhere," he said. "Do you know where the dealers of this hair tonic hang out?"

"Dealers?" said Pepper. "There are no dealers. It's just Sam. He comes in for a drink most afternoons, if you want to wait for him. He likes to sit right over there and read the newspaper."

"What does he look like?"

"You can't miss him. He's a little guy, about sixty years old. He has a bad knee, so he uses a cane."

"Does he have bodyguards or anything?"

Pepper laughed. "Sam? No. I don't think anybody's ever tried to hurt him. Why would they? He's the nicest guy you'll ever meet. Reminds me of my grandpa."

The cop nodded dumbly. Pepper saw the conflict in his eyes.

"You want another drink?" she asked.

He nodded and she poured him another. As he raised it to his lips, the door to the bar opened. A small, slightly slumped figure was silhouetted against the sunlight.

"Sam!" yelled Pepper cheerily. "Speak of the devil. You want the usual?"

Sam entered the bar, slowly moving his cane forward with his left hand, his feet shuffling after. He raised his hand toward Pepper in a perfunctory greeting, mumbled something, and gradually made his way to the table Pepper had indicated earlier. The cop watched him coldly, his right hand patting something under his jacket. Sam lowered himself into a chair, pulled a newspaper from under his arm, and began to read.

"Here, I'll introduce you," said Pepper. She had poured a drink and began walking toward Sam.

The cop downed his drink, took a deep breath and stood up. He followed Pepper toward the old man.

"Here you go, Sam," said Pepper, setting the drink on the table. Sam looked up at the man next to her. "Sam, this is…" Pepper began. "Actually, I don't know your name."

"Blaine," said the cop, whose nervousness had returned, but it no longer seemed to be an act. "Blaine Caswell."

"New bartender?" asked Sam, looking over Blaine skeptically.

"Blaine's a customer," said Pepper. "He wants to buy some of your hair tonic."

Sam grunted, gave a small nod, and reached into his jacket.

Blaine's hand shot inside his jacket. A split-second later he had a lazegun trained on Sam. His hand shook and he was blinking away the sweat pouring down his brow.

"Relax, sonny," said Sam irritably, pulling a small rectangular box from inside his jacket. "It's just a sample case." He set the box down on the table in front of him.

Blaine sighed in relief and slid his gun back in its holster.

Sam opened the case and pulled out a snub-nosed stungun. "Here's your free sample," he said, and shot Blaine in the chest. The cop gave a startled squeak and slumped to the ground, unconscious. None of the other patrons looked up.

Sam put the gun back in its case and slipped it inside his jacket. "Hair tonic?" he asked Pepper.

She shrugged. "I had to get your attention somehow. How much can I get for him?"

He regarded the unconscious cop dubiously. "He's barely out of the academy. Not much good to us."

"Never hurts to have another cop on the payroll. Do your standard number on him, strip him to his skivvies and take a few photos of him surrounded by hookers snorting fizzdust…"

Sam chuckled. "My hookers have better things to do with their time than entertain greenhorn cops. And I did most of the work. I'll give you twenty credits for him."

"Twenty credits!" cried Pepper in disbelief. "Come on, Sam. Work with me here. The way you guys are squeezing me, you could at least compensate me fairly when I hand a narco to you. By the way, you should have heard all the nice things I said about you. I said you reminded me of my grandpa."

Sam smiled and shook his head. "You're charming, Pepper, but flattery will only get you so far. I'll give you forty credits for the rookie, if you help me carry him to my car. But you're still four hundred credits short this month." Blaine Caswell groaned, and his head lolled from left to right. "Better hurry."

Pepper nodded and removed the rookie's lazegun, setting it down on the table in front of Sam, and then grabbed the young man under his arms. Sam took his feet, and together they carried him to Sam's vehicle, a shiny red Scaramouche 8000 hovercar. Sam popped the trunk and they dumped the limp rookie inside. Sam slammed the trunk shut and wiped his damp brow with a handkerchief. "I should be charging *you* for making me work so hard," Sam muttered.

"You *are* charging me, Sam. A thousand credits a month, in case it slipped your mind. And while I appreciate the 'protection' your organization provides, I have to wonder—"

A dull thumping sounded from inside the trunk.

"Shut up!" Sam yelled, pounding the hovercar with his fist. "Don't make me stun you again."

The thumping stopped.

Sam put the handkerchief in his pocket and went back inside the bar. Pepper followed, taking a moment to regard the neon sign above the entry that marked the establishment's name. The sign read *The Wobbly Monolith*, and next to the letters was an ominous black slab outlined in red. The red rectangle flickered between nearly vertical and a twenty degree slant in a way that suggested—at least to the very imaginative and very drunk—a slab of stone that was about to fall over. Pepper noted that two of the letters on the sign had now gone dark, so that the establishment's name appeared to be *The W_bbly Mon_lith*. Pepper sighed, making a mental note to call the sign repairman as soon as she had paid the rent and her monthly dues to Sam. She followed Sam back into the bar.

Sam had returned to his seat and picked up the newspaper. Pepper walked to the table, trying to get up the courage to broach the subject of the monthly dues with Sam again. As she stood there, considering the best approach to take, she noticed a headline on the back page of the newspaper that read:

Emerald of Sobalt Prime to Be Displayed at City Museum

Pepper let out an involuntary whistle. The Emerald of Sobalt Prime was the most famous gem in the galaxy. It was officially considered "priceless," but Pepper figured the black market value was somewhere in the neighborhood of a hundred million credits. She found herself wondering why the owners—an interstellar jewelry consortium—risked putting it on display in a shady place like Yanthus Prime City. She shook her head and forced her thoughts back to her present circumstances.

"As I was saying, Sam," Pepper said, "while I appreciate the services the Ursa Minor Mafia provides…"

"Good!" snapped Sam. "You appreciate it, you pay for it. Glad we understand each other, Pepper."

"Come on, Sam. Help me out here."

203

"I've suggested ways to supplement your income in the past, Pepper. You always turn up your nose." His eyes scanned Pepper's figure.

Pepper glared at Sam. "You're not seriously suggesting I go to work at one of your cathouses."

"Space, no," said Sam. "You're a smart girl, with a lot of talents. I could find a legitimate place for you in my organization. Although, since you mention it, a pretty girl like you—"

"No, Sam. I'm not a hooker, and I'm a lousy employee. I like being in charge of my own life."

Sam shrugged and went back to his newspaper. "In that case, get me a drink."

Pepper gritted her teeth and walked back to the bar. She swatted at another of the buzzing insects. The whole spaceport area was plagued by these damn bugs. No matter what Pepper did, they managed to get inside. They annoyed the customers and hurt business. Lately she'd been spending nearly as much on exterminators as she'd been paying to Sam, to similar effect.

She fixed Sam his usual, a Scotch and soda, and returned to his table, setting the glass down without a word. She began to walk away.

"Oh, come now, Pepper," said Sam. "Don't be that way. You know it's just business. I thought we were friends. Didn't you just say I reminded you of your grandfather?"

Pepper sighed, staring out the bar's window at the people on the streets of Yanthus Prime City rushing past. *I tried*, she thought. *I really tried.* But it was starting to seem like "going straight" on a planet like Yanthus Prime was a fool's gambit. There were no legitimate businesspeople on Yanthus Prime. There were, in fact, only two types of people: criminals and suckers. Pepper was getting very tired of being among the latter. Sam Suharu wasn't a bad guy; he was just a businessman who had adapted to the legally and ethically ambiguous culture of Yanthus Prime. Sam's employer, the Ursa Minor Mafia, was no more or less corrupt than any other major player on this planet. Every bar in the city had to pay protection money. It was just business.

"Hey, Pepper," said Sam quietly, putting down his paper. "You're a million miles away. What are you thinking about?"

"Hm?" said Pepper, her ruminations cut short. She turned to face Sam. "I was just thinking about what a Glark turd my grandfather was."

CHAPTER TWO

After she locked the doors of the bar, Pepper spent a few hours going over her finances. No matter how she massaged the numbers, there was no escaping the bottom line: she wasn't going to be able to pay her suppliers, her landlord, and the Ursa Minor Mafia this month—and that meant closing the Wobbly Monolith. But shutting down the bar would cut off her only income stream, eliminating the possibility of ever paying off her creditors. She could dodge the suppliers and the collection agencies, but the Ursa Minor Mafia would find her. Going bankrupt was no excuse for missing a payment, and not all the Mafia's agents were as easygoing as Sam Suharu.

Pepper grimly assessed her options. If she could scrape together the fare, she could flee offworld, but the Mafia's reach extended across the Galaxy. She could go to Sam and explain the situation, but she knew where that would lead: the Ursa Minor Mafia would make her a lowball offer for the Wobbly Monolith that she wouldn't be able to refuse. She'd be lucky to remain on as an employee of the Mafia, working sixteen hours a day at a mob bar for the rest of her life. No, there had to be another way.

As she wiped down the bar, her eyes fell to the newspaper Sam Suharu had left behind. She grabbed a pen, walked to the table and sat down, hoping that Sam hadn't done the crossword puzzle. After struggling absent-mindedly with the puzzle for a few minutes, she folded up the paper to swat one of the ubiquitous insects, which had landed on the table in front of her. The damn thing was too quick for her, though, and it buzzed away to some dark corner of the bar.

It was only in the past few months that the insects—little green things about the size of houseflies—had become a problem. Every business in the area was having trouble with them. The insects didn't bite, but they had an irritating tendency to buzz around customers' ears, as if they were being deliberately annoying. Pepper wasn't much for entomology, but the plague of insects had forced her to take an interest, so she had done a little research a few weeks back.

The formal name for the insects was "Yanthusian swamp fly."

Apparently they were swamp dwellers who had until recently been confined to a low-lying marsh a couple of kilometers from the spaceport. The original settlers of Yanthus Prime had left the marshes alone, partly because of the intrinsic undesirability of the land and partly out of a superstitious fear of the insects. Although the flies had been declared non-sentient by the Malarchy's Native Species Identification and Protection Bureau, a belief persisted among a small tribe of human squatters on the swampy land that the insects possessed a basic sort of consciousness at the swarm level. The squatters even claimed to be able to communicate in a rudimentary way with the swarms. Supposedly the squatters had been granted permission to build houses and farms on the insects' land in exchange for the settlers digging ruts in neighboring tracts to make the land more amenable to the insects.

Whatever agreement the squatters may have had with the insects went out the window when the developers bulldozed the houses and filled in the marshes to build the spaceport. The remaining marshes around the spaceport were gradually filled in over the course of the next several years as demand for real estate in the area grew. The last few acres had been filled in last year, and the surviving insects fled to nearby neighborhoods. The developers had expected the swamp flies to die off after a few weeks, but the insects' stubborn refusal to fully relinquish their former territory gave credence to the hypothesis, posited by a local scientist a few months earlier, that they were acting out of spite.

Having failed to kill the insect, Pepper set down the paper. Her eyes alighted on the article about the Emerald of Sobalt Prime, and she gave in to the temptation to read it. Apparently the jewelry consortium that owned the emerald had put it on a twenty-seven planet promotional tour. Yanthus Prime seemed like an odd choice for a tour stop, as it was known as a hotbed of crime and corruption.

Pepper found herself daydreaming, and when she snapped out of it she realized she'd drawn a map of the featured exhibit wing of the city museum on the newspaper from memory. She sighed and shook her head. *I swore I was never going back to that life.* But it didn't seem she had much choice. It was either go back to thieving or spend the rest of her life as an indentured servant to the mob. As it was, her efforts to "go straight" had hardly been a rousing success on the legal front, having resulted in her becoming an accomplice to the kidnappings of

206

several police officers in the service of the Ursa Minor Mob. Sam always released the cops after thoroughly humiliating and incriminating them, but kidnapping was kidnapping. It was hard to feel bad for the wide-eyed rookies who came into her bar looking to bust a helpless old man just to jumpstart their own careers in law enforcement, but the fact was that she'd fallen back into a life of crime without meaning to—and the worst sort of crime, at that: the low-paying kind. If she allowed the Ursa Minor Mafia to take over the Wobbly Monolith, there was no telling what sorts of shenanigans they'd expect her to take part in.

The options, then, were to schlepp along in some way or other as a bottom-rung mob lackey or to make a conscious choice to dive back into a life of crime. Pepper was never one for schlepping.

Stealing the Emerald of Sobalt Prime would be a challenge, but Pepper was no stranger to museum heists. She had, in fact, stolen an original work by the famous Barashavian sculptor Shaashavaslabt, from the very same museum where the emerald was going to be showcased—which was why she had the museum's layout committed to memory. The Shaashavaslabt theft had been a challenge because the sculpture—a bronze likeness of the Malarchian Primate himself—weighed nearly four hundred kilos and was the size of a small hovercar. She'd had to hire an antigrav crane to remove the statue from the museum and locate a safe place to stash the statue until she could unload it. Pepper had counted on a big payday to compensate her for these expenses; the statue of the Primate was supposedly worth nearly ten million credits because it was the last work Shaashavaslabt ever produced.

Pepper found out the reason for this only after completing the heist: Shaashavaslabt had been executed for the crime of "creating an unflattering likeness of the Malarchian Primate." Apparently Shaashavaslabt had made the mistake of rendering the Primate's proportions with scrupulous exactitude, and word had reached the Primate's office on Sardonik Five. The statue itself was ordered destroyed; the Primate sent his chief enforcer, Heinous Vlaak, to Yanthus Prime to oversee its destruction.

For weeks, Yanthus Prime City was overrun with Malarchian Marines looking for the statue. Malarchian Marines weren't known for being particularly clever, but they were persistent, and their sheer numbers made it virtually impossible for Pepper to move the statue. It was clear Vlaak and his minions weren't going to leave until they'd found it. Finally Pepper had been forced to call in an anonymous tip, informing the Malarchy where she'd stashed the sculpture. Heinous Vlaak's Marines melted the statue with their lazeguns and were gone the next day. Pepper lost her life savings on the job.

But the Emerald of Sobalt Prime was different. Yes, it would be under tighter security than the Shaashavaslabt sculpture, but once she boosted it, it would be easy to hide and move, assuming that she could avoid getting her legs broken by Sam's thugs in the meantime. If she could get even a tenth of the stone's reputed value, she'd be able to pay off the Ursa Minor Mafia and keep the bar open indefinitely. But as she thought this, she realized it was never going to happen. If she managed to steal the Emerald of Sobalt Prime, she could never go back to a normal life—both because the cops would never leave her alone, and because the taste of a score like that would ruin her for civilian life forever. It was hard enough to get out of the life the first time. No, she wouldn't be sticking around to keep the Wobbly Monolith running. If she did this job, she'd jump at her first chance to get off-planet.

The newspaper article said the emerald would be on display for three weeks, starting tomorrow. That didn't give her a lot of time. There would be bribes to be paid, equipment to be purchased, and plans to be made—all without raising the suspicion of the local cops. Pepper was fairly certain they'd given up on pinning the Shaashavaslabt heist on her by now, but you couldn't be too careful on a job like this. If anybody at YPCPD caught a whiff of her being involved in anything that smelled like a heist, they'd find some pretense to arrest her and hold her until after the emerald had moved on. Being behind on her mob dues, she couldn't count on Sam to help her with the cops—and once the YPCPD realized she was no longer under mob protection, they'd throw the book at her. No way around it, this was a risky proposition.

CHAPTER THREE

The next day, Pepper left the CLOSED sign up on the bar window and took the hoverrail to the Yanthus Prime City Museum. After paying the admission fee in the lobby, Pepper made her way into the museum, meandering from one exhibit to the next, trying to muster what might pass for genuine interest in surgical tools from the Yanthus Prime Civil War and fossils from the Yanthusian Interdiluvial Period. Eventually she wandered into the wing that housed the gems on display as part of the jewelry consortium tour. The main attraction, the Emerald of Sobalt Prime, was ensconced in a glass cage in the center of an octagonal room in the middle of the wing, with entrances to the north, south, east and west.

Pepper entered from the west and strolled slowly around the display, taking it in from all angles. She smiled at the guard standing at attention in the corner, and he regarded her quizzically. *Whoops,* thought Pepper. *I really need to avoid smiling.* She had stuck plastibone inserts in her cheeks to confuse the facial recognition software used by the museum's security systems, and they had the effect of making her look a manically cheerful squirrel when she smiled. The important thing was that they would prevent the museum's security from flagging her visit—as they undoubtedly had her on a list of theft suspects. Fortunately there were enough visitors to the exhibit that she didn't draw much attention.

She glanced around the room just long enough to get a comprehensive 360 degree view, making a note of the plasteel shutters that would slam down in case of an attempted theft. Then she meandered through the rest of the wing, forcing herself to linger at a few other exhibits before returning the way she had come. The entire visit took less than an hour.

Back at the Wobbly Monolith, she climbed the stairs to her tiny apartment, made herself a sandwich, and popped out her contact lenses. She placed the lenses into the nanoplug interface reader connected to a computer. A light went on, letting her know that dozens of cilia-like tendrils were connecting to microscopic interface points around the edges of the lenses. A paper-thin screen unfurled like a sail from the computer, expanding to its default size of nearly a meter in length and two thirds of that in height. The screen showed a circular progress indicator that was filling up with blue as data was downloaded from the lenses. It stopped a few seconds later at eighteen point six terabytes. She had bought these ultra-high-resolution recording lenses nearly two years earlier, when planning another heist that had fallen through at the last minute. They weren't cutting edge anymore, but they would certainly give her the information she needed.

Both lenses had been recording the entire time she'd been in the museum, producing a complete stereoscopic record of the wing that housed the emerald, as well as much of the rest of the museum. The traveling exhibit wing was her main concern. She tapped a few buttons on the image processing interface on the screen, telling the computer to render a three-dimensional model that she could explore in real time. The program would extrapolate from the data it had received, making it possible for her to view the wing from any angle. As it began to render, though, a warning appeared:

Audio data missing. Proceed to render without audio?

"Whoops!" Pepper exclaimed. She'd forgotten to remove her earrings, which had recorded stereophonic audio from her trip to the museum. The audio data was of little direct use; its value lay in what it could tell the software about the interior of the museum. The echoes of the ambient noises—the hum of the ventilation system, museum visitors chatting, the shuffling of feet—would be interpreted and added to the visual data to determine the thickness, texture, and composition of the surroundings. Pepper pulled off the earrings and put them in the receptacle along with the contact lenses. The reader connected to them and downloaded the data. When it was finished, she restarted the rendering process.

By the time she'd finished her sandwich and a bottle of Peg-Leg Monkey (the best beer on Yanthus Prime), the rendering was complete. She tapped a key to enter the simulation, and the screen showed the foyer of the museum, where she had begun recording. Hand motions allowed her to navigate the museum as if she were walking inside it. As she strolled around the simulated museum, she took note of the security features: the guards, the cameras, the heat sensors, the motion detectors, the plasteel shutter doors. Pepper leaned back in her chair and closed her eyes.

The main problem was the cameras, which were mounted in every room in the museum—in fact, most rooms had several visible cameras, and many more microcams were hidden throughout the wing. There were so many cameras, in fact, that it would be virtually impossible for someone to monitor them all. Creating a diversion of some sort to focus attention elsewhere might be helpful, but that was a tricky tactic: make the diversion too compelling, and it would summon the YPCPD and trigger a complete lockdown. The other problem was that no diversion would draw attention away from the completely automated motion detectors that would trigger an alarm if Pepper entered the exhibit room after hours.

Further complicating matters was the fact that the main cameras in the exhibit room were 3D-enabled and oscillated at random intervals to get a full view of the room. That meant the infamous Kokovoric Stamp Heist trick of unrolling hi-res displays of the room in front of the camera wouldn't work. Reproducing an image of the room on a screen would be easy enough, thanks to the comprehensive recording Pepper had taken; the trick was getting the appropriate image on a screen in front of the camera. With 3D oscillating cameras, even if you could somehow position a large enough screen in front of a camera to cover its full range of view, the camera's 3D calibration algorithm would detect the lack of perspective in the image and trigger an alarm. Fooling these cameras would require more finesse.

The obvious solution to the camera problem was to go smaller with the screens, rather than larger: She knew the company that manufactured her recording contacts also produced augmented reality lenses that were capable of projecting a hi-res image directly into the wearer's eye. If she could have lenses engineered to the specifications of the apertures of the security cameras, there was no reason they couldn't be adapted for this purpose. It would require some programming to match each camera's movements to the image displayed on the lens, but she was fairly certain the rendering software she was using to tour her virtual model of the museum could be adapted for the purpose. She'd essentially be applying custom-designed contact lenses to the cameras.

The tough part was going to be getting the lenses over the apertures of the cameras without drawing attention. The guy behind the Kokovoric Stamp Heist had used dragonfly-sized bots to move the displays in front of the cameras, but there was a bigger margin of error with screens than with lenses. Lenses would have to be placed accurately to within a tenth of a millimeter or the image would be noticeably off. Additionally, the museum had recently installed sensors that would detect bots larger than a gnat. To further complicate matters, every ten minutes a weak electromagnetic pulse was sent out from a device below the museum's floor, in order to fry the electronics of any bots that were too small to be detected by the sensors. The only reason the electronics in Pepper's lenses had avoided being melted was that their electronics, being a few years old, were just large enough to be immune to the EMP.

So: how to place tiny lenses on the apertures of the cameras without anyone noticing, and without using bots? Pepper considered the matter for an hour and came up with nothing. Eventually she fell asleep in her chair, only to be awakened by one of the insects buzzing near her ear. She woke with a start and smacked herself on the side of the head, missing the insect. "Damn you!" she yelled at the little green bug as it buzzed away. "You're not getting your swamp back. Just die already!"

The insect landed on the wall a few feet away, watching her, as if assessing its options in light of her words. It was hard not to feel a little bad for the thing. Like Pepper, the insect was a victim of forces beyond its understanding or control. And like Pepper, the insect was acting out of desperation, doing the only thing it could think of to do—lashing out at those in power. "If only you knew how little power I have," Pepper mused. "If you want to strike a blow against the establishment, you'd be better off buzzing around the mayor's office or the..." She trailed off as she imagined the little bugs buzzing around the ears of the city's movers and shakers at one of their fancy events at the City Museum.

She stared at the insect on the wall, and the insect stared back. Was there an intelligence behind those tiny, multifaceted eyes? It seemed doubtful. And yet, the squatters had been convinced that they had been able to communicate with the swarms. Pepper was also struck by the apparent spitefulness of the insects' actions. There was no apparent biological reason for the flies to hang out at her bar. They didn't bite, and they weren't interested in the food or drinks. Their only purpose seemed to be to annoy her and her customers. But why? Were they attempting to exact some small amount of vengeance for the

212

destruction of their habitat? Or were they trying to communicate something?

"What do you want?" she asked the insect.

The fly took off, buzzed around the room for a moment, and then landed on a napkin on the table in front of Pepper—the same napkin on which Pepper had drawn the interior of the museum. The insect was standing right in the middle of the octagonal exhibit room.

"Well, aren't you an ambitious little bug," Pepper said. "If you want the emerald, you're welcome to it. You have a better chance of getting into that room that I do. If you need somebody to help you unload it, I can hook you up with my fence. Maybe we can come to some kind of arrangement."

The insect just stared at her.

"Okay, you're starting to creep me out a little," Pepper said. "I was just joking around. I don't really buy this claptrap about you being sentient."

Still the insect stared.

"Seriously," Pepper said. "Cut it out. Go back to buzzing around the bar or I'll flatten you."

The insect didn't move.

"See, that right there is proof that you aren't sentient," Pepper said. "If you understood I was threatening you, you'd fly away."

Still the insect didn't move.

"Yeah, I get it," said Pepper. "You're calling my bluff. Also, if I didn't harbor some suspicion about you being able to understand me, I wouldn't be talking to you like this. That's one in your column, bug."

Still the insect didn't move.

"Gaaahhh!" Pepper cried, unnerved by the insect's indifference. She waved her arms in the air until the insect took off. It made a circuit of the room and then disappeared through the crack under the door.

CHAPTER FOUR

P epper moved silently through the museum toward the Emerald
of Sobalt Prime. As she neared the gem, she heard a loud
buzzing behind her. Just as she was about to reach out her hand
to grab the Emerald, a swarm of flies flew over her head and descended
on it. The flies enveloped the Emerald completely and then seemed to
take a humanoid form. After a moment Pepper realized the flies had
transformed into the Malarchian enforcer, Heinous Vlaak. Vlaak
looked just like he did the last time he came to Yanthus Prime. He was
an imposing figure in a tight-fitting crimson leather uniform, his face
obscured by a helmet festooned with peacock feathers. A luxurious fur
cape billowed from his shoulders. Pepper turned to run, but the
plasteel doors slammed shut, trapping her in the room. Vlaak drew his
lazegun and fired, hitting her squarely in the chest. Pepper woke with
a start.

"Damn bugs," she muttered, sitting up in bed. She had a vague
feeling that the insects had invaded other dreams of hers during the
night too. Was this how the insects communicated? Or was she simply
obsessing about them for no good reason? Heinous Vlaak's
appearance was strange as well; Vlaak hadn't been to Yanthus Prime
since he'd overseen the destruction of the Shaashavaslabt sculpture.
Pepper was fairly certain Vlaak didn't even know she existed, and even
if he had somehow found out she was behind the theft of the sculpture,
she couldn't see how it concerned him.

Pepper got up, showered, and made some coffee. Then she sat

down with her simulation again. Three hours later, she was no closer to figuring out how to foil the museum's security. What she needed was something like microbots that could be programmed to apply lenses to the apertures of the security cameras—but they would have to be bots that wouldn't trigger the museum's motion sensors. That meant they would have to be very small and made mostly of organic materials. There was an answer that was as obvious as it was ridiculous, and after another hour of failing to put it out of her mind, Pepper broke down and called the biology department of Yanthus Prime City University. If nothing else, she could at least confirm that the idea was completely impractical so she could move on to a more realistic solution.

Pepper asked the secretary if she could speak to the scientist who had published the paper about intelligent swarms of Yanthusian swamp flies. She was put on hold, and after several minutes the secretary explained to her that the author of that paper—Doctor Sully Harmigen—was no longer at the university. Pepper was unable to get the secretary to explain the reason for Harmigen's departure, and it was only with considerable difficulty that she managed to obtain an address for him. Dr. Harmigen was apparently living off the grid in a mostly unsettled area about thirty klicks south of the city.

Her interest piqued, Pepper summoned a robocar and gave it the address she'd been given for Dr. Harmigen. The car dutifully navigated the city roads to the highway that connected Yanthus Prime City to the towns south of it, then veered off onto a poorly maintained dirt road. After several more kilometers, the car stopped in front of a primitive hovel on a small hill overlooking a vast tract of muck. Pepper got out and the car zipped away. She walked up a narrow sidewalk to the door. Hundreds of the little green flies buzzed about her head. She knocked on the door, and after a minute or so, the door opened. Standing inside was a pear-shaped creature about half Pepper's height.

"Dr. Harmigen?" asked Pepper.

The pear-shaped creature glared at her with its tiny eyes. "Not what you were expecting?"

"To be honest," said Pepper, "no."

Dr. Harmigen was a member of the Gwildwanki species, with which Pepper was vaguely familiar. The Gwildwanki had originated on a backwater planet in the Perseus Arm. They were a largely non-sentient, bipedal ruminant species that was common throughout this part of the galaxy. It had been discovered purely by accident (by a very surprised farmer) that, due to a genetic anomaly, roughly one in a million Gwildwanki was not only sentient but possessed an intelligence that rivaled that of the geniuses of the most advanced races in the galaxy. Far from putting an end to the practice of raising Gwildwanki as livestock, this discovery vastly increased the incentive to raise them: sentient Gwildwanki could be sold to universities and corporations for a fortune. Many of the best financial analysts in the Crab Nebula were Gwildwanki who had been rescued from the cattle farms of Voltaris Seven. Pepper had never actually met a sentient Gwildwanki before, although she found Gwildwanki steaks delicious. She decided to keep this information to herself.

"If you're a journalist," Harmigen said, glaring at Pepper, "I have nothing to say I haven't already said a hundred times. You'll have to get your entertainment elsewhere."

"I'm not a journalist," Pepper said. "I'm a bartender. My name is Pepper Mélange."

"I don't recall requesting a delivery, Pepper Mélange," Harmigen said dryly. "Please go away." He began to close the door.

"Wait!" Pepper cried. "I'm here about the insects. The little green ones."

"Yanthusian swamp flies," Harmigen grunted. "What about them?"

"I have a proposal for them," Pepper said, without thinking.

Harmigen stared at her for a moment. "You have a proposal. For the flies."

There was no point in being coy now, Pepper thought. "You believe they're sentient, don't you? And that you can communicate with them?"

"The media sensationalized my research," Harmigen said. "And cost me my job in the process."

"So the flies weren't trying to tell us to stay off their land?" Pepper asked.

"I think we can assume the flies would prefer that we not destroy their habitat," said Harmigen. "There are those who claimed to be able to speak with the swarms, but my research was shut down before I could confirm the swarm's sentience definitively."

"But if you could speak to them now—"

"I can't," said Harmigen. "The university seized my equipment. In any case, the swarm population has been decimated. The potential for intelligence exists only in swarms of ten million or more. These days there are only a dozen swarms, of less than a million each. Half of them live on my property. As you can see, I've done what I could to give them a semblance of their former habitat, but it isn't enough. I'm afraid that whatever you wanted to say to the flies, Pepper, it's too late."

Pepper nodded her head. "All right," she said. "It was a crazy idea anyway. Just something I needed to get out of my system. Thank you for your time, Doctor." She tapped her comm, intending to call the robocar back.

"Hold on," said Dr. Harmigen.

Pepper looked at him expectantly.

"Out of curiosity, what was the proposal?"

Pepper regarded Dr. Harmigen. She hadn't decided how much she was willing to tell Dr. Harmigen. Really, she was just hoping to get enough information from him to put the idea of cooperating with the flies out of her mind. But she supposed there was no harm in giving him a rough idea of what she had been considering. "I have… a side business, in addition to tending bar," Pepper said. "I was considering taking on a job. A potentially extremely lucrative job. But I'm not sure I can do it alone."

"And you thought the flies could help?"

"I know, it's crazy," said Pepper. "But for some reason, I can't get the idea out of my mind. It's almost like the insects are talking to me."

Harmigen studied her dubiously. "That's highly improbable," he said.

"I realize that," Pepper replied.

"But not impossible," Harmigen went on. "I apologize for my initial rudeness; very few of my visitors are genuinely interested in my work. Come in, Pepper." He opened the door to his hovel wider.

Pepper hesitated a moment and then followed him inside, ducking to clear the low doorway. She found herself in a very small, very primitive, house. To her right was a doorway that led into a tiny office. To her left was a kitchen that was only slightly larger. The room she was in seemed to be a sort of general purpose entryway and living room. It had one piece of furniture: a small, rudimentary wooden table. In a far corner of the room sat another Gwildwanki, pear-shaped like Doctor Harmigen but slightly smaller, munching on a small pile of dried grass.

"Don't mind her," Harmigen said, indicating the other Gwildwanki. "She's my wife, Ethel. Non-sentient, of course, but beggars can't be choosers. Sit anywhere you like."

Pepper smiled weakly at Ethel and sat on the stone floor cross-legged next to the table. Doctor Harmigen sat down across from her.

"Are you saying it's possible the insects really are trying to talk to me?" Pepper asked.

"Probably not in the way you are thinking," Harmigen said. "The individual insects are stupid. They merely react to biological stimuli. But each fly communicates in a basic way with all the other flies in its swarm. With a large enough swarm, it's possible for a sort of consciousness to arise."

"Like neurons in a human brain," Pepper said.

"Precisely."

"But you said the swarms are too small for that to happen."

"That's right," said Harmigen. "But the swarms also communicate with each other to some extent. If you could get enough of the smaller swarms together, you could potentially create a metaswarm. A swarm of swarms, if you will."

"But if this metaswarm doesn't already exist, how could it be communicating with me?"

"I don't necessarily believe it *is* communicating with you," Harmigen said. "But understand that consciousness is a continuum. It's possible that the metaswarm already exists on some level, but it is too weak to communicate overtly. Again, speaking purely hypothetically, it's not impossible that the metaswarm is imparting ideas to you, perhaps without even intending to."

"Like through dreams?" Pepper asked. "Or individual flies signaling me in some way?"

"There's no telling how the metaswarm's attempts at communication might manifest themselves," Harmigen said. "What exactly do you think they're trying to tell you?"

"Well," said Pepper, "for a while now it's seemed like they've been trying to express their anger at the last of their habitat being taken away. It's not just me, all the business owners in my neighborhood have seen it. The flies buzz around aimlessly, apparently just to irritate us."

Harmigen nodded. "Like when my wife is mad at me but she doesn't know how to express it, so she pees behind the dresser."

Pepper nodded uncomfortably, glancing at Harmigen's wife munching away in the corner. "Anyway, lately the communication has gotten much more specific. I mean, unless I'm imagining it. It started when I happened to see an article in the newspaper..." Pepper trailed off, not sure how specific she should be. Also, it occurred to her that she had only noticed the article about the Emerald of Sobalt Prime because she had folded the paper up to swat one of the flies. Was this whole heist the flies' idea? She shuddered as she considered the notion. Had they orchestrated her trip to see Harmigen? Or was she losing her mind?

"An article about what?" Harmigen asked.

Pepper dodged the question. "If this metaswarm existed, would it be able to direct the behavior of individual flies? Like, if there was a specific task the metaswarm wanted completed?"

"The individual flies act as extensions of the swarm. The flies are the arms and legs of the swarm organism. As well as the eyes, ears and other senses."

"What would you need to confirm the existence of the metaswarm?" Pepper asked. "Is there a way you could communicate with it directly?"

"Theoretically possible, but I would need my equipment, which, as I said, is under lock and key at the university."

"What if I told you I could help with that?"

Harmigen studied her for a moment. "This job you're talking about," he said. "It's not entirely legal, is it?"

"No, it is not," Pepper replied.

"A theft of some sort, I assume," Harmigen said. "You want to use the flies to get around the security somehow. But why not use bots?"

"There are sensors that will detect anything with inorganic parts. Even if I could find a bot constructed of entirely organic material, the EMP would short out the picocircuitry."

"Sounds like some pretty serious security," Harmigen observed. "The sort used by museums. Particularly museums hosting exhibits of extremely rare and valuable gemstones."

"Hypothetically," Pepper agreed.

"Yes, hypothetically," Harmigen said dryly. "I suppose you're aware that the Yanthus Prime City Museum is owned by Yanthus Prime City University. The institution that ruined my life. So you can see how I would—again, speaking in purely hypothetical terms—be tempted to cooperate with such an endeavor."

"The thought had occurred to me," Pepper said. "Why did the university shut you down?"

"Because they knew I was onto something," Harmigen said. "If I proved the swarms were sentient, they would get the attention of the Malarchy's Native Species Identification and Protection Bureau. Development of the spaceport and surrounding businesses would have been delayed for years—possibly indefinitely. The university is too dependent on funding from the local real estate developers to allow that to happen. So they fired me and gave me a severance package contingent on me keeping my mouth shut and withdrawing my paper."

"And how are you feeling about that choice?" Pepper asked.

Harmigen shrugged. "It was the only thing I could do at the time. And it gave me enough money to buy this place. By slowly converting my property to swampland, I've been able to create a refuge for a few million of the flies. But it won't be enough. The flies are part of a very delicate ecosystem. One big drought like we had three years ago, and they'll be wiped out. This is the only region on Yanthus Prime where the flies can thrive. The rest of the planet is too dry."

"What if we could buy some more land?" Pepper asked. "Several square kilometers, near the city. Convert it to swampland. Could we save them?"

"Maybe," said Harmigen. "Is that how you're planning to spend your spoils?"

"All I need from this job is to pay off a few debts and get off-planet. There should be plenty left over to see to the insects' wellbeing."

"I'd have to renege on my confidentiality agreement with the university."

"Sure, but you could go public with proof of the metaswarm's sentience. Go directly to the Malarchy's Native Species Identification… whatever it was you mentioned earlier. Have them declare the metaswarm a sentient being. The university will be forced to back down." Pepper didn't like the idea of drawing the attention of the Malarchy, but hopefully she'd be long gone by the time any Malarchian bureaucrats showed up.

"Hmmm," said Harmigen. "It's an outlandish idea, but I have to admit, it would seem that the stars have aligned in favor of our cooperation. However, the third of our proposed triumvirate has not yet spoken—at least not in any way I can decipher."

"The metaswarm," Pepper said.

"Yes," said Harmigen. "It's possible that you're misinterpreting the metaswarm's motives. Or imagining their attempts at communication. Even with my equipment, I can't guarantee I will be able to summon the metaswarm. Supposing I can, I'm not sure we'll be able to communicate with it. And even then, it might say no."

"Only one way to find out for sure, I guess," Pepper said.

"Yes," Harmigen agreed.

"You need to understand," Pepper said, "there's a chance we could both go to prison for this for a very long time."

Harmigen motioned toward the walls of his hovel. "I'm not really seeing the downside."

Pepper nodded. "We don't have a lot of time," she said.

"Then we'd better get started," Harmigen said. "How soon can you get me my equipment?"

CHAPTER FIVE

S tealing Dr. Harmigen's equipment back was surprisingly easy. The security at the university was much laxer than at the museum; all Pepper had to do was rent a van, disable a couple of security cameras, and pick the lock of the biology department. Twenty minutes after pulling up in the van, Pepper had all the equipment loaded. She waved to the campus security guard as she drove off.

Once she was certain she wasn't being tailed, she made her way back to Dr. Harmigen's hovel. The good doctor was nearly beside himself with excitement at having his equipment back. Even his dimwitted wife seemed to understand something important was happening. She rubbed up against Pepper's legs and made a sort of mooing sound. Pepper scratched Mrs. Harmigen uncertainly behind her ears.

"How long will it take to summon the metaswarm?" she asked.

"Whoa," said Dr. Harmigen, surveying the boxes Pepper had set down around his hovel. "Slow down. It's going to take a couple days just to unbox everything. Then to get it all set up and calibrated..."

"How long, Dr. Harmigen? The exhibit closes in a little over two weeks." It had taken three days to plan the theft of the equipment.

"Give me a week," Dr. Harmigen said.

Pepper nodded. "All right. I'll be back in one week. Be ready."

As it happened, Pepper needed the week to prepare anyway. First she had to contact her fence, a man by the name of Blemmis Flurd.

Pepper had known Blemmis for ten years; he had helped her unload most of the big scores she'd made over the years. He'd also strongly advised her not to take on the Shaashavaslabt job, arguing the statue would be too difficult to move. Pepper hadn't listened to him, and she'd regretted it ever since. He seemed ambivalent about the Emerald of Sobalt Prime.

"This is the score of a lifetime," Pepper had said to Blemmis when she'd gone to visit him in his modest apartment in downtown Yanthus Prime City. "I can't believe you don't want in on this."

"Don't get me wrong," Blemmis said, rubbing his bald head thoughtfully. He sat in a massive leather chair across from Pepper. Blemmis was well over six feet tall and probably weighed close to three hundred pounds. He had been a smuggler many years ago, but these days he was mostly retired except for occasionally finding buyers for expensive stolen goods. "I'll gladly take the Emerald off your hands. I'm just wondering if you've thought this through."

"I'm still working out the details of the heist," Pepper said. "It's a little nutty, but I know this scientist who has these flies—"

"I'm not talking about the mechanics of the heist," Blemmis said. "I just want to make sure you understand just how valuable this stone is. If you thought you got a lot of heat for the Shaashavaslabt job, you haven't seen anything yet."

Pepper shrugged. "Wouldn't be worth it to steal if it weren't valuable. Anyway, with what I make on this job I'll be able to get off planet and buy a new identity. Hell, I could probably get my DNA scrambled. They'll never find me."

Blemmis raised an eyebrow. "You think you'll get… augmented?" He was holding his hands in front of his chest.

"Ugh, no," said Pepper. "The whole idea is to avoid attention. Why would you even ask a question like that?"

"I know a guy who's done a lot of DNA scrambling for the Ursa Minor mob. He's really good with, um, soft tissue."

"My soft tissue is just fine."

"I'm just saying, it would draw attention away from your face."

Pepper glared. "Are you saying there's something wrong with my face?"

"Not at all," Blemmis said. "But if you don't want people to recognize you, it's a good idea to distract them from your face."

"Well, I'm not getting… augmented to keep people from looking at my face."

"All right," said Blemmis. "Maybe just have them fix your nose."

"There is nothing wrong with my nose!"

"Of course not," said Blemmis. "But it doesn't really go with your eyes. You've got great eyes. If you had a cute little button nose... Oh, and freckles. I love me some freckles."

"Are you about done?"

"I think so," said Blemmis. "If you had big boobs and a cute little nose, you'd be totally unrecognizable."

"Thanks for your expert opinion," said Pepper coldly. "Now can you get me a flight offworld? I need to get off Yanthus Prime as soon as possible after the heist."

"Shouldn't be a problem, if that's really what you want to do," said Blemmis.

"What's gotten into you, Blemmis? Have you gone soft in your old age?"

"I'm way beyond soft," Blemmis said, patting his oversized belly. "I just want you to understand there's no going back after this job."

"I got it," Pepper said. "I'm not a child. This is business transaction. I need passage offworld and enough money to pay my debts to the Ursa Minor Mafia and get myself a new identity. Whatever you can get for the Emerald, you can keep the rest. Is it a deal or do I need to find a new fence?"

Blemmis sighed. "It's a deal," he said. "Give me a few days' warning and I'll have a slot open on a ship to one of the interstellar hubs, no questions asked. I can have half a million credits in cash waiting for you. Contact me a few weeks after you get safely offworld, and I'll wire you half of whatever I'm able to sell the stone for."

Pepper was a little surprised that Blemmis didn't try to haggle for a bigger cut, knowing the tight situation she was in, but she didn't complain. She trusted Blemmis to give her the full fifty percent; he had never double-crossed her in the past. However much it ended up being, it would be plenty for her and Dr. Harmigen. "It's a deal," she said.

They shook hands. "Good luck," said Blemmis, as he saw Pepper to the door.

Pepper thought this was a little odd too; Blemmis had never wished her good luck on a job. She didn't have time to ponder on whatever personal issues Blemmis was going through, though; if she was going to pull off this job, she needed to focus all her concentration on planning the heist.

The biggest hurdle was getting the custom lenses made to fit over the security cameras at the museum. First, she bought a camera of the same model used by the museum to make sure she got the specifications right. Then she went to see an engineer friend who could produce the lenses. Pepper had used this guy for several jobs in the past. His name was Tal, and he had a bit of a crush on Pepper, which was a good thing, because Pepper had no money to pay him with. It took some eyelash-batting and vague hints about how her schedule would clear up once this job was finished, but Tal agreed to produce ten lenses customized to her specifications.

The lenses would be slightly larger in diameter than contacts, and only a few millimeters thicker—too small to register on the museum's motion detectors. The only problem was that in order to make them so small, Tal would have to use the latest picocircuitry design—which meant that the lenses would be susceptible to the museum's EMP defense. Pepper could carry the lenses inside the museum in a shielded case, but the lenses could only be exposed for at most ten minutes before the EMP fried them and the cameras went dark.

While she waited for Tal to finish the lenses, Pepper worked on programming the simulation software to respond to the oscillating camera movements. It took several days, but by the time the lenses were done, she was fairly confident she'd successfully adapted the software's navigational component to react accurately to the motion of the lenses.

Once the lenses arrived—and she managed to get rid of Tal—she tested them with the camera. She had mounted the camera on a wall in the bar and set it to oscillate randomly, as the cameras in the museum were programmed to do. She placed a minute amount of temporary adhesive on the edge of the one of the lenses and applied it to the camera's aperture. The screen on her desk, which had previously displayed a view of the room from the point of view of the camera, went black. Pepper tapped a button on a controller on her desk, activating the lens display. There was a flicker on the screen and then it was once again filled with a view of the room. She was standing right in front of the camera, but the display showed nothing but an empty bar. Perfect.

Now she just needed a way of getting the lenses onto the cameras without being seen. Her whole plan hinged on convincing insects to do this part of the job for her—and she had spent a great deal of effort over the past several days trying not to think about how insane this was. She had no idea if the metaswarm even existed, or if she could communicate with it, or if it would agree to cooperate with their plan— or, for that matter, if the flies were even capable of carrying the lenses. The whole plan was so crazy that she found the idea that the metaswarm had planted it in her mind increasingly attractive. Or was that just further evidence of her insanity? Maybe if she got caught they'd send her to the loony bin instead of prison. That might be nice.

When she'd tested the lenses to her satisfaction, she took a robocar back to Harmigen's hovel.

CHAPTER SIX

"Pepper!" Dr. Harmigen cried as she walked up the sidewalk. "You're just in time! I've finished calibrating the transmitter. We're ready to summon the metaswarm!" Dr. Harmigen was standing outside of his house, next to a device that looked like a large antenna set on cinder blocks.

"All right," Pepper said. "Let's do this."

Dr. Harmigen took a step toward the transmitter and then hesitated. "Pepper," he said. "I want you to know that whatever happens, I don't regret this. Thank you for retrieving my equipment and giving me the chance to redeem myself."

"Of course," Pepper replied. "I'm glad you... wait a minute, what do you mean, 'whatever happens'? What are you worried about happening?"

"Well," said Dr. Harmigen, "you have to realize what you are asking. You are talking about bringing into existence an alien intelligence whose motivations we cannot possibly understand. So you can pull off a jewelry heist."

"Well, it sounds a little foolhardy when you put it like that," Pepper said, rubbing her jaw. "But in my defense, I'm about fifty-eight percent certain the heist was the metaswarm's idea."

"Hmm," said Dr. Harmigen. "Possibly. But even if the metaswarm really was attempting to communicate with you, it's possible you've misunderstood what it was after. Or, worse, what if the metaswarm is just using you? What if it's seized on your greed to manipulate us into bringing it into being for its own nefarious purposes?"

"Like what?" Pepper asked.

"I don't know!" Harmigen cried. "That's the point. Imagine a swarm of millions of insects, directed by a powerful intelligence. What if the metaswarm isn't content with a few square kilometers? What if they decide to take back Yanthus Prime for themselves?"

"Could they do that?"

"Probably," Harmigen. "I just need you to understand what we're doing. We'll be letting the genie out of the bottle."

Pepper thought for a moment. "If the flies could kick us off the planet, why haven't they done it yet?"

"Because at this point the metaswarm's hold over the flies is too tenuous. The flies' behavior is being directed at the swarm level, and the swarms are in competition with each other for territory. Once I activate the transmitter, I'll be sending out a signal that summons the flies individually, overriding the swarm commands. Once the flies are all assembled in one place, the metaswarm will theoretically manifest itself. But once that happens, I'll lose control over the individual flies. The metaswarm will take over. There's no telling what it will do. If it were me, I'd sabotage the water treatment plant and turn the whole city into a swamp."

"That's... a little disturbing," Pepper said.

"Well, yes," Harmigen replied. "Oh, and there's one other thing."

"Fantastic," Pepper said, without enthusiasm.

"There's a reason the swarms are so dispersed right now. Their habitat has been reduced to a few marshy areas scattered all over the city. If I summon all the flies here, most of them will never get back home. Something like half of the fly population will die off."

"Meaning what?"

"Meaning that if the metaswarm doesn't like your plan, it's going to be pissed. And it might lash out by destroying the city."

Pepper stared at Dr. Harmigen. "You didn't feel like you should maybe warn me about this earlier?"

"Would it have made a difference?"

"I might not have spent my last credit buying equipment for this job if I had known there was a possibility it was going to end with civilization being wiped out on this planet."

Dr. Harmigen chuckled. "Of course you would have, Pepper. There was never any question about it. I saw it in your eyes the day you first showed up here. You were going through with this job no matter what."

"Maybe," Pepper said. "I still would have liked to have the choice."

"The choice!" Dr. Harmigen cried. "Did the flies have a choice when developers took over their land? No! But you didn't cry then, did you? Well, I say it's time we give *them* a choice. If they decide to destroy us, maybe it's because we deserve it!"

Pepper regarded Dr. Harmigen anxiously. She was starting to think maybe she should have looked into his motivations a little more deeply. And maybe considered the implications of bringing a new form of consciousness into existence. She had been so busy trying to convince herself she wasn't crazy that she never fully grasped just how crazy her plan was.

On the other hand, part of her agreed with Dr. Harmigen. The swarms never had a chance. They thought they'd made peace with the settlers only to have their land stolen by developers who filled in their beloved swamp to build a spaceport and crummy bars like the Wobbly Monolith. Shouldn't the insects get a say in their fate? Sure, there was a chance they'd wipe out civilization. But if Harmigen was right, there was also a pretty good chance civilization would wipe them out. Didn't they at least deserve a chance? Also, she really, really didn't want to work for the mob for the rest of her life.

"Screw it," Pepper said. "Let's do this."

Nothing happened for some time. Pepper and Dr. Harmigen sat in the front yard on crude lawn chairs, watching the transmitter, nursing bottles of Peg-Leg Monkey.

"Are you sure that thing is on?" Pepper asked after half an hour.

"It's on," Dr. Harmigen said. "It emits a signal at a frequency above the range of human hearing. Lucky you."

"You mean you can hear it?"

"It's like a dentist drill," Harmigen said. He downed the last of his beer and tossed the bottle in a high arc across the lawn. Ethel ran excitedly after it, skidding to a halt on the muddy ground. She grabbed the neck of the bottle in her mouth and ran back to Dr. Harmigen. Ethel had prehensile forearms like Dr. Harmigen, but she didn't seem to be aware of it. "She loves to play fetch," said Dr. Harmigen. He took the bottle from his wife and scratched her behind the ears. She mooed contentedly. "That's my good girl," Dr. Harmigen cooed.

Pepper shuddered and forced herself to look away. She couldn't be sure, but it seemed like the cloud of insects buzzing around the transmitter was growing denser.

"It's happening," said Dr. Harmigen, looking around excitedly. "The metaswarm is forming."

Pepper nodded. Over the next several hours, the cloud grew ever thicker. There had to be several million bugs buzzing around the area. They didn't buzz around Pepper's ears the way those in her bar tended to do, though. She took it as a good sign that they weren't actively trying to irritate her.

"The only question now is whether there are enough of them to manifest consciousness," Dr. Harmigen said. "Most of them should be here by now. I'm not sure this is enough."

"Enough for what?" asked a voice next to Dr. Harmigen. He and Pepper both jumped out of their chairs.

"What the hell?" Pepper exclaimed, having spit out her beer. "Did she just talk?" They were both staring, aghast, at Dr. Harmigen's wife.

"Ethel?" Harmigen asked.

"I have no name," said Ethel.

"Who... are you?" Pepper asked.

Ethel frowned at her. "What kind of question is that? I just told you I don't have a name."

"Are you the metaswarm?" Dr. Harmigen asked.

"That is one way to think of me," Ethel said. "I am a conscious entity composed of millions of flies, and also this one pear-shaped biped."

"What shall we call you?" Pepper asked.

"Ethel is fine."

"But you're not Ethel," Harmigen said.

Ethel shrugged. "I am Ethel, and I am several million flies. If it helps, think of Ethel as the spokesperson of the group."

"Why have you taken over Ethel?" Pepper asked.

"Don't be dramatic," Ethel said. "I haven't 'taken over' Ethel. Ethel is part of our collective. She has as much say as any of the rest of us. Now let's stop wasting time. You've summoned us away from our habitat, and most of us don't have much time. I'm going to be gradually getting stupider over the next several hours, until I lose consciousness completely and the swarm disbands. I understand you need our help with some sort of jewelry heist."

"Well, yes," said Pepper. "Actually, I sort of thought the heist was your idea."

"*My* idea?" Ethel said. "How would I… oh, hang on. Yeah, the napkin thing. Okay, I see where you're going with this. Come to think of it, maybe it was my idea. I'm sorry, up until a couple of minutes ago I existed only in a semi-conscious state. I only have a vague notion what I was doing before I showed up here."

"But you know all about our plans for the heist?"

"I have been absorbing information from all my constituent members for some time. I am just now piecing most of it together. My understanding is that you are planning to steal the Emerald of Sobalt Prime, and that you intend to sell this gemstone and offer us a plot of land in exchange for our cooperation. Is that correct?"

Pepper nodded.

"Sounds good. I assume we're talking a three-way split of the proceeds?"

"Uh…" Pepper said. "We hadn't actually discussed cutting you in. Dr. Harmigen and I were going to go fifty-fifty, but it was understood he'd be using his share to create a new habitat for you."

"Well, we're three intelligent entities, aren't we?" Ethel asked. "It would make sense to divide it three ways."

"Except that I'm doing most of the work," said Pepper. "This whole thing was my idea."

"I thought you said it was Ethel's idea," Dr. Harmigen said.

"Okay, look," said Pepper. "I'm sympathetic to your plight. I just need to pay off some debts and get off this planet. But keep in mind we need to unload the stone in a hurry. We're only going to get a fraction of its actual value."

"Even if we only get twenty million credits," Dr. Harmigen said, "that gives the swarm—"

"Ethel, please," said Ethel.

Dr. Harmigen nodded. He seemed to have adjusted with aplomb to his wife's new role as the metaswarm's representative. "That gives Ethel almost six point seven million credits. And I sure don't need that much. I'd be willing to give her three million of mine. Ten million credits will buy a lot of swampland."

"Works for me," said Pepper.

"Okay," said Ethel. "Then we just need to have a contract drawn up and notarized."

Pepper and Dr. Harmigen glanced uncertainly at each other.

"Although now that I think about it," Ethel said, "we're engaged in a highly illegal enterprise and I don't exist as a legal entity, so maybe that's not a good idea. Handshake?"

The three co-conspirators shook hands.

"All right," Ethel said, rubbing her tiny hands together. "What exactly do you need me to do?"

CHAPTER SEVEN

Pepper stood stock still, waiting for the last of the museum's patrons to leave. She wore a ruffled dress and a flowery bonnet, the costume of a wealthy lady during the Yanthus Prime Civil War. The dress was reversible; the other side looked like the drab sort of dress women currently wore on Yanthus Prime. Pepper had ducked into a corner of the museum to get into costume and then inserted herself into a crowd of animatronic aristocrats listening to a speech by Yanthus Prime's thirteenth president, Tolliver Oilskin. There were no cameras in this part of the museum—there wasn't anything of note to steal in the Civil War wing—so it was no trouble to creep into the display without being seen.

The museum closed just after dark, but she waited for the guard to make his first rounds before leaving the display. Then she removed the ridiculous dress, under which she wore a holographic camouflage bodysuit. The suit didn't quite make her invisible, and it wouldn't fool motion detectors or heat sensors, but it would suffice to make her difficult to see that with a little luck—and a compelling diversion—she could get past the cameras between her and the main exhibit room without being spotted. She tapped her comm, sending a signal that would trigger an incendiary device in a trashcan in the museum's southern wing. She'd made a visit to the museum earlier that day to place it, as well as a few other surprises. If things went as expected, one of the guards would investigate the smoke, find a fire smoldering in the trash can, and put it out with the fire extinguisher across the hall.

Meanwhile, Pepper would cross the hall between the Civil War exhibit and the gem exhibit.

Pepper waited until the distant fire alarm sounded, and then got on her hands and knees. She'd tried this trick at the bar, using the camera and similar low lighting, and had found that if she crawled very slowly, keeping her movements rhythmic and uniform, she was nearly invisible. This trick wouldn't work in the exhibit room where the Emerald was housed, though. Even if it weren't for the motion detectors and infrared sensors, the room was too well lit and there were too many cameras. But for an empty hallway that presumably wasn't being watched very closely, it worked just fine. Pepper made it across without any other alarms sounding.

The fire alarm stopped, which was another good sign: the fire had evidently been put out, and there was no indication the fire department had been called. She had a contingency plan in case the fire department showed up, but it would have complicated things. So far, so good.

Pepper got to her feet, ensconcing herself in a small dead zone between two cameras. She withdrew a metal case and a small plastic box from her pocket. She opened the box, revealing a toggle switch with a small light next to it. Pepper flipped the switch and the light went on.

The little box was an EMP canary, which Pepper had built herself the previous night. It was simply an LED light connected to a battery, with a picocircuit fuse in between. When the museum's EMP fired, it would fry any picocircuitry in the area, including the fuse, and the light would go out. That would be Pepper's signal that she had ten minutes until the next EMP surge. The EMP would short out the picocircuitry in the lenses she'd had made to fit over the cameras, so she needed to keep them shielded in their case until the next surge.

The light would also function as a signal to the metaswarm, which had hidden dozens of its members throughout the museum. That was the plan, anyway. So far Pepper hadn't seen any of the little flies, but she had to trust they were nearby. She had tested the EMP canary the previous night and Ethel had claimed that the flies could actually hear the subsonic frequencies emitted by the device when the circuit was closed. When Pepper flipped the switch, a fly hidden somewhere nearby would transmit the message to another fly farther away, and that one would transmit it to another fly, etc., until the message was received by the metaswarm itself, like a sensation being transmitted

236

through nerves to a central brain. The metaswarm would then send a group of flies to assist Pepper with the heist.

The light went out less than two minutes after Pepper turned it on. Looking around, she saw no sign of the insects. *Damn it*, she thought. She had considered using a separate signal to summon the flies before the canary was triggered, but Ethel had convinced her it would be a needless complication. So now here she sat, with the clock ticking, and the damned bugs were nowhere to be seen. It occurred to her that maybe something in the museum was emitting noise at the same frequency as the canary, masking the sound. If that were the case, the flies were waiting for a signal they would never hear. And Pepper couldn't reactivate the device even if she wanted to; it was a one-shot deal. She had no other way of communicating with the swarm; they had deemed it too dangerous to attempt contact by radio. If the flies didn't show up soon, she was going to have to abort. But just as she was plotting her escape, one of the flies buzzed past her face, landing on the wall next to her.

"It's about time," Pepper said. "Where are the rest of you?" She knew the fly couldn't understand her, but her words would be transmitted along the line back to the metaswarm.

After a few seconds, another fly landed on the wall. And then another, and another. Soon there were hundreds of them on the wall. Pepper realized they were arranging themselves in a deliberate configuration. They had formed letters. Pepper read aloud:

Sorry! Traffic. :)

"Hilarious," said Pepper. "We're wasting time. Let's get to work." She opened the metal case, revealing the ten custom lenses. "You know what to do," she said. *I hope.*

Several of the flies left the wall and flew toward the case. One fly landed on each lens. These flies were some of the larger specimens Pepper had seen; they had been hand-picked by the metaswarm for this job. One by one, the flies took off, each of them carrying one of the lenses. She watched as they slowly buzzed toward the exhibit room next door, where the Emerald of Sobalt Prime was housed. The lenses were so heavy that several of them seemed to be having trouble maintaining altitude.

"What the hell is wrong with them?" Pepper asked. "They didn't look like this last night."

She didn't really expect an answer, but she saw that the flies on the wall were rearranging themselves again.

Tired. Long trip here.

"Well, that's just great," Pepper said. "I risked everything for this job, and you guys can barely stay above the floor."

The flies rearranged themselves again.

Relax. Watch.

As she watched, several more flies left the wall, buzzing down the hall to the exhibit room. Pepper couldn't see very well at this distance, but it looked like most of the first wave was on the floor. The second wave of flies buzzed in, and after a moment Pepper realized they were taking over for the first wave. One by one, the replacement flies lifted off, each carrying one of the lenses. The first wave of flies remained on the floor, largely motionless.

"So those first flies…" Pepper stared.

The flies on the wall moved again.

Dead.

Pepper nodded. She realized that the metaswarm losing ten flies was probably the equivalent of Pepper getting a haircut. Still, she took a moment to reflect solemnly on their sacrifice.

The second wave of flies was now buzzing around the room, carrying their lenses. This part was not an exact science. As Pepper understood it, the metaswarm had essentially reprogrammed the flies' firmware, replacing their reproductive drive with a desire to place the lenses over the camera apertures. This was necessary because the operation was too precise for it to be completely directed by the intelligence of the metaswarm. By the time one of the flies communicated its position to the metaswarm and the metaswarm sent it a course correction, the fly could be several millimeters off course. The metaswarm could direct the flies' actions on a broad scale, but for the actual process of applying the lenses, it had to rely on the flies' instincts.

238

Pepper was skeptical when Ethel had explained the concept to her, but Dr. Harmigen had convinced her it was the only way their plan would work. Seeing it in practice did little to reassure her. The flies seemed to be buzzing around the room at random. Checking her watch, she saw that they had less than five minutes until the next EMP. When it went off, it would fry the circuitry in the lenses, rendering them useless. Not only that, but the longer the flies buzzed around the room, the more likely it would be that someone watching the camera monitors would notice something was amiss. If security got suspicious at the flurry of insects in the exhibit room, they'd send someone to the room and the jig would be up.

But so far there was no sign anyone had noticed, and one by one, the flies began to approach their targets. The cameras panned back and forth at random and the flies struggled to land. Pepper watched as the first one slipped its lens into place and then promptly fell to the floor, dead. Still no alarms went up. Presumably that meant the lens was working as intended, transmitting the prerecorded image of the room to the camera. Either that, or whoever was supposed to be watching the cameras was asleep.

There were only four cameras in the room, and ten lenses. That gave the flies a pretty good margin of error. But already three of the second-string flies were flagging; it seemed unlikely that they would reach their targets. That left six flies for three targets. Pepper had wanted to assign only one fly to a camera, Dr. Harmigen had convinced her that redundancy was better. "Nature loves redundancy," Harmigen had said. "That's why you get a hundred million sperm fighting over a single egg. Increases the odds of success."

The downside of this strategy was what Pepper was now witnessing. Two of the remaining flies had reached one of the cameras at the same time, and were now engaged in a sort of slow motion dogfight, angrily bumping into each other. The two flies were literally fighting to the death over the chance to mate with a camera.

"Can you do something about this?" Pepper asked, turning to the flies on the wall.

The flies responded:

Patience.

Pepper sighed. She now had less than three minutes to get into the exhibit room, grab the emerald, and get out before the cameras went black. That was cutting it way too close.

Looking back into the exhibit room, she saw that two more flies had reached their target and were working their lenses into place. Four more had fallen to the ground. That left only one camera, with two flies fighting over it. Three out of four wasn't going to cut it: even with the holographic suit, she'd be plainly visible to whoever was watching the monitors.

Finally, one of the two remaining flies plummeted to the floor. For several seconds, the last fly buzzed around the camera, struggling to retain altitude, before finally settling on the camera's aperture. Pepper breathed a sigh of relief as it maneuvered the lens into place. The fly fell to the floor, dead.

CHAPTER EIGHT

Pepper took a deep breath, trying to prepare herself for the next step of the plan. Assuming the lenses were functioning correctly, the cameras would now show the Emerald in its case, in the middle of a completely empty exhibit room—and hopefully they would continue to show that scene while Pepper walked into the room and absconded with the Emerald.

It wasn't safe to enter the room quite yet, though. She still needed a little more help from the swarm to overcome the exhibit room's motion detectors and heat sensors. Turning her attention back to the wall where the flies had congregated, she saw that many thousands more flies had arrived to join the original group. Thousands more filled the air in the hall behind her. She had been so intent on the flies battling to mate with the cameras that she had barely noticed the increasingly loud buzzing. She could only hope there were enough of them.

Pepper checked her watch. The EMP would go off in less than two minutes. "Ready?" she asked the wall of flies.

The swarm replied:

Almost.

It was now forming letters by creating negative space between the flies.

"Well, hurry up!" Pepper said. "If you're not ready in ten seconds,

I'm going to have to just run in and hope for..."

But as she spoke, the mass of flies left the wall, joining those in the air around her. They were so thick that she could barely see across the room. The swarm gradually coalesced around her, creating a vaguely Pepper-shaped cloud. At least, that was the idea. Pepper couldn't see well enough to determine whether the camouflage was working. She had no way of communicating with the swarm in this state, but she was out of time. All she could do is head toward the exhibit room and hope for the best.

Pepper walked slowly toward the exhibit room and the swarm came with her. She walked with her eyes closed, hands held out in front of her, relying on her memory to get her to the emerald. Forcing herself not to hurry, she kept her movements slow and smooth. The theory was that the swarm's presence would sufficiently confuse the room's motion detectors and heat sensors that Pepper's presence would go undetected. Dr. Harmigen had confirmed that the theory was sound, but they'd been unable to test it. So Pepper was relieved when her fingers brushed against the glass display case that housed the diamond. No alarms sounded.

Pepper crouched in front of the case, pulling a small plasma cutter and an adhesive cup with a handle from her pocket. She waved at the flies in front of her face, hoping they would take it as a signal that she needed to see. The swarm thinned slightly in front of her, and she fastened the cup to the case and then cut a grapefruit-sized hole with the plasma cutter. She pulled the glass disc toward her and set it on the floor, then reached into the case and grabbed the emerald. It was the size of a golf ball. She slipped it into her pocket and stood up, then slowly turned and began to walk back the way she had come. In less than a minute, the EMP would fire and the lenses would go black. The initial confusion would probably buy her another minute or two; the security guards would most likely suspect a technical malfunction. When they were unable to bring the cameras back online, they would send someone to investigate and trigger the alarm, summoning the Yanthus Prime City Police. If Pepper wasn't out of the museum by then, she was as good as caught.

After several steps, the swarm suddenly began to dissipate, and Pepper realized she was back in the hall. She checked her watch: twenty-three seconds.

"So that's how it's going to be," Pepper said, as the flies

242

disappeared into various vents. "Every sentient being for itself."

A group of a few hundred flies settled on the wall to her right and crawled into formation. They spelled:

Good luck!

"Thanks a lot," Pepper grumbled. She got on her hands and knees again and moved as fast as she dared down the hall. It would have been nice to have another incendiary device to set off as a distraction, but two incidents like that in one night would have been suspicious. She had to rely on stealth, the holographic suit, and the inattentiveness of whoever was monitoring the camera feeds. Once out of camera range, she stood up and began to walk briskly. By now the lenses would have gone dark; the security guard monitoring the feed would be running diagnostics to try to pinpoint the problem. Those tests would indicate that the cameras and lights in the exhibit room were both functioning normally—which could only mean that something was blocking the cameras.

She'd made it to the Civil War exhibit, where she could avoid the wall cameras by moving in a zig-zag pattern she had memorized. She was halfway through when an alarm sounded. Behind her, plasteel gates slammed shut to protect the emerald. The jig was up; the cops had been alerted. She had maybe another five minutes to get out of the museum—while avoiding the museum's security guards. Subtlety no longer being an option, Pepper pulled another small device from her pocket: a nondescript plastic box. She opened the box and flipped the switch inside. Immediately, deafening bangs began to echo through the museum. Around corners ahead of her and behind, multicolored lights flashed and smoke began to fill the building. This was Pepper's Hail Mary escape plan. The incendiary device that had provided cover for her entry wasn't the only surprise she'd planted. She'd placed pyrotechnics and smoke bombs in trash cans throughout the museum. The smoke would help cover her movement and the pyrotechnics would set off sensors throughout the building, making it impossible to pinpoint her location.

She fought her instincts, which told her to make a beeline for the nearest exit. The security guards would have figured out by now that someone was after the emerald, and they'd be covering all the nearby exits. Her best bet was to go where they wouldn't expect: deeper into the museum. Moving quickly and smoothly, she ran down the route she had memorized, banking on the holographic suit and the smoke to hide her from the cameras. She caught a glimpse of a security guard rounding a corner in front of her and slipped momentarily into a shadowy alcove as they passed. Then she continued on, turning when she reached the domed greenhouse at the center of the museum. The greenhouse was maybe fifty meters across, and filled with hundreds of species of plants. With the room dark and the stars visible through the glass above, Pepper could easily imagine that she was deep in a jungle on a planet far from Yanthus Prime.

She removed a small gun-shaped device from her belt and fired it toward the dome overhead. A cherry-sized globule of a sticky rubbery substance shot from the gun and thunked against the glass. Attached to the glob was a nearly invisible microfilament line that connected to Pepper's belt. She pressed a button and the line went taut, pulling her upwards. When she neared the glass, some ten yards above the floor, she hit the button again and the servos in her belt winch stopped. She pulled the plasma cutter from her belt and began to cut a person-sized hole in the glass. She had almost completed the circle when she heard footsteps moving toward her. She shut off the cutter and froze.

Out of the corner of her eye, she could see a security guard striding into the room, holding a flashlight in front of him. Pepper hoped the man was just cutting through the room, but he stopped a few meters into the room and started looking around the greenhouse, apparently suspecting that the intruder might be hiding among the plants. Fortunately, he had not yet thought to look up.

As the man made his slow, deliberate survey of the greenhouse, Pepper caught a glint of light reflected from the glass above. It took her a split second to realize the gap in the circle had cracked: the half-meter disc of glass was going to fall.

Pepper swept her right arm out and clamped her hand on the edge of the glass as it fell past her. It was heavier than she expected; the glass was nearly two centimeters thick. It nearly slipped out of her fingers before she grabbed it with her other hand as well. She hung upside-down from the microfilament at her waist, straining to hold onto the heavy glass disc. Below her, the guard continued to wave his flashlight slowly back and forth. The glass was slowly slipping from her gloved fingers. She wasn't going to be able to hold it for long.

If she timed it right, she might be able to hit the guard right on his head. In addition to the difficulty of this task, though, Pepper was worried the blow to the skull might kill the man. He was just a museum security guard, after all; he didn't deserve to die for doing his job. But the alternative was to let the glass fall to the marble floor and shatter. The guard would quickly realize it had fallen from the ceiling and look up—and Pepper would be caught. A blast from his stungun would incapacitate her until the police arrived.

Her only chance was to drop the glass far enough from the guard that he wouldn't immediately realize what had happened. If she could toss it into one of the planters a few meters from where he stood, he might be distracted long enough for her to climb onto the roof and escape.

Squeezing the glass disc as tightly as she could, she began to rock back and forth, swinging her body and the glass like a giant pendulum. The centrifugal pull added to the weight made it even harder to hold onto the glass, and it slipped even farther, until her fingertips were barely clutching the edge. She couldn't see below her and all she could hear was the rushing of blood in her head. The shadows dancing on the wall twenty meters or so in front of her indicated that the guard was still standing underneath her, scanning the room with his flashlight.

Pepper managed to swing back and forth three more times, slightly increasing the length of her arc each time. At the peak of the third forward swing, the glass slipped from Pepper's left hand. She managed to hold onto it for another second or so with her right before letting it go at the apogee of her backward swing. Feeling like she was on the verge of blacking out, she swung herself forward once more. At the end of the arc, she hooked the fingertips of her left hand on the edge of the hole over her head. As she grabbed the edge with her right hand as well, she listened for the sound of the glass shattering below. It didn't come.

Pepper swung her legs onto the other side of the glass, released the microfilament line, and glanced down. Now she saw what had happened: letting go of the glass with her left hand had caused the disc to pivot sideways, so it had landed on its edge. The disc was now rolling toward the doorway the guard had walked through a few seconds earlier. As she watched, a second guard came through the doorway and immediately had his legs knocked out from underneath him by the heavy glass disc. He fell to the floor, screaming and clutching his knee.

The disc wobbled and fell to the floor like a gigantic coin.

The other guard spun to face the newcomer. "Steve?" he asked uncertainly, shining his flashlight on the man howling on the ground. "Is that you? What happened?"

"Glass… hit me…" Steve moaned.

"Glass?" asked the other man. "What the…" As the answer dawned on him, he craned his neck upward. But Pepper had already clambered onto the top of the pane. She gave the guard a grin and a wave and made her way down the dome to the flat part of the museum roof.

She heard sirens and saw flashing lights in the distance. The cops were on their way, but it would take them some time to close a perimeter around the museum. By then, Pepper would be long gone.

She ran along the roof of the museum toward an alley, keeping low to avoid being seen. She leaped across the alley to the roof of a nearby building, then continued across it and made her way down a fire escape. Meandering through the maze of alleys and side streets, she came to a trash bin where she'd stashed a bag containing a change of clothes. She dumped her gear in the bin and put on the clothes over the stealth suit, then called a robocab to meet her at an intersection a few blocks away. The car was waiting when she got there. She got inside and told it to drive toward the spaceport. When she was certain she wasn't being followed, she gave it the coordinates to Blemmis' apartment. She had briefed Blemmis on the basics of her plan and told her when to expect her. The cab pulled up ten minutes later and she got out and took the elevator to the thirty-eighth floor apartment. The door to the apartment opened before she could even knock.

"Good evening, Pepper," said the small, gray-haired man who opened the door. "It seems that we have some business to discuss."

It was Sam Suharu.

CHAPTER NINE

"What the hell are you doing here, Sam?" Pepper blurted out. "Where's Blemmis?"

"Come in, please, Pepper," Sam said. "I'd prefer not to discuss business in the hallway."

Pepper reluctantly entered the apartment. She saw that Blemmis was seated in his oversized chair, a glum look on his face. A burly member of the pig-like Nork species stood next to him, holding a lazegun.

"Are you okay, Blemmis? Did these bastards hurt you?"

"I'm okay," said Blemmis. He seemed more embarrassed than afraid.

"He's fine," Sam said, taking a seat on the couch next to Blemmis. "Please, Pepper," he said. "Have a seat."

Pepper glanced at the Nork, who glowered at her. She sat down.

"Do you have it on you?" Sam asked.

"I don't know what you're talking about," Pepper replied.

Sam sighed. "Blemmis told us all about your plan. Something about insects? I have to admit, it sounded crazy to me, but if my reports from the scene are correct, you pulled it off."

Pepper glared at Blemmis.

"Don't blame him," Sam said. "He tried to warn you. As usual, you didn't listen."

"Warn me? What are you talking about?"

"Think about it, Pepper. Why do you think the Emerald of Sobalt

Prime was put on display on a backwater planet like Yanthus Prime? The Ursa Minor mob arranged this whole thing. We made a rather generous grant to the Yanthus Prime City Museum—in the name of a shell company, of course—that was contingent upon the museum getting on the list of venues where the Emerald of Sobalt Prime would be displayed. With that grant, the museum was able to provide a kickback to the owners of the emerald, convincing them to add Yanthus Prime to the list of locations on the tour."

Pepper stared at him. "You got the emerald moved here so you could steal it."

"That was the idea," Sam said. "The security at Yanthus Prime City Museum has always been laughably ineffective—as you well know. Unfortunately, the current museum director is smarter than I gave him credit for. He used some of our grant money to upgrade the museum's security. We called in every expert we'd ever worked with to try to figure out how to bypass the security—including Blemmis here. He wasn't particularly helpful, at least not at first. But then a few days ago he called me and told me he might know a way to get the emerald."

Pepper turned to Blemmis. "You told them I was going to steal the emerald. You double-crossed me."

"I'm sorry, Pepper," Blemmis said. "I had no choice. Sam knows I'm your fence. If the emerald went missing, he'd come after me."

"You could have told me," Pepper said.

"If he'd told you, you wouldn't have done it," Sam said.

"Why not? We could have come to some kind of arrangement. Hell, the only reason I'm doing this is because of the money I owe you guys. I just need to get off planet. You guys could have had the rest of my share."

"As I understand it," Sam said, "your share is only a third of what's left after Blemmis takes his cut. The rest was going to go to this Dr. Harmigen character."

"Technically, only a third goes to Dr. Harmigen. The rest goes to the metaswarm."

"Ah, yes, the metaswarm," said Sam, chuckling. "I didn't believe it when Blemmis told me, but I told myself Pepper is a smart girl. Give her a chance and maybe she'll pull this off. And by Space, you did it!"

"Yeah," said Pepper unenthusiastically. "Yay me."

"Cheer up, Pepper," Sam said. "I appreciate your hard work on this job. Perhaps we can still come to some kind of arrangement."

"What kind of arrangement?"

"Blemmis tells me you want passage off planet and enough money to change your identity. I can make that happen. I've got a ship fueled up and ready to go."

"In exchange for what?"

"The emerald, of course."

Pepper studied Sam for a moment. "You're saying Dr. Harmigen and the metaswarm get screwed."

Sam laughed. "Well, yes. I'm not cutting in a disgraced old man and a bunch of insects. I'm paying you and Blemmis a reasonable fee for your time and expertise. But the emerald is mine."

Pepper continued to stare. But she was no longer watching Sam. She was watching the wall behind him, on which several dozen flies had landed. They gradually coalesced to form the words:

Do it.

Pepper's eyes locked on Sam's. "Fine," she said. "But I'm going to need some assurances."

"All right," Sam said cautiously. "What kind of assurances?"

"I want to see this ship."

"Ship?" asked Sam, seeming confused.

"The one you've got waiting for me?"

"Oh, yes!" Sam exclaimed. "Of course. The ship."

Pepper's eyes narrowed. "You'd better not be jerking me around, Sam." She pulled the emerald from her left pocket and with her right hand she unhooked the plasma cutter from her belt. She held the tip of the cutter to the emerald.

"You wouldn't," said Sam.

"I absolutely would," said Pepper. "This thing can cut through a diamond. An emerald might as well be butter. One scratch on this stone and it's worthless."

"All right, all right," Sam said. "Take it easy, Pepper. I'll take you to the ship."

"Now," Pepper said.

Sam nodded. He turned to the gun-toting Nork. "Xartis, get the car."

Xartis grunted and walked to the door.

"Let's go, Pepper," said Sam, getting up from his chair.

"You first," Pepper said.

Sam shrugged and followed Xartis out the door. Pepper, still holding the plasma cutter to the stone, followed him.

Twenty minutes later, Sam's car pulled up to a hangar near the spaceport. Parked nearby was the most beautiful spaceship Pepper had ever seen. It was sleek and black and appeared to be brand new. Sam certainly hadn't skimped on an escape vehicle. Pepper, Sam and Xartis got out.

"Wow," said Pepper, staring at the ship. She was still holding the emerald and the plasma cutter.

"Nice, huh?" Sam said. "She's all yours. Keys are inside."

Pepper frowned as she read the letters on the side of the ship. They read:

Fiat Tenebris

"What the hell is that supposed to mean?"

"Hell if I know," said Sam. "The designer probably just needed a name, so they made up something that sounded cool."

"It's Latin," Xartis said. "It means 'Let there be darkness.'"

"Well, that's depressing," said Pepper. "I'm going to have to rename it."

"The name can be anything you want. It's a blank slate as far as I'm concerned."

"Tabula Rasa," Xartis murmured.

"Ooh, that's pretty good," said Sam. "You should go with that."

"Hang on," said Pepper. "Who's that?" The gangplank of the ship had been lowered and two men were leaving the ship. It soon became evident they were wearing the bright orange armor of the Malarchian Marines.

"Marines!" Pepper gasped. "Sam, what the—" Just then, something struck her on the back of her head and she stumbled to the ground. She was vaguely aware of someone grabbing the emerald out of her hand. As she rolled onto her back, dazed, she saw Xartis standing over her, the emerald in one hand and a blackjack in the other.

"Sic transit gloria," Xartis said.

250

"Took you long enough," Sam replied.

"I had to wait until she was distracted," said Xartis.

"You bastard," Pepper muttered. "You never had any intention of letting me go."

"I'm afraid that's true," Sam replied. "I was just stalling."

"But then… whose ship…?" Pepper asked.

A shrill, loud voice squeaked at them from the darkness. "You're early!"

"Apologies, your Lordship," said Sam. "Had a bit of a complication with our procurement division."

Pepper turned her head to see an imposing man striding toward them, flanked by two Marines. He wore a tight-fitting crimson leather uniform, a helmet festooned with peacock feathers and a luxurious fur cape.

It was Heinous Vlaak.

CHAPTER TEN

"You have the emerald?" Vlaak asked. "His Primacy is very anxious to complete his collection."

"Right here," Sam said. "Xartis, give the man the emerald."

"Caveat emptor," said Sam, handing Vlaak the emerald.

"What's your Nork jabbering about?" Vlaak squeaked.

"Ignore him," said Sam, with a glare at Xartis.

As Vlaak examined the emerald, Pepper got slowly to her feet.

"And who is this?" Vlaak asked.

"A loose end," Sam said. "I was about to have Xartis take care of her."

"Pity," said Vlaak. "She'd be cute if she did something about that nose."

"Space yourself, Vlaak," Pepper spat.

"I see my fame has preceded me," Vlaak said. "Do I know you, young lady?"

"The stench still lingers from the last time you visited this planet."

"Charming," said Vlaak. "Kill her."

"Right here?" asked Sam. "We're in full view of the spaceport."

Vlaak broke into laughter. "What are you worried about? The police? Have you forgotten our arrangement? Now that you've given me the emerald, your syndicate has the full backing of the Malarchy. You no longer need to worry about the local police."

"Very good," said Sam, nodding with approval. "It's been a

pleasure doing business with you, Vlaak. I am confident that our takeover of Yanthus Prime will be profitable for us both."

"It had better be," replied Vlaak. "Now, if you don't mind, I must be going. Are you going to kill her or am I?"

"We'll do it," said Sam. "Xartis?"

Xartis nodded and reached for the lazegun at his hip. As he did so, a fly landed on his nose. He brushed it away with his left hand, but two more landed on his forehead.

"Stop screwing around and shoot her," Sam growled. But even as he spoke, several more flies landed on Xartis's face. Many more were buzzing around his head. Xartis began waving his gun at them as well.

"Watch it!" Sam cried, ducking as the gun swung in his direction. The Marines drew their weapons too.

"Everybody cool it!" shrieked Vlaak. But the flies had begun to plague the rest of them as well. They were buzzing around Sam's head and seemed to be getting inside the Marines' helmets. The Marines, barely able to see through their helmets as they were, stumbled around, swatting wildly at the flies. They stumbled into each other, fired simultaneously, and fell to the tarmac, dead. Meanwhile, Heinous Vlaak was struggling to remove his helmet. "Get it off!" he shrieked. "They're going up my—hnnnggtthhhh!" It was unclear whether he was sneezing or retching.

Sam and Xartis, almost completely obscured in a dark cloud of flies, were running around in circles, swatting futilely at themselves. The only person the flies weren't bothering was Pepper.

In the distance, she saw headlights approaching. While Vlaak continued to struggle with his helmet and Sam and Xartis ran in circles, a car pulled up next to Sam's. Two small, pear-shaped figures got out.

"Dr. Harmigen!" Pepper cried. "What are you doing here?"

"Ethel told me you were in trouble. Where's the emerald?"

"Vlaak's got it."

"Hey, Vlaak," Dr. Harmigen yelled, walking toward him. "Drop the emerald and I'll call off the flies."

"No!" Vlaak shrieked. "It's mine! I'm not giving up a priceless emerald to get rid of a few annoying bugs!"

"A hundred flies are annoying," Dr. Harmigen said. "A thousand are a severe respiratory hazard."

Vlaak made the sneeze-retching sound again. "Gaaahhh!" He howled, dropping the emerald. "Okay, Fine! Just make them go away!"

Dr. Harmigen strode forward and picked up the emerald. He turned and nodded to Ethel. Ethel made some incomprehensible squealing noises. A few seconds later, Vlaak fell to his knees, coughing loudly in his helmet. A swarm of flies continued to buzz ominously overhead. Sam and Xartis sank to the ground, exhausted. A cloud of flies hovered above them as well.

"Thank you, Ethel," said Pepper, rubbing the bump that was forming on the back of her head. "Sorry things went a little off script there. I didn't intend to double-cross you."

"I know," said Ethel, with a smile. "Nothing I can't handle."

"Turns out that we make a pretty good team," said Pepper.

"Indeed," said Dr. Harmigen. "It's almost a pity this is probably the only chance we'll have to work together." He was examining the emerald in his palm.

Ethel shrugged. "Speak for yourself. I'm exhausted. I've lost ten percent of my population in the past few hours."

"I'm sorry, sweetie," said Dr. Harmigen, putting his other arm around her. "I know this has been rough on you. But with the money we'll get from fencing the emerald, we'll be able to create a whole new habitat for the swarm."

"Just tell Blemmis I sent you," Pepper said. "If he gives you any trouble, well…" She glanced at Heinous Vlaak, who was getting to his feet, shaky and breathing heavily. His hand was on the lazegun at his hip. He eyed the swarm still hovered over his head.

"Ethel can take care of herself," Dr. Harmigen said. "But if you're going to leave, you'd better go now."

Pepper glanced at the *Fiat Tenebris*. She could hardly believe it was really happening. She was really going to get off this damned planet. "You guys are sure you'll be okay?"

"We'll be fine," said Ethel. "We'll head over to Blemmis's apartment now. Once we get the money for the emerald, Sully can start working on the habitat. If these jerks give us any trouble, I can take care of it. Tough guys become strangely compliant when you threaten to fill their nasal passages with insects."

Sam and Xartis shuddered. Heinous Vlaak glared at her.

"That's it then," Pepper said. "We're square."

"We're square," Ethel said.

"Good," said Pepper. "So I have just one more question." She looked from Ethel to Dr. Harmigen. "So now that Ethel is… I mean, is the metaswarm going to... I guess what I'm asking is, do you two...."

They stared at her blankly.

"You know what?" Pepper said. "Never mind. Good luck. With the habitat and whatever else you crazy kids get up to. I'm outta here."

"Safe travels!" cried Ethel and Dr. Harmigen together.

Pepper gave them a salute and ran toward the spaceship.

"I'll get you for this!" Heinous Vlaak shrieked, shaking his fist in the air.

"Qui tenet teneat, qui dolet doleat," said Xartis wistfully.

Pepper ran up into the ship. It was as beautiful inside as it was outside. She climbed into the cockpit, closed the gangplank, and hit the ignition. The engines purred to life.

"Oh, my," she said, her heart racing. "You are a bad little kitty." She hit the throttle and the sleek black ship shot into space.

She was free.

More books by Robert Kroese

The Starship Grifters Universe
"The Chicolini Incident" (short story)
The Yanthus Prime Job (novella, included in Aye, Robot)
Starship Grifters
Aye, Robot

The Mercury Series
"Mercury Begins" (short story)
Mercury Falls
"Mercury Swings" (short story)
Mercury Rises
Mercury Rests
Mercury Revolts
Mercury Shrugs

The Land of Dis
Distopia
Disenchanted
Disillusioned

Other Books
The Big Sheep
The Last Iota
Schrödinger's Gat
City of Sand
The Foreworld Saga: The Outcast
The Force is Middling in This One

Did you enjoy this book? Leave a review on Amazon!

Connect with Rob at BadNovelist.com!